FUTURELAND

THE NIGHTMARE HOUR

ALSO BY H.D. HUNTER

Futureland: Battle for the Park

FUTURELAND

THE NIGHTMARE HOUR

BOOK TWO

WRITTEN BY

H.D. HUNTER

ILLUSTRATED BY **Khadijah Khatib**

RANDOM HOUSE 🏠 NEW YORK

All rights reserved. Published in the United States by Random House Children's Books, a division of Penguin Random House LLC, New York.

Random House and the colophon are registered trademarks of Penguin Random House LLC.

Visit us on the Web! rhcbooks.com

Educators and librarians, for a variety of teaching tools, visit us at RHTeachersLibrarians.com

In association with

Library of Congress Cataloging-in-Publication Data is available upon request.
ISBN 978-0-593-47946-9 (trade)—ISBN 978-0-593-47948-3 (lib. bdg.)—
ISBN 978-0-593-47947-6 (ebook)

Printed in the United States of America
10 9 8 7 6 5 4 3 2 1
First Edition

For Charli

For Rob; Brooklyn's Own

FUTURE TREK

FUTURE SEAS

THE BLACK BEAT

WONDER WORLDS

WORD LOCUS

OBSIDIAN
IMAGINARIUM

MINES OF
TOMORROW

GALACTIC
GALLERY

REALM OF
REALITIES

SPORTS
SUMMIT

THE WALKER WAYS OF LIVING
New Year's Eve—Year 2038
By Cam (and Mom and Dad)

1. Always make time for each other.
2. Family business is family business.
3. Do the best you can.
4. Speak your mind and don't hide your feelings.
5. Be grateful to those before you.
6. Be considerate of those coming after you.
7. Be yourself and dream big.
8. Walk the walk and keep your promises.
9. Stick together. No matter what.
10. Always keep it moving.

CASE CLOSED

ATLANTA MYSTERY

The New York Crimes
SOUTHMORE ARRESTED

Blaise Southmore, fugitive and former head of ADRC, was arrested earlier this week. He has been on the run since the Futureland fiasco in Atlanta. Southmore is being held without bond at Maximus State Prison. His charges include intellectual property fraud, kidnapping, and cybercrim

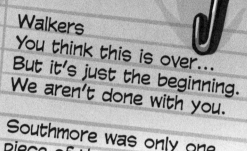

Walkers
You think this is over...
But it's just the beginning.
We aren't done with you.

Southmore was only one piece of the puzzle. A very small piece.

We will come for you. In fact, we already have one of your own on our side.
We are many.
We are everywhere.
We are...limitless.

THE ARCHITECTS

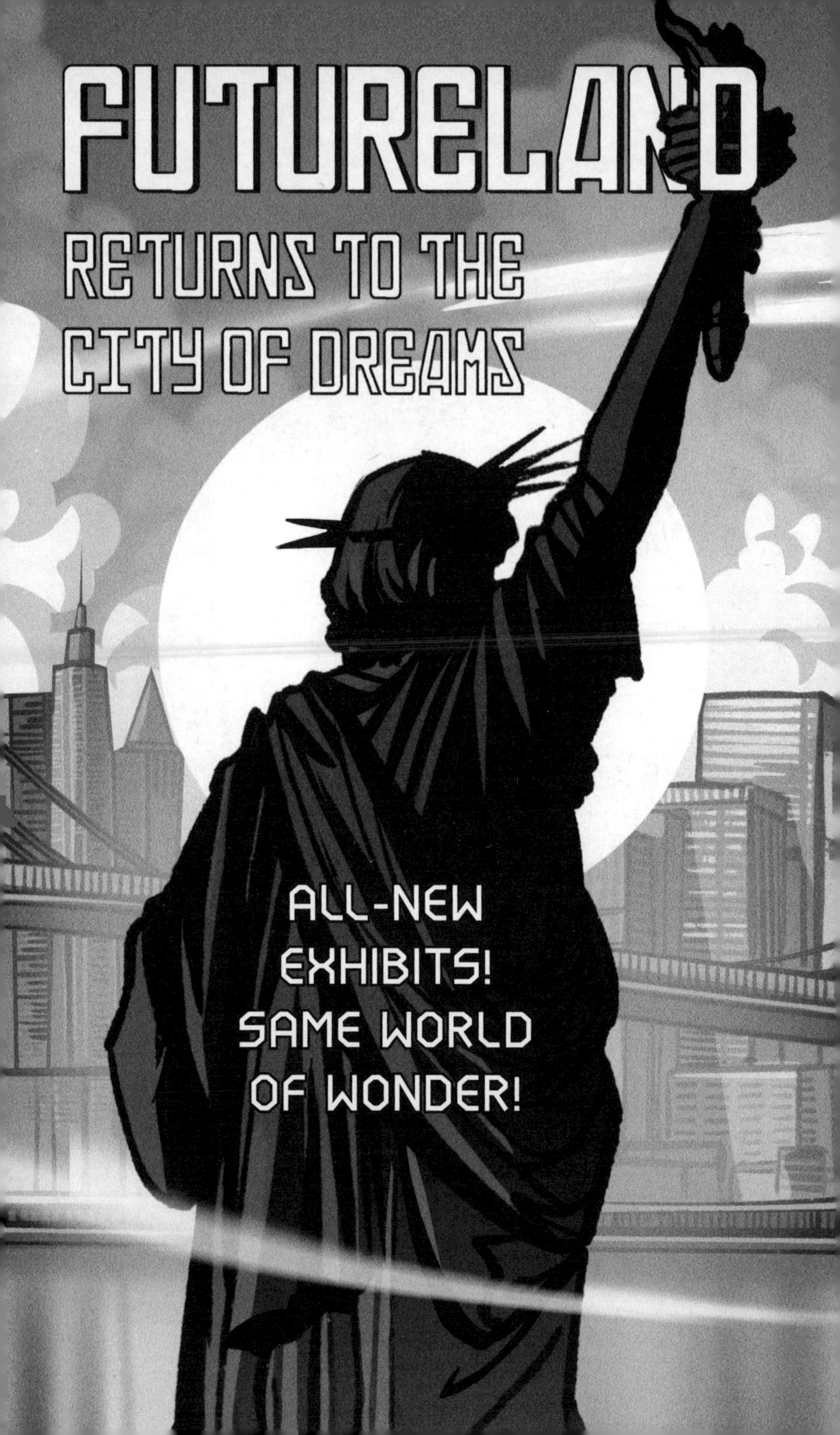
FUTURELAND
RETURNS TO THE
CITY OF DREAMS
ALL-NEW
EXHIBITS!
SAME WORLD
OF WONDER!

PLAN B

VOICE ONE: Do we still have a trace on the Walkers?

VOICE TWO: Absolutely. We've stolen enough of their data to continue our plans.

VOICE ONE: What are they up to? Are they staying in Atlanta? Should we strike again?

VOICE TWO: It's hard to tell. We are monitoring their conversations for any decisions they make.

VOICE ONE: And have we received any word from Southmore since he was captured?

VOICE TWO: I'm afraid not. He is on a strict lockdown.

VOICE ONE: Very well, then. I think it's time we move on to plan B.

VOICE TWO: Oh, goody! Plan B!

VOICE ONE: Yes. Time for us to send in someone who can get the job done. One of our finest. One of our cruelest. Someone not even *we* can fully control. . . . We told the Walkers this was only the beginning. Now it's time to show them.

VOICE TWO: I'll get a message out right away.

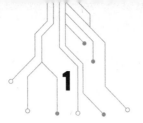

GOOD MYSTERIES

Saturday, January 23, 2049
Midnight

You know, good mysteries don't just fall out of the sky onto your lap.

You usually have to hunt for 'em. Sniff 'em out. Put the clues together like a real investigator. I guess I always had a feeling I could be a detective. I love figuring stuff out. Good mysteries are kinda like . . . a holographic trading card! You turn it this way and that, and each time it catches the light, you see something a little different. You gotta be able to look at a picture from all angles and see what no one else can see, even if it's right in front of them.

After everything that happened in the last few months, I know that solving mysteries is the life for me. It feels like I finally know who I'm supposed to be.

I'll admit, when me and my family landed in Atlanta five months ago, we got more than we bargained for. An evil corporation led by a really bad dude named Southmore hacked our park's technology. He made the Futureland revs and attractions glitchy and dangerous, and then he started kidnapping kids who visited the park. Can you believe he even made evil rev copies of my parents?

He wanted to frame my family and shut down our park so he could use our technology to start his own creepy city. But we stopped him. Totally pow, wham, whomped him outta the park! Even his own robot henchmen turned on him. But I didn't do it alone. It was me, my new crew I met at Eastside Middle School, and Dooley—my best friend and the smartest rev ever.

The best thing about friends is that they can turn good mysteries into great ones. I don't know what I'd do without them.

"What would you do without us?" Rich said, shaking his head at me. The five of us crouched behind a glowing bush off the beaten path of Futureland's walking trails.

"Hush up, Rich!" Earl whispered. "We're supposed to be hiding."

A group of revs with bright orange eyes and Futureland uniforms walked slowly past our hiding place. They peered side to side as they made their silent nightly rounds. We all crouched lower to stay out of sight.

"CJ—are those Watchers?" Angel asked.

I nodded. "Yeah, they're doing their last check of the park, to make sure nobody stayed behind after the doors closed. They'll be gone in a second. Then we can move."

"What are we looking for, anyway?" Yusuf asked.

"You'll see." I smirked. I waved for my crew to follow me as I bounded from behind the bush. We took off running through the park, headed to the nearest Jet-Blur pod station.

We placed our feet on the Jet-pads, and two metallic black orbs, big enough for us to crawl into, arrived within seconds. Me and Rich took the first one. Yusuf and Angel went for the second one, and little bitty Earl squeezed between them. He'd do anything to stay close to Angel.

I programmed our pods to travel to the same location, deep within the park to an area that visitors hardly ever encountered.

Our pods landed gently in a clearing surrounded by fog and shadows. I stepped out and felt a leaf crunch softly under my foot.

"CJ . . ." Earl's voice quavered. "Where are we?"

"This is the back of the park. Between the Mines of Tomorrow and Future Trek."

"Mines of Tomorrow? Isn't that that scary place where you almost got trapped by those creepy cave-revs?" Rich asked.

"Well, yeah," I started, "but this part of the park is empty. No one comes this way. There's nothing out here."

"Then what's that?" Yusuf pointed.

Through the fog, I spotted the outline of a large metal cylinder, like an upside-down cup, as tall as the lowest tree branches. It didn't sparkle or make any sounds—simply camouflaged into the darkness surrounding it.

"The perfect place to hide something," I said.

We stepped toward the cylinder, circling it and chattering with each other in low tones.

"CJ, is this something your parents made?" Angel asked. "Why did they put it all the way out here?"

6

"I'm not sure," I said. "I noticed it on my locator scanner the other week, but my parents haven't said anything about it. It could be anything. Maybe even something Southmore left behind."

"Creepy," Earl said. "I don't want to relive that all over again."

"This thing is probably just junk," Rich said. "Storage or something your parents wanted to put out of the way. It's not dangerous. Look at it. It's not even turned on."

Rich whacked the side of the cylinder with his leg like he was playing kickball. Immediately, a blinding column of light blasted upward through the trees from the center of the dome.

"Rich, no!" I tried to move toward the machine, but the ground under me started to rumble. I tumbled backward. My heart thudded as my eyes darted between my friends. *I have to get them outta here. I have to keep them safe.*

I pushed myself up off the ground, but someone grabbed me from behind. When I tried to shout, my breath got caught in my chest. I wriggled and kicked, but I couldn't break free. What was happening?

Boom. Boom. Boom. Boom.

My heart pounded. I started to get dizzy. I screamed out, but the person holding me covered my mouth.

7

My mind raced. *It's Southmore. Southmore is behind this. He's back to finish the job. Him and his evil, corrupted revs.*

The column shining out of the top of the cylinder disappeared, leaving us in total darkness for a couple seconds. Then soft lights beamed down into the clearing through the surrounding trees, and I opened my eyes to get a look at the villains.

Watchers. Futureland's very own security revs. Wearing typical Watcher outfits—dark clothes, hats with low brims. You might even mistake them for regular park guests if you didn't know what to look for. That made it easier for them to do surveillance in all of Futureland. But what were they doing *here*?

My Watcher held me so tight I still couldn't turn around, but I heard multiple sets of footsteps crunching behind me, getting closer and closer. Within seconds, Mom, Dad, and Uncle Trey appeared in the clearing and stood in the middle of all of us.

"Cam. What on earth are you doing?" Mom asked. Her face tightened, stern. Her back-length locs were wrapped in a bright purple silk headwrap.

"Um, exploring?" I said, my voice muffled by the Watcher's hand still covering my mouth. Mom shook her head in disappointment. My heart tumbled. I snuck a glance at my friends, my skin prickly with embarrassment.

"Let them go," Uncle Trey barked at the Watchers. The park's security-revs turned us all loose and faded back into the woods surrounding the cylinder.

"You're pretty deep in the park," Uncle Trey said. "Got your friends out here, too. After closing. Gotta be more careful, kid."

"How many times have we told you, Cam—you can't just sneak around wherever you want. We had no idea where you were." She gulped. "Futureland is . . . It's different now. We have to be more careful."

"I—I don't know," I stammered. "I found this thing. I thought . . . I thought maybe Southmore—"

Mom sighed and walked over to me, kissed me on the forehead, and rubbed a smudge of dirt off my cheek. Dad joined us at her side, rubbing his bald head like he always did when he was stressed.

"Come on, Big Man. Let's head back to the condo. And y'all—" He turned to my crew. "Your parents have called us looking for you. It's time for y'all to get home, too."

I huddled with the crew. Sometimes when I stayed in the park too late with my friends, Mom and Dad would have to drive everyone home and apologize.

Other times Pierre, Rich's personal chauffer, would take everybody home and my parents would lecture me about safety and respect.

"Actually, Stacy," Uncle Trey said, "why don't y'all take the rest of the kids and I'll hang back with Cam for a bit. Want to talk to him about something."

Mom nodded, and she and Dad set off, shuffling my crew to the front of the park like a row of ducklings. I waved goodbye and my stomach tightened with the fear that maybe their parents wouldn't let them come back. All I wanted to do was keep my friends close. I closed my eyes and exhaled. Uncle Trey squeezed my shoulder.

"You okay?" he asked.

I shook my head. "I didn't *really* think it was Southmore, you know. We were just adventuring. . . ." I gulped. "What if my friends get in trouble?"

"It'll be okay," he said. "Your parents will smooth it out how they always do. I know it's hard. You used to have Dooley around twenty-four-seven. Now when your friends are gone, you're all alone. I know you want to keep them here as long as you can, but—"

"She was my best friend," I mumbled. "She saved Futureland, and it's not fair. Just because her code got a little messed up, she had to be taken offline."

Uncle Trey frowned and rubbed my shoulder again.

"I know, I know. I wish I could fix it. Wish there was something I could do to make it how it was before. But until we figure things out, you have to more careful, Cam. We're pretty sure the park is safe. But we still don't know how bad we were hacked. In the meantime, please just listen to your parents. Do what they say."

I frowned and crossed my arms. "There's so many rules now. Curfew. Can't go here, can't do that. Futureland used to belong to the whole family. You guys trusted me to handle anything in here. Now it's like this isn't even my home. It's like I'm . . . trapped here."

Uncle Trey took a deep breath. He opened his mouth to speak, but I don't think he could find the words. We stood in silence next to each other for a couple seconds before he changed the subject.

"Hey." He nudged me, pointing to the huge metal cylinder in front of us. I had almost forgotten it was there. "You wanna know what this is?"

"I thought I was in trouble. Supposed to go back to the condo," I grumbled.

"If that's what you want," he replied. "I mean, if you're not Futureland's number one kid-approved destiny tester anymore, then just say that."

My eyes widened. "This is a new destiny?! I knew it! I *knew* it was something special!" My chest swelled with pride.

11

Uncle Trey laughed. "Good hunch, kid. Those detective skills coming in strong. Now, let's hurry up before your parents start looking for us again." He extended his arm toward the metal building.

"The future awaits you."

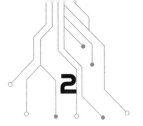

THE HOLO-PAL

Saturday, January 23, 2049
1:00 a.m.

All right," Uncle Trey said as we entered the building. "Close your eyes, and don't open them until I tell you to."

"Okay, sheesh! You're bossy like Mom," I joked.

"Nuh-uh. I'm the good twin. I'm nothing like your bigheaded momma," he said.

"Y'all got the same head, though," I replied.

"Hers bigger." We both laughed as Uncle Trey tied one of his pocket bandannas around my eyes and led me into the cylinder.

"Here we go, almost there," Uncle Trey said. He held my hand and guided me through the space. I didn't recognize the smell or any of the sounds inside. Uncle Trey's excitement coursed through me like static as we shuffled into the building, and my heart pattered with anticipation. Finally, we came to a stop.

"Here it is, Cam. Here it is."

I snatched the bandanna off and looked around eagerly. We had entered an empty room with a column of light beaming down from the ceiling, big enough for one person to stand in.

"Uhh, an empty room? Wow. This is what's been keeping you busy lately, huh? Working around the clock and having our chef-revs bring you all those peanut butter and blackberry jam sandwiches. Way to go, Uncle Trey." I snickered.

He rolled his eyes and chuckled. "Very funny. Oh, it's empty now, but it won't be empty for long!" Uncle Trey replied. "Go stand in the light."

I squinted, suspicious. "*You* go stand in the light."

"Ugh. Nephew, this isn't a prank! I'm serious."

Uncle Trey was a *known* prankster, and he had been on a winning streak ever since the police released him and he returned to life in the park. He had programmed the assistant-revs in my dad's lab to slap him on the butt every time my dad asked for them to "give him a hand." He had swapped out all of my mom's macro-wave instant coffee droplets with different nasty flavors. When my mom thought she was getting

14

a delicious coffee flavor, she got medicine instead. Or licorice. Or the worst: hot dog–flavored water. He wasn't going to get me.

"Nah, Unc. I'm sorry. You can't be trusted."

"Fine, look!" Uncle Trey walked over to the beam of light and stood directly underneath it. He twirled around and jumped up and down. Nothing happened.

At first.

After a few seconds of him jumping up and down, the column of light flickered and then a crackling sound shot through the air. The entire inside of the dome went dark. I couldn't see Uncle Trey. I couldn't even see my own hand in front of my face.

"Uncle Trey?" My heart raced. "Uncle Trey!"

The lights in the dome returned, including the undisturbed column of light covering Uncle Trey. He held his hands up to calm me down.

"It's okay, nephew. It's okay. Just a small power surge. This thing uses a lot of energy. I'm still working on that part. But everything is fine. Sorry for scaring you."

I exhaled deeply. "I'm okay. I just . . . every time something goes wrong I think . . . I just worry that—"

"That lightning is gonna strike the same place twice." Uncle Trey's face softened with empathy. "I know it's scary, Cam. But it's in the past. Not everything is a bad omen. Accidents happen."

I nodded, finally setting my breathing back to normal.

"See? It's perfectly safe." Uncle Trey pointed to the light beam. "Now, please. Come stand in the light. I worked really hard on this, and you're the first person I want to see it in action."

"Okay." I made my way over to the beam of light. Uncle Trey tapped some commands onto the hologram screen projecting out of his tablet, and the column started to rotate. It filled with shimmers of different colors, like a strobe light. The colors spun rapidly around for a few moments before slowing down. Then I heard a familiar voice.

"Body scan completed and subject recognized. Beginning Holo-pal process for 'Detective' Cameron Walker."

"Itza?!" I shouted, smiling.

The voice chuckled. "Mm-hmm. How's it going, Detective?"

I looked back at Uncle Trey. He smiled proudly at me. "I know we're closing down Bright Futures, but I just couldn't part with Itza. Everybody loves her."

I turned back around as the colors began to circle me faster and faster.

"Itza, what's happening?" I asked.

"We'll be all wrapped up in a second. Just be still, if you don't mind."

"Right, sorry."

"Doubling and extrapolation process completed. Beginning final step. Cameron Walker, what is your favorite animal?"

"Huh? Like, *animal*? I guess dogs are pretty cool."

"Think bigger!" Uncle Trey yelled from the back of the room.

I rubbed my chin and put my mind to work. Animals scrolled in my mind until I remembered the nature documentary that Angel and I had watched in science class last quarter.

"Sooo . . . I saw this TV show that was talking about caracals, these big cats with long, pointy ears that live on the other side of the world. They have super hearing and can jump ten feet high to catch food."

"That's perfect!" Uncle Trey shouted.

"Animal identified. Profile created. Please stand by as we produce your Holo-pal and their Holo-pet."

The column of light disappeared, leaving the room in darkness except for a few sparkling gems rotating around me. I felt Uncle Trey's hand on my shoulder as he guided me to step backward. The spots of color spun faster and faster, and a new column sprang down from the ceiling, so bright I had to shield my eyes. The floor beneath us began to rumble a bit, rattling the metal platform and making a loud clinking sound.

"That doesn't sound so good," Uncle Trey said. He stepped forward toward the platform, but a final rumble and big *BOOM* knocked him backward into me, and we both fell down. The new column of light and all the little gems disappeared. We scrambled over each other to stand in total darkness. The room started to light up, and when my eyes adjusted, I saw someone in front of me. Two someones.

A boy. And a cat. A *big* cat.

The boy was tall—a few inches taller than me. He had the beginnings of a mustache resting on his top lip. His hair was in locs just like mine, but his were longer, hanging down past his shoulders. He wore a pair of giant rainbow-tinted ski goggles set up on his forehead and a Futureland T-shirt. Skinny arms stretched out of his sleeves. I looked him in the eyes and noticed, just below the left one, a star-shaped birthmark. He smiled and winked at me.

"What's up, Cam?" he said.

I stepped face to face with him and put my palm up to his slightly larger palm. The biggest difference between us was his skin. It was purple. And swirly. Like a galaxy was spinning inside his see-through body. The caracal sitting next to him had the same hues on its coat, and it growled when I stepped up to the boy.

"Easy, girl," he said, soothing her, patting her on the head.

"Um . . . Uncle Trey . . . what is this?" I asked with a tremor in my voice.

"It's your Holo-pal." He beamed. "How do you like it?"

I couldn't break my gaze from the boy's eyes, which were a soft brown with creases in the corners. He stared at me and petted the caracal until its low growl turned into more of a purr.

"This," Uncle Trey began, "is our new attraction. Your mom *finally* let me come up with an idea for guests, after all these years. And, nephew, I think I've got me a good one with this. I think it's the one!"

"I just— Wh-what?" I stammered. "How?"

"How do they work? Good question! See, after the thing with Southmore, everybody wants to know about park security, right? Our guards aren't enough, our Watchers aren't enough, et cetera, et cetera. Plus, we have to close Bright Futures no matter what, which means we need a new attraction. So I had this idea— what if every kid gets a guide when they come to the park? Like the buddy system."

I nodded. I had to admit, it was an interesting idea.

Uncle Trey paced back and forth as he explained. "Only, what if the guide is *you*?" he continued. "A slightly older version of you. Who better to watch your back than someone who thinks and acts just like you? With a few intelligence mods by way of your mom's brilliance, of course. These holograms will travel around with park guests and help look out for them."

Uncle Trey kept going, growing more excited with every word.

"Everybody is going to get these new, special wristbands your mom has been working on—Futurelinks— that will project their holograms for them. As long as they wear them in the park, their buddy will be available. Looks like Itza didn't need to give you a new wristband, though." He examined my wrist. "The exhibit must be synced up to the data in your Futurewatch. Even though these Holo-pals don't have rev bodies, they can still interact with the environment in the destinies. Now, I'm not gonna lie, I threw Holo-pets in there for fun. But I—"

"He looks just like me," I interrupted in amazement.

"Huh?" Uncle Trey said. "Well, yeah! He *is* you. You'll probably look just like this when you grow a few more inches and get your first little peach fuzz. Minus the sparkly skin, of course. It's kinda like looking into a future mirror. Cool, right?"

"So cool." I stared at my Holo-pal in wonder.

"Speaking of the skin," he explained. "Had to make them so we could tell the difference between Holo-pals, human guests, and revs. Gave 'em some pretty gnarly colors. That was your dad's idea. Well, go ahead. Don't be shy. Meet him—er—yourself!"

Gulp. I looked up at the Holo-pal and waved, a little shy. "Hi, I'm Cam."

"Haha, of course you are, dude." He smiled down at me. "I'm Cam, too."

"Oh, snap," Uncle Trey said. "We should probably fix that. You should give him a nickname or something. That way nobody gets confused. I'll enter it into the system."

I surveyed my Holo-pal up and down, my eyes finally settling once more on his eyewear. "Nice goggles."

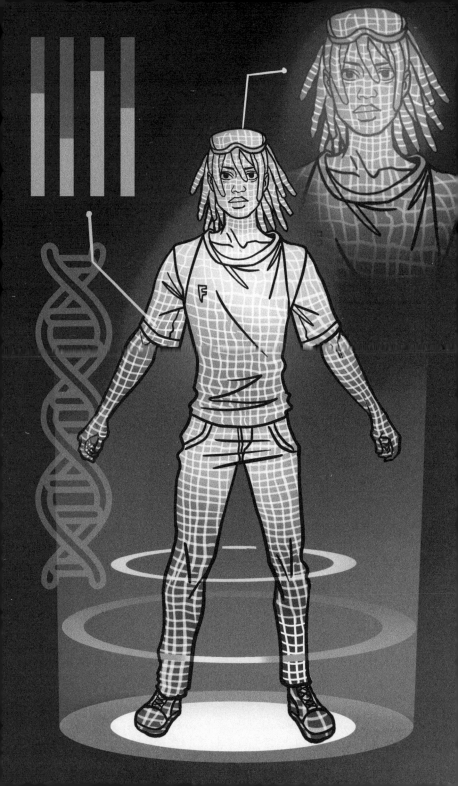

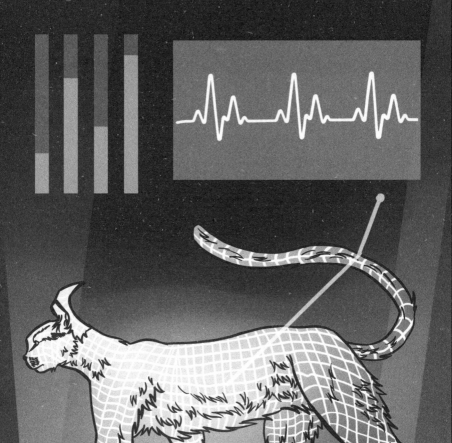

5'9"
5'4"

GOGGLES
140 LBS

CAM
100 LBS

"Huh?" He looked up as if he'd be able to see something on his forehead. He chuckled and moved his hands up to feel around for the protective shades, then grinned. "Sweet."

"'Goggles,' huh? I guess you get your creativity from your mom, not your dad, but that's fine. Whatever you want!" Uncle Trey said, logging the information in his tablet. "Done deal. All right, Itza. Terminate program."

Goggles and his pet caracal faded away, their shimmering exteriors scattering through the rest of the light in the room until they were gone.

"Wow, Uncle Trey." I raised my eyebrows, impressed. "This is going to be a hit."

He looked down at me and smiled, tenderness spreading across his expression. "You really think so? I worked so hard on it. You really like it? Like, really?"

"Really," I said. "Why the big secret, though? Why hide it back here in the park wilderness?"

"Ugh!" He threw his hands up in annoyance. "Your parents didn't want me showing you the new tech until all the bug fixes got approved and implemented. They're still being extra sensitive about *everything* in here. I think they're scared something will happen to you."

My heart dropped at the thought of my parents keeping me out of Futureland developments, even if it was for my own safety. I had always helped. Always.

"I keep telling them we've got to keep you involved in everything or this park won't stand a chance," Uncle Trey continued. "But the Holo-pals and Holo-pets are just about ready for public use. I had to get my nephew in on the surprise. Let's just keep it our little secret for now." He stroked his beard and smirked.

"Thanks, Unc." We hugged. He gripped me tight and picked me up off the ground, squeezing me until I could only use a small amount of breath to laugh.

"Okay, okay! Too tight! Too tight!"

Uncle Trey laughed and put me back down. We turned to leave the secret chamber housing Futureland's next great attraction. But before we made it to the door, he stopped, put his hand on my shoulder, and stooped down to eye level with me.

"Look here, nephew," he started. "I . . . I want to thank you. I couldn't have come up with this idea without you. Your imagination inspires me. Keeps me young. I hope you don't mind, but . . . I overheard your parents talking about Dooley and—"

The sound of her name made me wince. I put my eyes to the floor and began to fidget.

"I heard them say that you didn't want another rev companion. Maybe it's too soon. Maybe forever is too soon. But whatever you decide—"

Uncle Trey grabbed my chin and lifted it up, locking our gazes once again.

"Whatever you decide, I support you. Everybody handles grief differently, and there's no right or wrong way. Losing a friend is the hardest thing in the world. All we can do is honor their memory and live our lives in ways we know would make them proud. But you still need somebody to watch your back. And *that's* why I came up with the Holo-pal. I'm gonna keep thinking of ways to honor Dooley, no matter what. But if you end up wanting somebody to talk to, or hang with, or anything—then you got Goggles and that scary-looking cat. And, well, haha, you got your old uncle, too. But that's already understood."

I couldn't stop the tears from rolling down my face. Uncle Trey stood up and pulled me into him. I muffled my sobs up against his chest, soaking his Eastside High T-shirt that still fit after all these years. He rubbed my back and held me tight until I calmed down. I wiped my eyes and looked up at him.

"Thank you, Uncle Trey."

It was great having him around again. He waved me off with a grin, massaged the back of my neck with a big, strong hand.

"Naw, nephew. Thank *you*."

3

RESEARCH

Sunday, January 24, 2049
6:00 p.m.

Today's adventure? Testing the new, motion-controlled Jet-Blur pods. My parents made a special suit that lets the pods follow the movement of your body. A sleek black second skin with shiny metallic gold threaded into it. A nifty Futureland emblem right in the center of the chest. With my Future-vision goggles on, I felt like a new kind of explorer.

A kind the world had never seen.

I leaned to the left and the pod did the same, barely dodging one of the jagged cliffs under Future Falls before zipping directly under the crash of water. When I straightened my body and lowered my hands, the pod smoothly dropped down to skim the water's surface. It left a spraying stream behind, like a Jet Ski. I smiled and waved to the koi-revs and eel-revs at the bottom of the falls. Then I leaned back and raised my arms, sending the pod straight up into the air at lightning speed.

Fastest Jet-Blur pods ever? Maybe. Probably. Definitely.

I gently landed the pod at the top of the falls, removed my goggles, and hopped out. Even after everything, Futureland hadn't lost any of its beauty. Not to me, anyway. From the bluff of Future Falls, with the calming sound of rushing water filling my ears, I could see rev-birds soaring and hundreds of flowers blooming. I could feel the breeze in my hair and the sun on my skin. I loved it here. I couldn't help but think Dooley would've loved it, too.

I closed my eyes.

This was my happy place.

Deet deet deet da-deet-deet da-deet.

Well . . . it *had been* my happy place. Ugh.

Deet deet deet da-deet-deet da-deet!

I walked back over to the Jet-Blur pod and fished around for my Futurewatch. The watch kept *deet-deet*ing until I found it, and all the while, I was hoping that maybe it was Uncle Trey, or Dad, or even Grandma Ava calling. But when I grabbed the watch and slapped it on my wrist, Mom's hologram face started to come into view.

"Hi, Cam-Cam," she said, with a soft voice and a softer expression.

"Hey, Mom," I mumbled. I wrung my hands as a spiral of butterflies fluttered in my stomach.

"You all right out there?" she asked hurriedly. "Are you safe? Do you have a rev with you?"

I sighed. "Yeah, everything is fine. Just . . . uh . . . just . . ."

I stumbled over my words. I wanted to tell her how I really felt, but I couldn't.

"I'm good," I said. "Just testing out the new motion-control suit for the Jet-Blur pod."

"Oh, neat." Mom exhaled. "How is the suit?"

"A little tight." I scratched my head and avoided her gaze.

"Got it," she said. "I can adjust it. Should probably put a tracker in it, just to be safe. So we can always know where you are." A few seconds of awkward silence passed between us.

My parents had become so overbearing since we defeated Southmore. They got more strict, more paranoid, and rushed all the time. I knew it was their way of trying to keep me safe, but I didn't like it. I felt farther from them than when they were actually gone— you know, that time they got replaced by replica revs as a part of Southmore's evil plan.

30

"Well, anyway . . . ," Mom started. "Your friends have been calling. They said they couldn't get you on your watch. So they called the condo . . . twenty-three times. I think you should probably call them back."

I sighed. "Yeah, okay. Sorry. I'll give them a call. Thanks, Mom."

"Cam?" she said before the transmission ended. "It's going to get dark soon. You need to be inside the park by the time the streetlights come on."

"But, Mom, I'm supposed to get pizza with the crew. It's fine. I'll keep my locator on and——"

"No buts, Cam," she said. "I'm serious. We've got to keep you safe."

I sighed. "Okay."

Her face disappeared from the hologram, and I rushed back to the pod. I had my regular clothes in the back, so I activated the pod's stealth mode to change clothes. When I got to the Guest Hub, I left the pod and practically leaped into the zero-gravity beam, floating down to the ground. I put one foot over the other as fast as they could move toward the gate surrounding Centennial Olympic Park. I spoke into my watch.

"This is Skyboy, en route to cheesy pepperoni deliciousness. Estimated time of arrival on foot? Eh, maybe ten minutes. Sorry I'm late."

"Let's get a round of applause for this guy!" Rich shouted as I made my way into Pizza Mania, our favorite place with the most delectable pizza in town. In a few short months, it had become the crew's official meetup spot. Rich, Angel, Yusuf, and Earl were already in a booth with one mostly eaten pizza, clapping sarcastically as I walked through the door.

"What's with you? You don't wear your Futurewatch anymore?" Rich held up his wrist, displaying the Futurewatch I had given him and all my other friends so we could always stay in touch. I stopped right in front of him and held up my wrist, showing my watch.

"I got it. I was just busy for a little while. Relax, Christopher."

"Don't call me that!" Rich growled. Everybody laughed.

I slid into the booth next to Angel and Yusuf and gave them hugs, then fist-bumped Earl and Rich across the table.

"We saved you some pizza," Earl said between chews.

I eyed the remaining pizza on the tray and raised my eyebrow at Earl. "Barely."

"There's another one coming." Angel laughed.

Right on cue, a rev with sandy-brown hair and thick eyebrows brought out a hot, fresh cheese pizza. Uncle Trey had donated the rev to Ms. Madison, Pizza Mania's owner, who'd been running the place for over thirty years. She waved from behind the counter, the glare from the bright lights reflecting off her thick glasses.

"Here you go, Cam," the rev said, the rims of its eyes glowing orange. "This one's on the house." They smiled before turning away.

"Thanks!" I knew it was going to burn my tongue, and I didn't even care. I grabbed a slice and started chomping away, sucking in air between bites to balance out the heat.

"Sooo . . . ," Angel said, raising her eyebrows.

"Huh?" I huffed through pizza-mouth.

"Stop playing around, CJ!" Yusuf laughed. "Why'd you call us here? Is there another mission? Another mystery we need to solve?" He eyed me eagerly.

"Thankfully not," I said. "I just wanted to see you guys. Hang out. Talk about something normal."

Yusuf's shoulders sank.

"We were just discussing plans for the research field trip," Earl said.

"Research field trip? What's that?" I asked.

Angel shook her head. "You don't read your syllabi, do you?" I shrugged and chewed.

"Eastside Middle makes students do a group research trip ever year," Rich said. "You're supposed to go somewhere interesting and write down your observations. Explore a new environment and compare it to your home. You know, boring school stuff."

"The best part is that you get to choose your own groups for it," Yusuf said.

"It's due at the end of February, right before spring break," Angel said.

"This sounds pretty cool," I said, thinking of all the places I had traveled before arriving in Atlanta. How cool would it be to write about Thailand, or Greece, or Norway?

"Yeah, but we can't agree on where we should go." Angel frowned. "Wherever it is, we want to do something together. What are our options again, Earl?"

Earl looked down at a grease-stained piece of paper. "Yusuf wants us to go to Macon, Georgia, to visit the Georgia Sports Hall of Fame. He said he had a blast last time he went there."

"Won't work," Rich said. "I've already been. And

34

it says in the syllabus that only one group member is allowed to have already visited the destination before."

"Rich said we can come with him to Lake Lanier on his mom's boat," Earl added.

"No way," Angel said. "That place is haunted. That's why none of us have ever gone."

"It's not that bad!" Rich protested.

"And me," Earl chimed in. "Well, I think we should go to Memphis."

Everyone paused, looking confused.

"What? I heard they have great barbecue."

Angel rolled her eyes. "Anyway, as you can see, CJ, we're really struggling. Do you have any ideas?"

"Hmm." I thought hard for a second. Maybe I could get my parents to take us somewhere. But then again, they were always so busy with the park. They probably wouldn't even have time. And I didn't know Georgia well enough to offer any suggestions. I frowned and shrugged. "I'm sorry. I don't really know."

"What? Aw, come on, man," Yusuf said. "You've been to so many cool places. There's gotta be some mysteries and adventures somewhere. We could go solve one together."

I narrowed my eyes at Yusuf. That was the second time that day he had talked about coming with me to solve a mystery. Yusuf was busier than all of us between volunteering at the mosque, basketball, and helping care for his siblings. Did he even have time to solve cases?

"Nobody wants to be solving mysteries all the time," Angel said. "No offense, CJ."

"None taken."

"This trip is for *learning*. We can't get distracted. But anyway, just keep thinking, CJ. After everything that happened the last few months, we could all use a fun trip. Maybe we can even go to a beach. Get some rest and relaxation. Get in touch with la tierra."

"Angel's right, CJ," Rich said. "You came to Atlanta in August. It's been almost five months and you already had your parents stolen away from you and replaced with revs, lost your uncle for a little while, got the technology in your park hacked . . ."

"Had to rescue multiple missing kids from an evil millionaire," Angel said.

"And stop his plan to use your mom and dad's inventions to create some kinda weird fancy city," Earl said.

"On top of all that, you had to adjust to going to public school for the first time," Yusuf said. "And dealing with all that homework Ms. Patel likes to give in math class." He shook his head.

"Yeah," I said, taking in the weight of it all. "And I lost my best friend."

Everyone got quiet. Angel put a gentle hand on my back. The crew was right. When you started to count it up, it was a lot. Ever since we'd come to Atlanta, thing after thing after thing had gone wrong. In fact, only one thing went right from the beginning—meeting my friends, the crew. I felt lucky to have them.

"If you ever need to talk, we're always here for you," Yusuf said. Everybody around the table agreed.

"Thanks, y'all. I think the research trip sounds like a great idea for all of us," I said. "I'll think about it some more and talk to my parents."

"Sounds great," Angel said. "But hurry up and ask them. We only have about a month."

"Now that's what I'm talking about!" Rich said. "We *almost* have a plan. Time to celebrate. Hey, Ms. Madison! Can we get another order of pizza? Put this one on Cam's tab!"

Deet deet deet da-deet-deet da-deet.

Ugh!

I grunted in frustration and looked out the window of Pizza Mania. It wasn't even sundown yet. I lifted my watch to ignore my mom's call, but I realized that it wasn't my watch beeping at all. I looked across the table and noticed Yusuf fiddling with his wrist.

"Yusuf . . . is that your Futurewatch?" I asked. "Who else could be calling it? All of us are here. . . ."

"Doesn't look like a Futurewatch to me." Earl craned to get a good look.

Yusuf rose from the booth so swiftly and powerfully he almost toppled our water cups. Like something mechanical sprang him out of his seat.

"This is, um . . ." He hesitated. "It's a— Never mind. I gotta go. See y'all later."

We all watched, confused, as Yusuf hustled out of the booth toward the Pizza Mania exit.

"You got basketball?" Rich yelled after him.

"Yeah . . . basketball." Yusuf barely turned his head before bounding out of the restaurant. I watched him cross the street and break into a full sprint westward.

Away from Eastside Middle—the opposite direction of the basketball gym.

NEXT STOP, NEW YORK

Monday, January 25, 2049
6:00 p.m.

W hew, Cameron, baby. Let's sit on down on that bench right there for a while. Grandma is tired." Grandma Ava hobbled over to the park bench and plopped down. I sat next to her and put my head on her shoulder. She fished some birdseed out of her purse and started to scatter it for the ducks walking around us.

"I ain't givin' these birds none of my good bread, shoot," she said. I chuckled.

Since Futureland was closed for operations on Mondays and our lives were mostly back to normal, I spent every Monday after school at Grandma Ava's house. It had quickly turned into one of my favorite things about living in Atlanta. Getting to know her, hearing her old stories about my mom and Uncle Trey, and even about things she didn't fully remember. She told funny jokes and made delicious baked goods. I loved her.

"So, Mr. Man, how are things in your world? What you feeling these days?"

"Well, things are mostly okay," I started. "But not how they used to be. Been spending a lot of time with Uncle Trey. He makes me laugh. But my parents . . . they're so worried all the time. Barely want to let me walk around Futureland alone. They don't include me in all the new developments anymore. It doesn't even seem like they're having fun."

Grandma Ava shook her head. "What y'all went through as a family was traumatic, baby. They acting the way they acting because they want to protect you. Your face and name have been all over the news. That could make you a target for anybody wanting to do you some harm. The more you know, the more power you have. And I'm willing to bet it's still some people out there want to take that power."

I hung my head. "Yeah, I know. I guess I just wish I could change things."

"Things change us more than we change them," Grandma Ava said. "But we *can* move forward with our head high. Now, tell me about something *good* that's been going on."

I smiled. "Well, the crew was teaching me about some kinda research trip group project that the school does. We're trying to plan where we want to go. Still figuring it out, though."

"That sounds nice," she said. "How y'all going to manage that with you so far away?"

"Huh?"

"You know. When you leave? Will your friends come to you, or will you come back to Georgia and travel somewhere with them?"

"Grandma! Quit playing around. What are you talking about? Leaving?" My pulse started to race, and my stomach felt queasy.

Grandma Ava's eyes widened to twice their usual size. "Oh, baby. They haven't told you? Goodness gracious. Me and my big mouth . . ."

"Who? Told me what?!"

Grandma tossed the rest of the birdseed to the swarming ducks and stood, grabbing my hand. "Let's go home and call your parents. It's almost dinnertime. We need to have a family discussion."

"Cam." My dad palmed the top of his shiny, bald head nervously. "There's really no easy way to say this. . . ."

"We wanted to tell you sooner. We were just working out exactly how," Mom added.

Grandma Ava scoffed from the corner. She reclined in her sofa chair, quietly knitting. My heart pounded as I waited for my parents' next words. I already knew what was coming. But I wanted, more than anything, for it not to be true.

"We've got to leave Atlanta," Dad said.

My heart tumbled all the way into my gut. "This isn't fair." I clenched my teeth and crossed my arms. I could feel a tiny vein in my forehead throbbing. "You said . . . you said I could stay the whole school year. We just got here. I *just* made friends."

Dad dropped his head in shame. Mom stepped in.

"I know, Cam-Cam. You're right. But that was before . . . everything. Our reputation here is shaky now. People are canceling their Future Passes. . . . There are lawsuits—"

"Heyyy, family! What's up? What's with the long faces?" Uncle Trey burst through the door carrying two big tubs of ice cream at the worst possible time.

"We just told Cam the news," Dad said.

Uncle Trey set the ice cream down and held his arms limp at his sides. "Oh. Right. Sorry, nephew."

"You knew, too?!" I hollered.

His eyes darted between my mother and father. "Wasn't my place to say, kiddo."

"I can't believe this!" I pushed back from the table, standing in front of my parents. "You told me we would stay! How I needed to get used to being on the ground and have a life outside Futureland. I finally started to fit in and now we just have to leave? We didn't do anything bad. We saved Futureland! We saved the city! Why do we have to go?!"

My mom came around the table and tried to wrap me in a hug, but I shied away. She crossed her arms and leaned down, face to face with me.

"Cam, I know this is hard to understand. It's not fair. But it's what has to happen. Our job as parents is to make the best choices for the entire family. We didn't plan it this way. But the decision is final."

I crossed my arms, too. "Fine," I spat. I stood up and brushed past Mom. "May I be excused? I need some fresh air." I started walking toward the front door, not even waiting for permission.

"Cameron, wait!" I heard Grandma Ava's voice but kept going. I flung the door open and stared right into the abdomen of a tall person. They wore brown pants, heavy black boots . . . and a white lab coat. I slowly raised my eyes to see their face and saw . . . him.

Woody. The rogue lab assistant rev who had been missing ever since we defeated Southmore in the park. His tufts of reddish hair, his freckles and thick glasses. He sneered at me.

I screamed and stumbled backward into the house once again. Uncle Trey and Dad rushed to the door to confront Woody while Mom dove for me. Grandma Ava rose from her chair.

"Cameron! What on earth is going on with you?" she asked.

I uncovered my eyes and looked toward the door, where Uncle Trey had the lab assistant snatched up by the collar. I looked at his face and realized it wasn't Woody at all. He wasn't even a rev. He was a regular man who probably worked in a regular lab. He whimpered, holding his arms up to shield himself, a white paper bag clutched in his left hand.

"I thought . . . I thought it was Woody," I rasped. "I thought Woody came back to get me."

Grandma Ava stomped over to the door and smacked Uncle Trey's hands off the man. He straightened up his shirt, took a deep breath, and handed my grandma the bag.

"This ain't no Woody. This is Jonathan. He work at the pharmacy. Coming to deliver my medication." She turned to Jonathan. "I'm so sorry, young man. My grandson just got confused. Can I offer you anything before you go? A cold drink?"

"Uh, n-no, ma'am," he stammered. "I've had enough chills for tonight. Sorry for the disturbance."

Jonathan hustled off the porch, back to his car parked on the street, and drove away. Uncle Trey closed the door behind him, and the room grew silent between all of us.

"I think we've all had enough chills for tonight," Dad said. "Momma Ava, Stacy and I will stay here with Cam tonight, if you'll have us. We can finish this discussion in the morning."

I stuck my fork into some kind of mystery meat nugget and maneuvered it around my lunch tray. My body and soul felt heavy, words piling up inside me that I knew I'd have to say eventually. But I didn't know how.

"Cameron, my dear, you've hardly touched your meatloaf surprise." Rich nudged me and laughed. I

gave him a dry half smile back and kept toying with the unidentified substance.

"Uh-oh," Earl said. "Those are CJ's bad-news shoulders."

Rich's eyes got wide. "You're right. I should have noticed before. Definitely bad-news shoulders."

"I do not have bad-news shoulders!" I protested.

"Yeah, you kinda do," Angel chimed in.

"What's going on, CJ?" Yusuf said.

I took a deep breath and sighed. "I have something to tell y'all. When I found out, you were the first ones I wanted to call, but I couldn't get my words together. Still can't."

"You can't come on our research trip?" Angel said.

"No, no. Well . . . yeah, kinda. It's just—"

"Look, Cameron Jabari Walker," Rich started. "We're your friends. You can tell us anything. It doesn't have to be pretty. It just has to be real. Whatever it is, we'll face it together."

I looked around at the group, everyone beaming at me with earnest support. I smiled weakly, swallowed a hunk of meatloaf surprise, and set my fork down. I leaned back and dropped my shoulders.

"Ugh. Okay. I don't know any other way to say this, so I guess I've just got to be honest. Here goes." I took a deep breath. "I found out last night that . . . well . . .

I'm going have to do virtual learning the rest of the year."

Come on, Cam! That's not the whole story. Say what you wanna say!

"Oh," Earl said. "Because of, like, the park and stuff? Gonna be busy, huh?"

"Well, no—"

"That's sorta a sweet deal," Rich said. "I wish I could do virtual school. More like video game marathon. Heh-heh!"

The whole crew started buzzing with ideas about the half-truth of my situation. Except Yusuf. He looked at me intently, seeing the fear of the secret in my eyes.

"You're moving, aren't you?" he said softly. "Eastside lets students do virtual school if they move away in the middle of the school year." The group's chatter died down to silence. Everyone turned to look at me, confused.

"Yes. I'm moving." I said the horrible truth and clamped my eyes shut so I didn't have to face my friends' expressions. "Me and my parents and my uncle. We're leaving again. Going to New York." After a second, I opened one eye, slowly, to a squint. Angel, Earl, and Rich stared at me with blank faces.

Then they burst out laughing.

"You're a trip, CJ!" Angel hollered, holding her stomach.

"You know how when somebody is so *not* funny that they become hilarious?" Rich said. "That's you! Man, the way you said that!" He imitated a nasally voice that sounded *nothing* like me: " 'I'm moving.' Oh, man. Comedy!"

"That's *not* how I sound," I told Rich.

Earl stared at me, and his expression flattened. "You're not joking, are you, Cameron?" he asked.

I shook my head.

Angel and Rich calmed down for half a second, and then the frenzy started. The part I'd been afraid of since the very beginning.

Leaving? Why? You just got here!

This is terrible!

You told us you'd be here all school year!

This isn't fair. Why can't you stay?

My friends said all the things I'd said to my parents since I learned their plan. I explained it to the crew the same way they'd explained it to me: Futureland was okay, for now, but the whole ordeal with Southmore had really done a number on our reputation. There was some kind of public relations company in New York that had agreed to help my parents restore people's

48

faith in the park. It was in our best interest to go and work closely with them until Futureland was back in everyone's good graces.

My parents knew it wasn't fair for me to have to leave school after promising I would stay for the whole year, so they applied for virtual learning permission with Eastside. Above all else, Mom and Dad had made it very clear that staying in Atlanta was *not* an option. At least not right now. Too much had changed.

Walker Way of Living #10: Always keep it moving.

A sad kind of quiet fell over our whole crew. Suddenly, nobody was very eager to eat the rest of Eastside Middle's infamously bad lunch.

"Well, this stinks," Rich said. "Can we throw some kind of going away party, at least? When do you leave?"

That was the part I *reaaaally* didn't want to talk about.

I sighed. "That's the thing. We're supposed to leave soon. Like really soon."

Yusuf leaned in, listening.

"How soon?" Angel asked.

"I don't know exactly, but they're in a rush. They say the faster we get to New York, the faster we can fix everything with the park . . . and hopefully get back to normal."

"Tuh. Guess I actually have to do my share of the research project now." Rich rolled his eyes.

"None of us have ever been to New York, but I still wish we could come with you, CJ," Earl said. "Live inside Futureland and never go to school and forget all our worries."

"Wouldn't that be something." Yusuf's eyes glazed over in a daydream.

I took in Earl's words. There was a time when my life looked exactly how he described, and I was happy. But that's not the life I wanted anymore. I wanted this one. On the ground. In Atlanta, with my friends. I pushed my tray away from me, folded my arms on the table, and plopped my head down.

"Yeah, Earl, if only. If only."

A PARTING GIFT

VOICE TWO: Master! Master! There's been a development.

VOICE ONE: What is it?

VOICE TWO: The Walkers. Our tracking bugs show that they're preparing to set off from Atlanta. Their course is charted northeast. It appears that they are headed to New York City.

VOICE ONE: Are you serious? Don't joke around with me.

VOICE TWO: Joking isn't a part of my code, master.

VOICE ONE: Ha! How perfect. The Walkers have no idea what they've gotten themselves into. This will be even easier than I thought. They're flying right into our trap.

VOICE TWO: I can't wait to crush them.

VOICE ONE: Not too hasty. We've got to be smart about this. We can't have any mistakes like last time. Make the call. The Walkers are going down.

VOICE TWO: Yes, master.

VOICE ONE: Get on that computer and do what you have to do. Wouldn't want them to leave Atlanta without *a parting gift*, now would we?

VOICE TWO: No, master. I'll take care of it.

SOARING

Monday, February 1, 2049
6:32 a.m.

I was running, bounding through the darkness, piercing orange eyes all around me, watching. No matter how far up I climbed in the sky-high Wonder Worlds tower, I could never reach the top. Whispers of my name, hundreds of them, hissed so loudly they drowned out my thoughts. My ears got stuffy and my vision went blurry, but not too blurry to see the creepy rev with the heavy boots and stained lab coat.

Woody, my mom's former lab assistant.

He grabbed me by the neck. He was much stronger than I was—than I could ever be. I clawed at his hand, but he just squeezed tighter, and tighter, and tighter. Dooley appeared, clutched in his other hand as he held us over the tower ledge. I tried to scream for her, but no sound came out. I kicked and thrashed, but it was no use. Woody sneered and tossed Dooley over the ledge with an evil smile, like she was nothing more than a puppet. Tears rolled down my face. My lungs—they were full. I couldn't hold in the scream any longer. Soon, I would implode.

"AHH!"

I awakened with a start, scrambling to sit up in my bed while I gasped for air. A dark figure crouched at the edge of my bed with a hand on my leg. I yelled again and grabbed one of Dooley's purple sneakers from its resting place on my nightstand, chucking it at the shadow that was trying to steal me away in the night.

"Ow! Cam, it's me!"

I tapped the light switch on my comms box and illuminated the room. Dad stood at the foot of my bed, rubbing a steadily growing knot on his forehead from where the sneaker made impact. Mom rushed into my room and stood next to him, tightening her robe and straightening her satin bonnet down over her long locs.

"Is everything all right?" she said. "I heard screams."

"One was his, one was mine. Boy's got an arm on him," Dad said.

I breathed a sigh. I had been having the same nightmare ever since I lost Dooley. Every few nights around the same time, deep into my slumber. I'd always wake up around the same hour, with the moon high and the condo dark and quiet. "Sorry, Dad."

"That's all right. I didn't mean to startle you. I wanted to wake you up a little early. Got something to show you."

I slipped on my fuzzy house shoes and shuffled out of the room behind my dad. Mom went back to bed. Dad led me up to the stairs to the observatory, an area between the condo and the park where you could look out and get a 360-degree view of the world below, as far as the eye could see.

"Need these?" he asked, offering me a pair of Future-vision goggles. I shook my head and pulled my own special pair out of my robe pocket—the same ones Dooley had altered for me months ago, with advanced features—and slipped them on. I hardly ever left my room without them.

"Down there, those are the Great Smoky Mountains. We're flying over Tennessee and North Carolina now. Can't beat this sunrise. Beautiful, isn't it?"

I looked out on the mountains—miles and miles of green hills dusted lightly with snow. Some splashes of color left over from autumn made the scene look like a painting.

"Yeah," I grumbled, twiddling my thumbs. A week

earlier, I had adopted a rigid scowl that I was determined to preserve for as long as possible. But inside, my heart ached.

Dad tried another angle. "Did you have a good last week in Atlanta?"

I scrunched up my face. "All I could think about was the moment I would have to leave."

Dad sighed. "You're still mad at us?" he asked.

"I don't know, Dad." I exhaled all the air inside of me. "I don't know how I feel. I'm mad because everything is changing. You and Mom act different now. Like you want to put me in a bubble and shield me from life. I finally made friends and I don't even get to keep them. I'm tired. It just feels like nothing is going right for me."

Dad nodded, quiet for a moment. "You know, I keep having nightmares, too," he said.

"About what?" I asked.

"Losing you, Cameron. I've never been so scared in my life as I was when Southmore forced Dooley to abduct us. Before our brains got scrambled and my memory got fuzzy, all I could think about was you, and how we wouldn't be able to keep you safe."

"But I *was* safe. We solved the mystery, and everything ended up fine—"

"Just because you survived doesn't mean you were safe, Cam. And it's not your job to solve mysteries that dangerous. I know you have a dream . . . but you're only a kid. My kid."

I looked at my dad. He took off his Future-vision goggles to wipe at his eyes with his sleeve. My heart softened.

"I think this whole detective thing is great, I do. I support you. But it's not your *job*. Not yet. You're a kid, Cam. Your job is to be a kid. To have fun. To learn and grow and not have to worry about the worst parts of the world. You understand?"

I nodded.

"I'm your dad. My job is to make sure you feel loved. To help you become the person you want to be. And most importantly, to keep you safe. When we got stolen . . . I couldn't do my job, Cam. And I can't let that happen again. Me and your mom will do whatever it takes to keep you safe. That's what matters most to us. That's something we can't fail at again."

I stewed on my dad's words for a moment, my thoughts swimming and twirling like a school of fish. I trusted Dad, but I didn't feel any less sad about leaving.

"If my job is to be a kid, then why aren't I having fun?" I asked. "Why don't I feel happy?" I wrung my hands as I looked out at the fog rolling over the mountaintops.

Dad sighed. "Because things are hard. But I need

you to trust me. I'm sorry all this has been so rough on you. You don't deserve it. But sometimes, I have to make the decision that nobody is happy with right now so that everything can be better later."

I frowned. "I don't understand, Dad."

He looked over to me and smiled gently, put his arm around me, and rubbed my shoulder. We both looked out over the forever-stretching mountain range as the park continued to soar.

"I know, son. But you will. You will. Just trust me until then."

We stayed in the observatory for a while, watching the landscape change in silence. When we got to Washington, DC, we flew low enough for Dad to point out the museums, the monuments, even the home he lived in as a kid. Then the sun rose above the hills, a deep orange glow brightening the horizon.

I wanted to believe all the things Dad said about making the right decisions to protect me and our family. I tried to think positively as the warm sun on my face relaxed me back to sleep.

But as soon as I closed my eyes, I was running, bounding through the darkness, piercing orange eyes all around me, watching. My ears got stuffy and my vision went blurry as the creepy rev with the heavy boots and stained lab coat grabbed me by the neck again.

Buzzcorp, Inc.

Creating buzz about your business!

Futureland Public Relations Plan:

In order to fix the image and reputation of Futureland, we recommend a combination of the following strategies:

- Temporarily relocate park for a fresh start; somewhere Futureland is already known and loved.

- Launch a new and exciting destiny for visitors to experience.

- Invite visitors to free, family-oriented events inside the park.

- Design a social media campaign to show how kind and thoughtful the Walkers really are.

- Consider coordinating a giveaway. Something technology related. Wearable devices are very popular these days.

6

REUNION

Monday, February 1, 2049
9:14 a.m.

Honk! Honk! Honk, honk, honk!
Bwoop! Bwoop! Bwooooooop!

Ayo, what's that?! It's mad big! It's like an alien ship or something.

Come on, bro. You the last one in the city who never seen Futureland?

Ughhhh. New York was always so loud, especially in the mornings.

Wait—New York? We had arrived!

I rolled over and checked the time on my comm-box. 9:14 a.m. Dad must have carried me back to bed after I fell asleep in the observatory. I put my pillow over my face, but I knew better. I *never* went back to sleep once I woke up in New York City. There was just too much life outside, too much adventure . . . and even if I didn't like admitting it—too much fun.

I hopped out of bed and slunk over to the window. I stared down at the ground and all the people gathering to marvel at Futureland or pausing to take a look on their way to work. Kids, elders, adults—it didn't matter. The world's most magnificent theme park captivated everyone's attention. From my window, I noticed a lady in a bright red coat with bright red hair looking straight up at the park. But she wasn't taking pictures or pointing like most folks.

She was staring. Right at me.

At least, that's what it felt like. But that was impossible. Nobody could see inside Futureland from the outside without Future-vision goggles. I grabbed mine off the desk to get a closer look at her. She held her gaze, piercing green eyes facing straight up toward the condo portion of the park. I moved to the side a bit to see if she angled her head. She remained still. But her mouth curled up slightly in a devious smirk. My blood ran cold.

"What are you looking at?" I said under my breath.

Just then, the lady turned on her heel and walked away like nothing had happened.

Maybe it's all in your mind, Cam. You're only half awake.

New York was our new start. Everything would be fine. I just had to trust and be patient. Like Dad said. I wiped the sleep from my eyes, yawned, and made my way into the kitchen.

Alejandro and Aurielle, our chef-revs, had left me a breakfast plate on the warmer. An egg and cheese croissant sandwich with orange juice and fresh fruit. My parents and Uncle Trey were probably already on the ground starting their full day of meetings with the public relations people. Before Atlanta, Mondays had meant a whole day for me to help in the park. But now I'd have to do virtual school until the end of the day, and then see what was left to help with in the evening. Maybe I'd at least get to see my friends on camera.

I carried my plate back to my room and put on some music. I took a bite of my croissant sandwich before putting the plate on the bed, twirling around, kicking out my legs, and waving my arms to the groove. Angel had been teaching me some dance moves before I left Atlanta. I was determined to master a few of them. Maybe my parents would even let me visit for Eastside Middle School's spring dance.

I swallowed a bite of my sandwich, turning back around to reach for the rest, pausing when I looked at my plate. Some of my fruit was missing.

Or was it?

I thought I had more fruit than this when I left the kitchen. Maybe I was still groggy from an early and unexpected wake up. I drank down most of the orange juice and kept dancing for a little while, but when I turned again to eat more of the sandwich, I froze.

Somebody had taken a bite out of my croissant sandwich. A *big* bite.

"Music off," I called out. I stood still in the room, trying to listen for anything moving.

Hey! Be careful with that thing!

"Yusuf!" I yelled. He tousled my hair. It had only been a week since I had seen him, and it already felt like he was a couple inches taller. Those basketball kids, jeez.

"What are you— How are you—" I stopped to gather my breath. "What is going on, man?"

Yusuf sighed, scratching his head nervously. "Okay, look. I know it's going to sound ridiculous, but . . ." He started to pace back and forth in the room, then stopped. "Wait—are we the only ones here?"

I nodded. "My parents are on the ground all day for meetings."

"Good, good. Okay. So . . . I snuck into the park."

"Obviously. But why? And *how*?"

"It wasn't hard, I just had to time it right. My Futurewatch still has the extra park privileges you installed while we were investigating Southmore. After you told us your parents were making you leave, I made my decision. I came into the park one night and stayed after closing, like we do when we explore. I would have stayed hidden longer. But I got hungry."

We both looked at the empty plate.

66

"There's plenty of food here," I said. "We can keep you fed until we get you home. I should probably un-install those privileges, too. Thanks for reminding me."

Yusuf's eyes bulged. He rushed over to me and grabbed my hands. "Home? Please, CJ. I can't go home. I'm supposed to be here!"

"But, Yusuf . . . that's outrageous! What about your family? The mosque? Basketball?"

"I'll be going to the mosque and playing basketball for the rest of my life," he said. "But when will I ever have another chance to go to *New York City*? The city of dreams. I love solving mysteries with you. When you told us you were leaving, this little voice in my mind kept telling me I *had* to come with you, no mat-ter what. I couldn't just let you leave Atlanta without somebody to watch your back."

A bad feeling crept up into my brain from the pit of my stomach. Something wasn't right. I frowned. "I don't know, Yusuf. I think my parents are going to be really upset that you came all this way without them knowing. And your parents are probably worried sick. I think we should tell them so we can fix this whole thing before it turns into a big problem."

Yusuf's eyes pleaded with me. "Come on, CJ! I al-ready told my parents I was coming with you and your family to New York. Just for a little while. Just until

spring break. Remember that voice changer on the Futurewatches you gave us?"

I palmed my forehead, already seeing where he was going with this.

"I just recorded a sample of your mom's voice from one of her interviews online, then blended it with my own voice to create a message to my parents," he said. "I said y'all had invited me to come to New York for a month. That y'all would feed me, take care of me, show me around, stuff like that. They were so grateful. Eastside said I can do the next month online, too. My parents didn't want me to miss this opportunity."

"Yusuf," I sighed.

"CJ. Ya want to be a good friend, right? Well, cover for me on this one. Ya needed us to keep so many secrets for you when you first came to Atlanta. And we did. Everything was fine, wasn't it? I only need ya to keep one teensy-weensy secret. Come on, man. Be a friend."

I felt torn. On the one hand, alarm sirens were blaring loudly in my brain that hiding Yusuf in Futureland would only cause trouble. This wasn't some innocent secret or part of a mystery investigation that needed to stay confidential. And his decision didn't exactly make sense. Everybody in Atlanta loved Yusuf—he had a good life at home, with sports and volunteering.

Leaving to solve mysteries just didn't really seem like something he would do. . . .

But Yusuf had a point, too. Since day one, I'd trusted the crew with my most private information. They never turned their backs on me, and even when things were uncertain, Yusuf had been the first one to come to my rescue. He was a great friend. Didn't I owe him?

Brrring! Brrrrring!

"Ah!" I shrieked when I realized what time it was. I leaped past Yusuf and over the bed, ripping through my book bag furiously. "Is everything okay?" he asked.

"It's fine!" I pulled my tablet from the bag in a hurry. "But I've got to log on to school. Science class starts in five minutes!"

Yusuf looked at his wrist. "Oh, man, you're right. Okay. Let me grab my stuff. I've got science, too. I guess we've already got group project partners figured out, huh?" He chuckled. "So, wait—does this mean I can stay?"

I projected the class video feed onto my wall-o-gram from my tablet. Me and Yusuf would need to keep our cameras turned off, at least for today. I wasn't ready to answer any questions about him being in Futureland before I figured out how to break it to my parents.

"I don't know," I said. "My parents won't be home until tonight. We'll figure this out after school. Do some things in the park. By the time they get back, I'll have a plan. Then we can go from there."

"Cool," Yusuf said. He typed swiftly on his laptop, logging on to the virtual classroom portal. I noticed the neon-green band on his wrist.

"Hey, what's that?" I asked. "Is that the same fancy watch you had at Pizza Mania?"

"Huh? Oh!" Yusuf replied, tapping his wrist. "It's, uhhh, I forget the name of it. Some kinda wristband. My mom gave it to me. She said her manager at work had an extra one and wanted me to have it, because of sports and stuff, you know? I don't know exactly how it works yet, but it's, like, supposed to track your activity and fitness and stuff."

"Oh, okay," I said with a nod. "Well, it looks pretty cool. I like that color."

"Yeah, me too. Ain't no Futurewatch, though."

Our classroom video stream began, and Mrs. Espinoza, our science teacher, appeared, her nose directly in the camera. She was a short woman with big hoop earrings and a million fancy scarves. She always tied them around her forehead to help hold up her massive top bun. Mrs. Espinoza clamped a digi-pen between her teeth as she scrolled on the tablet, probably taking attendance.

"Cameron Walker," she said. "Good to see you. Actually, I shouldn't say see you, since your camera is off. But at least you're here. Will you be gracing us with your lovely face today?" She yawned as she asked the question, dropping the pen from her mouth.

"Um, hi, Mrs. Espinoza," I answered, making sure to speak up so she could hear me. "I can't use my camera today. I'm having technical difficulties."

"Oh, I'm just so sure you are," she said. "The most advanced technological setup that any of us has ever seen, but Futureland hasn't figured out webcams, huh? Oh well. Maybe we'll get a chance to see you again before you start sprouting gray hair." The kids in the room laughed.

"I'm here too, Mrs. Espinoza!" Yusuf called. She smiled at the sound of his voice.

"Oh, Yusuf, honey! I already marked you down as present, you're all good. I'm so glad you're in my class again this semester! Look, don't worry about that camera if it's a hassle, okay? Just do your thing, and if you need any extra help, then we can set up a chat after school."

I raised my arms and soured my face in disbelief.

There was obviously some favoritism going on here. Yusuf muted his microphone and leaned over to me.

"She's a really big basketball fan," he explained. "Her son plays on the team, and she wants me to pass him the ball more. His jumper is broke, though."

"Ahh, got it."

Mrs. Espinoza started the lesson. "All right, my little Einsteins. By choice or by accident, you have found yourself in Eastside Middle's *only* elective science course. You could have taken art, or music, or even been sweating through your T-shirts and underwear in gym class. But you're not. Welcome to Technology and Society: Human Innovation."

"Is this the class you signed up for?" I whispered to Yusuf.

"Yeah, man," he said. "I love Mrs. Espinoza. I take whatever she teaches."

"I don't remember choosing this as one of my options."

He shrugged. "Maybe they swapped you in once you switched over to virtual. Relax, man. She's nice once you get to know her. And her classes sound hard, but she's good at making it easy to understand. Besides, we'll get to take it together, so I can help you."

"Good point." I nodded and focused on my screen again as the lesson began.

Mrs. Espinoza continued. "In the syllabus, I mentioned we'd be talking about hearing aids today. They're a very important and misunderstood advancement in biomedical technology—that is, science we use to make our lives healthier and better."

Yusuf was right, Mrs. Espinoza really did make this stuff interesting. I never thought I'd learn so much about eyeglasses, hearing aids, asthma pumps, and other stuff. As she kept teaching, I glanced over at Yusuf. He furrowed his brow and took detailed notes, hanging on Mrs. Espinoza's every word.

I tried to hold back a smile. Yeah, sure, this situation was a mess. I had no idea how my parents would react, and Yusuf would probably have to go home right away. But I couldn't help but feel a little happy that he was here. My friend. In New York with me.

For the first time in weeks, I felt a little less alone.

7

SOMEBODY'S WATCHING

Yusuf and I switched our devices off and set them aside. School hadn't even been out for five minutes before a flood of messages pinged onto both of our Futurewatches.

> **RICH:** wats up, y'all. tryin' to head to West Lake Park?

> **ANGEL:** Why don't we go to East Lake? It's closer.

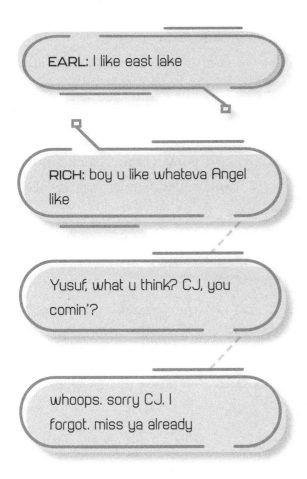

EARL: I like east lake

RICH: boy u like whateva Angel like

Yusuf, what u think? CJ, you comin'?

whoops. sorry CJ. I forgot. miss ya already

Regret and jealousy stung in my chest as I read the messages. I swallowed, feeling like a pebble got caught in my throat. It hurt to see the crew making plans without me. Was it gonna feel like this every time I looked at the group chat?

"Should I respond?" Yusuf asked me. "I didn't tell any of them that I was leaving with you."

I smacked my forehead. "Why not?!"

"Because you weren't supposed to know. Or else you would have stopped me. And they would have told you before I had a chance to sneak onto the ship."

I sighed, once again feeling uneasy—and a little suspicious—about Yusuf's decision-making. Something didn't feel right.

"You gotta respond somehow," I said. "At least for now. Let's keep up the secret until we figure out what to tell my parents."

"We're not gonna tell your parents, remember?" Yusuf said. He flicked the hologram of our chat off his watch face and into the air in front of him. He studied it for a moment, composed his message, and hit send.

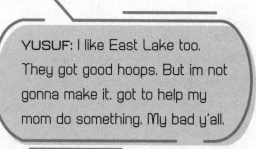

YUSUF: I like East Lake too. They got good hoops. But im not gonna make it. got to help my mom do something. My bad y'all.

My face must have dropped when I looked at the message, because Yusuf put his hand on my shoulder. I looked at him. "Yusuf, what's really going on? Is everything at home okay?"

Yusuf's expression darkened.

"Everything is fine, CJ," he said sternly. "I already explained it to you. Why do you keep asking me the same question? What do you want from me?"

A hot flash of embarrassment blanketed me. "I'm sorry, Yusuf, I—I didn't meant to—"

"My folks work hard to take care of me and my siblings, but they don't make enough for vacations. When you told us you were leaving, coming with you was the first thing that popped into my head. It's like my conscience was telling me to *go, go, go.* I felt like I had to listen."

My jaw still hung slightly ajar from the quick change in Yusuf's demeanor, and my heart hurt for him. He had never snapped at me before. Maybe I *was* being a bad friend. I guess I had never really thought about what it feels like to be trapped in one place, since I had spent my entire life on the move. Yusuf did all the right things and never complained. But he never really got any rewards or got to celebrate.

I yearned for my old life back. Yusuf was hoping for a new one.

"Hey!" I tried after a moment of silence. "What do you say we head into Futureland?"

"Really?" Yusuf asked. He perked up and his eyes brightened.

"Why not?" I said. "We still have, like"—I checked my watch—"three or four hours before my parents get home. That's plenty of time. We can go have some fun and think of a plan to explain how you got here."

"You're not worried something could go wrong?" he asked. "You're *always* worried about what could go wrong."

I smiled, put both hands on his shoulders, and looked into his eyes. "What could go wrong? What could be more dangerous than the things we've already faced inside that park?"

Yusuf beamed.

"You're right," he continued. "Besides, you could just program a rev or a Watcher or something to look out for us? If we fall on our heads, then they'll carry us back in here and get us an ice pack. And if your parents come home and our heads are busted, they'll have to take care of us before they get mad that I'm here. It's like order of operations or something."

We both laughed.

"You just reminded me of something," I said.

I flicked through screens on my Futurewatch until I found what I was looking for. I tapped a few times and stood up, pulling on my sneakers. "Come on. Follow me."

"So we're doing it?!" Yusuf asked.

"Come *on*!" I repeated with a laugh.

I took the first few steps out of my bedroom and stopped short, noticing something familiar outside the window. I moved close to the pane and stared

79

out. I saw *her* again. That woman in her red trench coat with her bright red hair, staring up at the park. I swallowed.

"You good, CJ?"

I narrowed my eyes and pointed out the window. "This lady . . . she keeps coming by here. She won't stop staring."

"Huh? Who?" Yusuf asked. He crowded next to me and peered out the window. When he caught sight of her, he blinked and stood a bit straighter.

"Her? It's probably nothing. She's most likely just a big Futureland fan, excited for it to open. Come on, let's go to the park."

"Yeah," I breathed, struggling to break my gaze from the lady. "Yeah, you're probably right."

We rushed out of the condo and took the elevator up to the park level before entering. I bet we looked like two tiny ants up against the huge orbs of each park destiny. We walked through the park, empty for now, but still inviting as ever.

We passed the Millennium Marketplace that sold lumi-gum and star-cookies. In a few days, it would be shrinking, floating, and relocating to make sure every Futureland guest could get as many sweet treats as they could eat. Next, we sidestepped the stage for the

Future Theater. I could almost hear the parade-revs jamming in my mind. We passed the posts the griot-revs would assume in just a few days to spin their marvelous stories. The greeter-revs would be right beside them, inviting guests to experience all Futureland has to offer.

I led us into the dark chamber, tapping some buttons on my Futurewatch before flicking on the lights. As the room slowly brightened, Yusuf jumped back, grabbed my shirt, and pointed. "Aye, man! Who is that?!"

The boy with purple galaxy skin turned toward us and smiled. His caracal purred and rubbed up against him.

"Don't worry!" I said to Yusuf. "He's cool. He's with us. Hey, Goggles!"

Goggles strode smoothly over toward us and put up a peace sign. "What's up, Cam?" he said.

"Not much, man," I answered. "What's up with you?"

"Just taking it easy, dude." He adjusted his goggles.

"Yusuf, this is Goggles," I explained. "He's going to watch our back while we play in the park. Goggles, this is my friend Yusuf, from Atlanta. He's gonna hang out with me today."

"What's up, man?" Yusuf said. He stretched his hand out to dap Goggles up, but his fingers swiped right through the hologram. The caracal growled.

"Awkwaaard," Yusuf drawled, pulling his hand back. "I get it, though. He's a . . . um . . . pretty much like a . . . Cam? Okay, I don't get it. What is he?"

I snorted, laughing. "He's my Holo-pal. It's a new program my uncle Trey made. He's like me, but older. And purple. And with a big cat." The caracal curled up at Goggles's feet, and I grinned. "All the guests will have the option to make one, so nobody has to walk around the park alone. For safety, just like you said."

Yusuf whistled. "Ahhhh. Yeah! That's what I was trying to say," he said, and smiled eagerly. "So, can I get a Holo-pal?"

"Yeah, we'll get you one," I said. "But let's do it on opening night so Uncle Trey doesn't suspect anything. For now, it's just you, me, Goggles, and . . . Hey, Goggles, what's your Holo-pet's name?"

"Her name?" Goggles rubbed the few hairs on his chin. "She doesn't have a name."

"I think you should name her," I said. "Every kid should be able to name their own pet." I squatted down and observed the majestic purple caracal. "But to me, she kind of looks like a—"

"Sarafina," Goggles said.

"Whoa." My eyes widened. "That's exactly what I was thinking!"

"Me too, dude," he said. "Supercool. Sarafina it is." Sarafina purred, drawing her ears back.

"Aye, this is weird," Yusuf said. "He really *is* like you. But purple."

I flashed a sly grin at Yusuf. "Now that we're all together," I said, "you ever been surfing?"

His eyes lit up. "No way! We're going surfing?"

"Let's do it. Goggles, you ready?"

"Totally."

Me, Goggles, Yusuf, and Sarafina skipped across the park and caught a Jet-Blur pod to Future Seas. Goggles and Sarafina stepped right into their own pod, settling in neatly like they'd done it a thousand times. We made it to Future Seas and changed into our surf gear. A short video about surfing basics played and Yusuf locked in on the virtual instructor's every word. As the video played, his leg bounced so rapidly in excitement I could feel our bench shaking beneath me. I smiled.

"I've never been surfing," he said. "But it always looked cool on TV. I'm so ready to try."

"It's a lot of fun. But take your time, and don't feel

bad if it doesn't come to you all at once," I warned. "The water can be kinda gnarly. Goggles and Sarafina—can y'all stay on the beach and look out for us?"

"No doubt," Goggles said. "Sarafina can hear just about everything that goes on within a mile. If one of y'all wipes out, we'll send help."

When the video ended, we left the viewing room and stepped out into the open air of the Future Seas beach. Yusuf closed his eyes and took in a big breath before rushing to the water ahead.

In Future Seas, you got a good mix of clean waves, A-frames, the occasional bomb, and even some chunder if you requested it. Last time Futureland docked in Los Angeles, a lot of surfers would come practice specific moves here with customized wave conditions.

Yusuf took off and charged what may have been the first good wave he saw. He didn't get raked over as he paddled out. When the wave peaked, he made the drop on its left shoulder as soon as it peeled.

I'd never seen anything like it from a rookie. Me and Goggles clapped and hollered in astonishment. Yusuf whooped as he glided onto the shore and threw us a shaka with each hand.

He really was the most athletic kid I had ever seen.

He'd taken a huge risk sneaking into Futureland. But I couldn't help but smile seeing him that happy.

Three distinct chimes rang out in the silence of my room. I opened my eyes to see Yusuf still asleep at the foot of my bed, snoring like a grizzly bear.

"Oh no. No, no, no!" I jumped over Yusuf and rushed to the wall-o-gram near the door of my bedroom. I spotted three locators—one for Mom, one for Dad, and one for Uncle Trey—slowly moving across Central Park, making their way home to Futureland.

"We overslept!" I yelled, pulling the pillow from beneath Yusuf's head and hitting him with it.

"Huh?! What's going on?" He rolled and toppled over onto the floor, wiping the drool from his chin.

"My parents and my uncle—they're home!"

"Cool!" Yusuf said.

"*Not* cool!" I cried out. "They still don't know you're here. And we didn't make a plan. What am I supposed to tell them?"

"Umm, just tell 'em I came to visit?" Yusuf said.

"What?!" My mind was spinning. "No, no, no.

That's not going to work. They'll ask so many more questions. I'm not ready." I paced back and forth, wringing my hands. "I need more time to think about this—you have to hide."

"What?! Hide where?"

Ding, dong, ding! The condo chime sounded, and my parents' footsteps clonked up the stairs alongside Uncle Trey's deep voice.

"The closet!" I pushed Yusuf backward into the walk-in closet in my room and shut the door.

"CJ! What am I supposed to do in here? What if I get hungry?"

I rushed back to the bed and grabbed the plate of sandwiches that we had made after surfing. Then I reopened the closet and pushed the plate into his hands. One of the sandwiches dropped, but I caught it before it hit the ground, and shoved it into Yusuf's mouth. I slammed the door right as he let out a muffled *thank you!* through his mouthful of food.

"You're welcome," I hissed. "Now be quiet!"

Just in time. I heard my parents enter the apartment and settle into the living room. They shuffled around, talking in low tones. I cracked my door just a bit to look out at them. My mom's beehive of dark brown locs was pulled together tightly, with just a few blond tips free and dangling. She sported an emerald turtleneck sweater and a peacoat, with some heels that made her tower even higher over my dad than she usually did. I stepped out of my room into the chilly air of a New York winter that my parents had brought in with them.

"There he is!" Dad said, shuffling over and pulling me into a handshake-hug hybrid. He sported a tight-fitting sweater and a matching knit cap covering his bald head, with gray slacks and black loafers. His fuzzy beard brushed up against my face as we separated. My dad was trying to copy Uncle Trey's new beard, but my mom hated the look of it. She begged him to cut it every single day. Uncle Trey burst through the side door with a handful of envelopes just as my mom tried to maneuver into the kitchen.

"Oh, whoa, whoa! Watch where you're sliding, baby sister. I guess you never really grow out of clumsiness, huh?"

"Trey, shut up," Mom said. "And *stop* calling me baby sister. I'm older than you."

"Only by a few minutes," he said. "But you're still clumsy like a baby, so I think it fits."

Uncle Trey followed behind her as she left the room, throwing shadow punches behind her. The punches stopped after a few seconds, though, when Mom turned around and raised her fist with a look in her eyes that told all three of us that *this* punch might not be so playful.

"Hi, family, bye, family," Uncle Trey said as my parents settled into the living room. I stood a little bit away, back toward the kitchen.

"Headed out. Got a date," he added with a wink.

"Trey," Dad started. "Before you go, can we talk about . . . the thing?"

"Sounds like grown-up stuff," I said, turning to go.

"No, Cam-Cam. Stay," Mom called after me. "I think you should see this, too. It's a part of what we have to deal with, with the park. It's important that you're aware. Trey, do you have that recording you were talking about?"

"Yeah, let me pull it up." My uncle Trey cast a wall-o-gram from his Futurewatch onto the living room wall. It showed a stuffy-looking man with a bad hairpiece and a suit on, readying his mouth to grumble about something. This had to be the local news.

Today, New Yorkers gathered in Times Square for a one-of-a-kind giveaway. Though the gifts came a little after Christmas, Hanukkah, and Kwanzaa, I have no doubt they inspired excitement and cheer for everybody there.

The video recording cut to Times Square, where

hundreds and hundreds of people stood around, cheering and waving their arms in the air.

In somewhat of a Secret Santa–type maneuver, an unidentified group distributed over one thousand brand-new Haventech LifeBuddy wristbands to the crowd gathered there. All for free.

The Haventech LifeBuddy wristband wasn't set to release to the public until later this year.

I squinted at the image of the wristbands. They looked familiar.

The LifeBuddy is the latest in a series of competitive technology that monitors a person's daily activity. It includes a fitness tracker, a sleep monitor, to-do list reminders, and much more. The mirror-mode feature allows you to project a visual of yourself from the wristband so you can check your gym progress or make sure nothing is stuck between your teeth before a hot date! But the most exciting component of the LifeBuddy is a sleep-learning feature called hynopedia.

No official word yet, but rumors are spreading that there will be more Haventech giveaways at local community centers before the month ends—

Uncle Trey paused the news report and looked at my parents. No one spoke.

"What does it mean?" I asked.

Mom sighed. "J.B.?"

Dad removed his hat and looked blankly at the carpet. He ran his hand over his smooth head repeatedly, searching for words. Uncle Trey picked it up where no one else could.

"That wristband—that's Futureland technology, Cam. Same function, just a different design. Your mom has been working on that for two, three years. We finally found a use for it with the Holo—uhh, with one of the new exhibits." He winked at me slyly. "But your mom came up with that design a long, long time ago."

That must have been why the wristbands had looked familiar to me. Probably saw it in some old files around the lab. "How did Haventech get it, then?"

"That's our question, too, Big Man." Dad stepped in. "And what we're a little afraid to find out."

"But we *have* to find out," Mom said. "Cam, there's no way to tell the extent of the damage that Southmore's hack caused to Futureland. To our technology. To our business. We've recovered revs and we're working on this ridiculous marketing plan, but it's impossible to know how many of our files were copied. I wouldn't be surprised if more and more of our designs start to show up for sale. Southmore's people probably want to make a profit off them."

"But I don't understand," I said. "Isn't that illegal? They can't just take it. You came up with it first, right?"

"It's not that simple, baby," Mom said. "Legal battles never are."

"So, what do we do?" I asked.

"Your father and I have to talk to our lawyers," she answered. "We've got to talk to our ethical hacking team *again* and see if we can find out anything else about the Southmore breach. We've got—we've got to do a lot of things, sweetie, but most of them aren't your concern."

She took my dad's hand in hers, darted her eyes nervously from him to me, then tried to smile her nervousness away.

"Dad and I are going to be very busy, but Uncle Trey will be here for anything you need. You two are in charge of Futureland park operations as of today. J.B. and I need to focus our efforts on making sure there still *is* a Futureland to operate." She sighed.

"And that starts tomorrow, with the beginning of the public relations plan," Dad said. "Shaking hands, kissing babies, and giving out free Future Passes all over the city." He took a deep breath and exhaled.

"Actually," Uncle Trey said, frowning, "it starts tonight. With this." He stopped skimming a freshly opened letter over the top of his reading glasses and held it up. "Stacy, did you tell the city about the invisibility feature?"

"What?" Mom said, sounding a little panicked. "No, of course not, I— It's not even fully tested. What are you looking at? What is that?" She reached for the piece of paper.

"We have an invisibility feature?" I asked, shocked.

"Only for emergencies," Dad said.

"Came in with today's mail," Uncle Trey told Mom as he handed her the envelope. "Got the mayor's office seal on it and everything."

My uncle continued as Mom read over the letter.

"There's somebody around here that knows a lot more about us than we've told them," he said. "Somebody has been watching. And I'm willing to bet they still are."

City of New York
Office of Beautification and Aesthetics
C. Whitebourne

Bureau of Tourism
January 31, 2049
Dr. Stacy Walker
Airspace: 40.7817° N, 73.9664° W
New York, NY 10024

Re: Notice to implement immediate invisibility mode in accordance with NYC aesthetics standards.

Dear Dr. Walker:

This notice is the first and final prompt for you to immediately engage the invisibility feature of your airship, currently settled above Central Park's Great Lawn. We became aware of the ship's capability to camouflage with natural skyscape from a confidential informant. We request that you utilize the invisibility feature at all times aside from park operating hours. If you fail to comply with this notice, the airship will be grounded and seized for breaking airship code SF14-053GA. There will be no further warnings.

This is a final notice.

Regards,

C. Whitebourne
C. Whitebourne

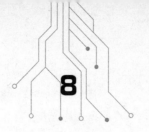

FUN CITY

Friday, February 5, 2049
7:00 p.m.

Well, me and Yusuf had done it.

We'd made it to Futureland's opening night in New York City undetected by my parents. Now it was time for the big reveal. We would "accidentally" run into Mom, Dad, or Uncle Trey inside Futureland. They'd be surprised to see him there, and then we'd tell them that he came on a surprise trip to visit family. I'd be all like:

Can he pleeease stay for the weekend, Mom and Dad? I miss my friends so much!

Of course they'd say yes. After that, he'd "miss his flight" or his train or his ride home or whatever and need to stay with us for a few days. Blah, blah, blah.

We didn't have the whole thing figured out, okay? But we had enough.

It had been a quiet week—much quieter than usual. But, with the invisibility feature enabled on the park, no crowds gathered on the sidewalks to stare at the shimmering black glass exterior of Futureland. No people stopped on their way to work. No senior citizens swore up at the massive "alien ship," shaking fists at it for almost giving them a heart attack, hovering over their beloved city.

I hadn't seen my parents for most of the week after the Haventech family meeting. I'd moved Yusuf into the spare bedroom that I had converted into my detective office. Mom and Dad knew that special room was off-limits. I love Uncle Trey . . . but he wasn't the best babysitter. He'd pop in to check on me every once in a while, just to make sure I was alive. Keeping a secret from him was a breeze.

Whenever my parents would come home from their meetings, Yusuf had to sleep in my closet, but it was only for a couple of nights, and he didn't mind. During the day, he'd taken advantage of his unlimited access to Alejandro and Aurielle's infinite cooking catalog. I'd never seen somebody eat so many falafel balls. After school, we'd work on the park maintenance to-do list for a little while. Then we'd play around before hiding him and doing it all over again. Everything had been going smoothly.

Too smoothly. So, I should have known that opening night would be a mess.

"Look, Yusuf," I said. "Hold still in there, all right? I've gotta wheel this thing through the kitchen and living room to get up to the park. No funny business, okay?"

"I'll be quiet as a mouse," he promised with a wink.

Yusuf tucked his head back beneath the top shelf of the lab supplies cart, and I draped a big plastic tarp over it so that you couldn't see him from either side. All we had to do was make it to the park from my parents' lab underneath the condo. Once we were inside the park, Operation Yusuf Surprise would commence. The plan was guaranteed to work, unless . . . Yusuf sneezed, or yawned, or fell out of the cart before we made it through the condo to the elevator. Then our cover would be blown. And we didn't have a plan for that.

"Don't stress it, baby," I heard Dad say as I quietly wheeled the cart into the kitchen. "We have other options. I'll make some custom art. We'll get people back on our side. They'll love Futureland again. I promise . . ."

"But, sweetheart, how?" Mom cut in, barely above a whisper. "How are we supposed to promote Future-land and restore its good name when we're not even allowed to let the park be seen during the day? People don't trust things they can't keep track of. Somebody is doing this on purpose, J.B. Somebody knows how bad this will hurt us. That notice—"

I turned the corner into the hallway that led to the living room, and a wheel on the cart creaked before getting stuck. I felt Yusuf's weight shift inside the cart and grasped it tightly to steady it.

"Cam!" Dad called, clearing his throat. "Hey, buddy. You heading down for the opening? What ya doing with that cart?"

"Oh, um." I turned to look over my shoulder with what I hoped was a convincing smile. "There's a . . . little leak. A leak I saw earlier in Word Locus. I was just going to tighten a couple of valves before guests start arriving."

"That's my baby, taking initiative!" Mom said. "I guess my bigheaded brother has been teaching you a few useful things during the day, huh?"

I nodded, turning back to the cart.

"Do you need any help?" My dad stood up to make his way around the couch. "Somebody to hold the flashlight? I can come down with you."

97

"No!" I practically shouted. I cleared my throat. "I mean, no thank you. I was hoping to just head down there before y'all and Uncle Trey came down. Knock it out quick. You know how chaotic opening night can be."

Dad stopped approaching. "Boy, do I. But that chaos is all for you and Trey tonight. Me and your mother are wiped out. We're going to stay in and get some rest."

"Wait, really? You're not kicking off opening night?"

"Nope," Mom said. "We told you—you and Trey run the park now, until further notice. If y'all want to say a few words or something before the destinies start spinning, go ahead. No pressure. We've been to New York plenty of times. People know what we're about here. At least, they used to know. . . ." Her voice trailed off as she slumped back into the couch, sipping from her wineglass.

"Got it," I said. "Well, we won't let you down! It's going to be a good opening night, you'll see. You guys get some rest. I'll tell you all about it in the morning."

"You sure you don't want a hand?" Dad took another half step in my direction.

"I'm good, Dad." I smiled.

"All righty then, Big Man." He smiled back. "My

boy. Growing up. You may want to put some oil on that wheel, though. Squeaking a little bit."

"Will do!" I yelled as I rushed the cart through the rest of the hallway and into the elevator. As soon as the doors closed, Yusuf popped his head out from under the tarp and smiled wide. "We did it."

I shoved his head back under the tarp. "Hush. Not yet. Just a couple more floors up."

Guests started arriving soon after Yusuf and I made it into the park. They watched the opening night video in the Guest Hub before flooding the Jet-Blur stations and walking trails. I checked to make sure Uncle Trey wasn't close by, then quickly kicked the side of the cart to get Yusuf out.

"Ow!"

"Whoops," I said. "Sorry." Yusuf rolled out from under the cart, stood up, and brushed himself off. He shook me by the shoulders and started jumping up and down. "We made it!"

I smiled. "Yeah, we did."

"Where to now?" he asked.

"Let's just see what's going on."

We started to stroll around the park. There was nothing—and I mean *nothing*—like Futureland on opening night. The sounds, the sights, the energy—it was amazing.

Smells of lunar fried dough, chocolate rockets, and space-tunnel funnel cake wafted through the air from the Millennium Marketplace. The smells spread along park walkways, enticing guests to take a look, or better yet, take a bite. Uncle Trey's beautiful array of glow-in-the-dark plants swayed gently beside the calm waters of the Future Ring in the distance. A few visitors who had already secured their floats started to slowly cruise around the park's neon waterways.

The music pulsating from inside the Black Beat competed with the music that blasted from the Future Theater. Maybe I could get Mom to program the parade-revs to do a special guest appearance *inside* the Black Beat one day. Booming bass drums, crashing cymbals, lively horns, and electric vocals rang out from both areas as Yusuf and I weaved through them.

But the award for the most soulful sounds went to the lead singer from Future Theater. Everyone nearby stopped dead in their tracks when the parade-rev jumped out of formation, hit a spin, and belted out a series of magnificent riffs and runs. The rev sang a Futureland song I had never heard before.

The future's green, the future's blue
I wanna dance on the moon with the future you

Into outer space and back again
My past, my present, and my future friend

The crowd went totally wild with whistles and cheers. The lead singer of the parade-revs—a stout rev in a red costume with dark sunglasses—took a bow and gestured toward the band so that guests would show them some love, too. The cheers didn't stop, even after all the revs shimmied onto their platform and shrank down, down, down to a tiny little cube. They lifted into the air and zipped away, headed to deliver another showstopping performance somewhere else in the park. Yusuf and I cheered with the crowd.

And that's when things got interesting.

Little by little, we started to see them—Holo-pals. And their Holo-pets, too. Guests started emerging from the center of the park accompanied by slightly older, more sparkly, shiny versions of themselves. Not to mention all sorts of creative hybrids of animals we *thought* we recognized. A tall girl with a red mohawk and platform boots walked by with a neon-yellow twin and a miniature dragon. The Holo-pet breathed little puffs of holographic fire. We saw all shapes, sizes, and colors of holographic human projections. Beside them? Waddling multichromatic crocodiles, atomic antelopes, and phosphorescent pandas. All the guests had Futurelink bands on their wrists, too.

"It's open! It's open! Can we go?" Yusuf asked. "Can I make one?"

"Yeah!" I said. "Let's head there now."

We ran and skipped until we reached the center of the park—the new destiny's official location. The outside was decorated with a radiant block-lettered sign that read THE HOLO-PAL. A greeter-rev waved us in with a warm smile, but before we entered, a newly designed griot-rev stopped us.

The rev had long braids, each a different color, all falling to reach the back of their knees. Their makeup was made up of blushy shades of orange, red, and blue with a splash of glitter across the face. The individual specks glinted at every touch of the park's lights. The rev stood about my height and wore a green cargo jacket and white sweater underneath, with groovy, patterned bell-bottom pants and high-top canvas sneakers. They stopped Yusuf and me gently, with a mischievous look in their eye.

"Hey, hey, two young fellas like yourself happen to be in the mood for a good story? It's all about this place." The rev pointed a thumb over their shoulder toward the entrance. "But really . . . it's about you."

Yusuf smiled and looked at me. Before I could respond, a voice called out from behind us.

"I would love to hear a story!" We turned to see a woman with red hair holding hands with a young boy who looked like he could be her son. I thought I recognized her, but . . . but some people moved to block our view before I got a better look.

"Of course," the griot-rev said to the woman. "Every time you walk into the future, you walk right into the past at the same time. Every story we create, creates us."

"Come on, CJ! So many people are coming!" Yusuf tugged me past the griot into the Holo-pal chamber. I glanced back over my shoulder twice to get another look at the red-haired lady, but she'd disappeared behind a crowd of people.

When Yusuf and I made it into the chamber, only a few kids waited in front of us. I could hear Itza's voice helping guests establish their profiles and launch their companions. More innovative projection and animal pairings walked past us until Yusuf's turn came. He hopped up on the platform, centered in the cylinder of light as it became opaque. I could still hear Itza, but none of Yusuf's responses. Uncle Trey had added a privacy update since he'd given me the demo. Smart.

I projected Goggles and Sarafina from my Future-watch so they'd be ready to meet Yusuf and his new pals when they arrived. After a few moments, the cylinder turned transparent. Yusuf stepped down from the platform, and behind him came two other beings.

If Itza's body scanning had any kind of crystal ball qualities, then Yusuf was due for another growth spurt very soon. Yusuf's Holo-pal stood nearly a whole head taller than him with broad shoulders and thick arms, and instead of Yusuf's signature afro, the boy had his hair braided into chunky cornrows that hung down by his shoulders. His skin was a magnificent silver, speckled with all the colors of the rainbow. He wore a black hoodie and matching basketball shorts, with some crew socks and high-top athletic sneakers. The only thing shining brighter than his skin was his smile. Well, and his pet, too—an animal I'd never seen, like either a big mouse or a tiny squirrel, perched on the Holo-pal's shoulder.

"Welcome back. Who do we have here?" I asked Yusuf.

"CJ, Goggles, Sarafina—meet Sana and Ali," he said. "Oh, Ali is the small one."

"Hi, y'all." I waved. "Hi, little Ali." I moved in closer to the cute rodent and tried to rub its head with my index finger, but it scurried to Sana's other shoulder before I had a chance. Its electric-blue fur was streaked with a shimmering silver that matched Sana's glowing skin.

"Haha. Yeah, he's a little shy," Sana said in a voice that sounded like Yusuf's but deeper. "But don't mind it—he'll warm up to you. Sugar gliders are actually very family-oriented animals. Just give it a little time."

"A sugar glider, huh?" I laughed and looked at Yusuf. "Man, you really know a little bit about everything, don't you?"

"Learned about them last year in Mr. Evans's class." He shrugged and smiled. "CJ, now that the gang's all here, let's roll out and have some fun!"

"For sure!" I said, turning for the exit before stopping short. I spun back around and studied Yusuf's wrists. "Um, did you get a Futurelink band? My uncle said our projections wouldn't be able to leave this chamber unless guests have a wristband to project them. And the Futurewatch I gave you last year doesn't have the right software for it to work."

"Um . . . Itza said I didn't need one," Yusuf said.

"Huh?" I raised an eyebrow. "That can't be right."

"Seriously," he said. "Something about 'adequate preexisting technology.' Whatever that's supposed to mean. See for yourself—let's walk out of here and see if Sana and Ali disappear."

Me, Goggles, Sarafina, Sana, Ali, and Yusuf shuffled toward the door. When we exited, an eerie quiet made the hairs on my neck stand up. I stopped, confused.

There was nobody waiting outside to get into the Holo-pal chamber. Where had all the people gone? We turned around and scanned the area for the griot with the cargo jacket and multicolored braids, but we couldn't find them anywhere.

"That's weird," I said. "Griots usually hold one post for an entire night. And where did everybody else go?"

"The Holo-pal chamber is probably only taking a certain amount of people tonight," Yusuf said. "Didn't your uncle say he was still testing? Might have taken the griot away to fix a glitch, too."

"Well, yeah. He *did* just get it up and running. But the park just opened. And the griot was working just fine. . . ."

"When *we* saw them," Yusuf insisted. "But we've been in there for at least thirty minutes."

"Yeah. Yeah, I guess so."

An uneasy feeling spread through the pit of my stomach. *Intuition.* I heard Dooley's voice in my head, reminding me to trust my gut. I shut my eyes to try and squeeze the sound out.

All the music and voices in Futureland became muffled. I felt dizzy and warm all of a sudden, like the first time I experienced the Atlanta humidity. By the time I opened my eyes, Yusuf stood in front of me, calling my name over and over again.

"CJ . . . CJ! Are ya good, man?"

"Yeah." I swayed a little on my feet. "My bad. I just got a little dizzy."

"I'm going to run to the Millennium Marketplace and get ya something to drink. Ya need to stay hydrated. I'm taking Sana and Ali with me. They haven't disappeared yet, bro. And look—the light on my fitness band is blinking. Maybe they connected to this thing somehow."

It was true. A dim glow illuminated all the way around Yusuf's gift, and individual lights beneath the silicone exterior blinked every few seconds. I had no clue what it meant—but the band was definitely doing something.

Is that . . . is that a Haventech band? Like the ones Uncle Trey showed us from the news? It had to be. Now it made sense why I had recognized the wristbands from the TV news. I hadn't seen any schematics from my mom's lab. I had seen a real live Haventech band on my own's friend's wrist.

"Yusuf, where'd you say your mom got that band from?"

"Her manager at work," he said. "Gave it to her to

give to me. For sports and stuff, remember? I guess it can do other things, too."

"Where does your mom work?" I asked.

"Um . . . I don't really remember." Yusuf scratched his head. "She changes jobs a lot. But she works in an office. Like, helping all the managers and stuff. Like, um . . . like an assistant."

I closed my eyes again and pressed my thumbs into my temples, the throbbing fast and furious. The warmth spread over me again.

"I'm going to get ya that drink, bro," Yusuf said, sounding concerned. "Stay right here."

Yusuf bounded away, and as he left, he passed the fuzzy outline of a lady and a boy walking toward the Holo-pal creation chamber. I blinked away my dizziness and tried to focus on them. It was the same lady from before—behind us in line at the Holo-pal chamber. Something about her looked funny to me. Maybe it was the way she walked—she stood very straight and stiff, with her hands resting perfectly at her waist, fingers interlocked.

Every couple of steps, she slowly panned her head from one side to the other, like she wanted to see everything in front of her, in every direction. Each step ended with a little bounce as she went from one foot to the next. The boy followed along. Every few steps he coughed violently, and she patted him on the back to ease his ailing.

The lady didn't look like she came to Futureland to have fun. She just . . . stared at things, admiring them. She and the boy stopped directly in front of me with their matching natural red hair and green eyes. The woman grinned slightly with an eyebrow half raised.

"Hello, young man," she said. "Is this the proper location for the . . . oh, what is it called again, honey?" She nudged the boy.

"The Holo-pal chamber," he mumbled, then coughed.

"Yes! Have we arrived at the proper destination to create our own Holo-pals?"

I tried to ignore my thumping headache and put on a welcoming face. "Yes, this is the place. Everything you need is right inside. But wait"—I snapped my fingers, suddenly remembering—"I think I've seen you before. Do you sometimes stand beneath the park and look up at it from the street?"

The lady frowned. "Me? Oh, heavens no. This is my first time visiting your magnificent park. Maybe you have me mistaken with another redhead." She chuckled softly and smiled with half her mouth.

My head pounded as I rubbed my temples. "My apologies," I said. "Well, ma'am. I'm afraid you won't

be able to create a Holo-pal for yourself. As of right now, the exhibit is only designed for youth guests. Between you and me, this is our first time launching it. But the next update should expand to include adults."

The woman gave an intense frown, the way a sad clown does.

"Aww, well, that is just devastating news. I am obsessed with what the Walkers have done here. Just plain obsessed. Humans, robots, some things in the middle—it's really fascinating. How delightful would it be if all of us were a little more like machines? I probably wouldn't need so many cups of coffee to get going in the morning!" The woman cackled out an unrestrained laugh and patted the boy's head. He winced at her touch.

"Anyhoo," she continued, "how exhilarating this all is! I can feel the excitement in the air inside this park. It's inspiring. So different from the boring day-to-day of *out there*." She pointed over her shoulder toward New York City. "Sometimes I wish the entire world could be one big playground." She gestured at Futureland all around her. "I am so elated that Futureland has decided to visit New York again. Lately, this place has gotten a bad rap—but I still think it's a fun city. I am certain that Jordan will enjoy accessing his own Holo-pal. Isn't that right, honey?" She looked to the coughing child again. "If I may ask a question—do you all ever do any spooky theme nights in the park? I *do* love a good scare, myself."

I rubbed my chin. "No, but you can submit suggestions online."

The woman smiled. "Thank you, young man. Have a splendid night."

She pushed past me and into the exhibit, nearly leaving her son behind. With the half step of space between them as they entered the creation chamber, I gently took Jordan's wrist as he followed his mother.

"Hey," I whispered. "Are you okay?"

Jordan looked me squarely in the face. His eyes were green with little gold flecks in them. They kinda reminded me of Dooley's. He had a mysterious expression and dark bags under his eyes that made me think he hadn't slept in days. He made a snarling face at me and ripped his arm out of my grip.

"I'm fine," he growled. "Don't touch me."

I put my hands up in apology. "Sorry!"

Jordan pushed past me just like his mother had and walked up the ramp into the chamber. As soon as he disappeared, Yusuf appeared with two bottles of light-year liquid—Futureland's special super-hydration formula—and two fizzy flows, my favorite. I thanked him and grabbed an LYL, chugged it. The drink went down smooth like water with all the flavor of tropical fruit punch. Delicious.

After a couple moments, my head stopped thumping and my body felt much cooler. All of us, including the Holo-pals and pets, started walking away from the entrance of the Holo-pal creation chamber, headed nowhere specific.

"Who was that boy you were talking to?" Yusuf asked.

"Huh?"

"With the red hair?"

"Oh," I said, snapping back to reality. "I don't know. Some kid with his mom. They were trying to find the Holo-pal chamber, but they were both kind of weird. I could have sworn I saw his mom before . . . outside the park."

"Looked like something funny was going on. You good?" he asked.

"Yeah, I'm fine. Futureland brings in thousands and thousands of people from all over the world every year. If I have learned one thing, it's that people are just different. Sometimes I expect people to act a certain way and they don't, but I try not to take it personally." I looked back at the Holo-pal chamber, where more excited kids were gathering. "Futureland needs to be a welcoming place. Where everyone can feel safe. Not like we're judging them."

"That's a good way of looking at it."

"Yeah." I thought for a moment, then laughed a little. "Like one time, we were in Houston, Texas, and—"

WHAM! VRMM. VRMM. VRMMMMM.

A loud slamming sound rang through the air, followed by complete darkness. The radiant destinies, the bioluminescent plants, and the glowing Holo-pals all blacked out. As hard as I peered through the dark, I couldn't find one light anywhere. Some guests burst into laughter. Some burst into screams.

The park became a mess of confusion. People shuffled around and pushed past one another. I almost fell to the ground but found myself toppled over right into Yusuf's arms.

"I got you, CJ."

He pulled me aside, and we kept our arms linked to stay close to one another. My brain tried to kick into problem-solving mode. The total power switch was located in Galactic Gallery, all the way at the top of the park. It would take me forever to get there, especially with a power outage, because the Jet-Blur pads wouldn't work.

But how could there be a power outage?

"This doesn't make sense," I said to Yusuf.

"Huh?"

"This whole park, it runs on an endless supply of

113

solar-lunar energy. Even keeps it floating in the air. My mom designed it herself."

"Then how could we be out of power?" asked Yusuf.

How? What could've happened? All I could think of was that maybe Uncle Trey or one of the revs had tripped a switch or popped a cord accidentally. As my pulse started to quicken, I hoped with all my heart for that to be the case, because I couldn't stomach thinking of the only other option. My mouth became cotton at the thought.

It's happening again. Someone, or something, is controlling the park.

I turned toward Yusuf. We had only been covered in darkness for about a minute and a half, but it felt like a century. The wristband on his arm glowed brightly and spun with all kinds of colors. I looked down at my own Futurewatch, tapped its face. Nothing. Even *stored* energy was failing. Something was sucking all the energy out of everything in Futureland. But somehow, Yusuf's band still worked. *What is going on?*

"Um, CJ?"

WHAM!

Another ear-shattering slam rocked the ground underfoot. Guests screamed louder and fell over one another as they rushed toward the exits. Yusuf and I leaned up against a lumi-pop stand for stability. A couple seconds after the slam, all the lights came back on, and for a moment, everybody stopped moving.

Everybody except the revs.

Every rev I could see stood slumped with their head down. But when the lights came on, they powered back up, donning their signature service smiles. Their orange eyes spun rapidly as the software containing their personalities and their storylines rebooted. All of them started to move, in sync with one another.

And all of them moved backward.

When my mom designed rev bodies, she modeled them after humans. You know, like, we can walk forward easily but moving in reverse feels pretty funny for most people. If you've never tried to run backward while keeping your eyes on a charging gorilla-rev during a Future Trek safari—don't. Trust me.

Never ceasing to smile, each rev bent at the waist and thrust their hips back. They swung their legs behind them and stomped into the dirt, smashing into exhibits and stands and colliding with one another. Even after a rev ran into something else, they didn't stop moving—just kept trying to propel themselves backward. Kept smiling. Yusuf tapped me on the shoulder. His gaze was fixed to the right of us, his mouth agape. He pointed a few yards away.

Goggles, Sarafina, Sana, and Ali. They had left our sides and were moving backward, too. They had hitched, jerky movements, just like the revs. Their holograms glitched—fading and coming back into focus as they struggled to move. I looked around and noticed everyone else's Holo-pals doing the same thing.

I could hardly believe my eyes—or my ears. A ghastly tune played through the speakers, and it took me a moment to realize what it was.

The Futureland soundtrack was playing in *reverse*. Over the guests' shrieks and the dysfunctional reverse revs, I heard the songs my dad composed—eerie, messed-up versions of them—playing through the Futureland speakers. The musical notes playing backward made the songs sound off-key and out of tune. Like music from a haunted circus. The kind of place where the clowns might snatch you, all the animals have red eyes, and the rides won't let you off once you get on.

The revs moved backward for about ten seconds before the lights flickered again, and almost as soon as it all had started, it was over. Suddenly, the revs stood upright and began to move smoothly, normally. Their creepy smiles transformed back into their usual warm expressions. They picked up toppled stands and started to repair things they had broken.

Buzz, buzz.

116

I looked down at my Futurewatch. Back online with a barrage of messages.

MOM: Cam, where are you? Are you okay?

DAD: Big Man, come back up to the condo. We're shutting down for the night.

UNCLE TREY: Kiddo, you all right?

I didn't have a chance to respond before I heard Mom's voice—the most soothing voice in the family—coming through the Futureland comms system.

Attention, all guests. This is Dr. Stacy Walker, founder of Futureland. Sorry for the inconvenience and the little scare. Futureland is experiencing a power glitch

117

and we're going to close the park early tonight. All of your Future Passes will be refunded with tonight's admission and loaded with a free future visit. Please proceed in a calm, orderly manner to your nearest Jet-Blur station. Be safe getting home and check your news streams for further details on tonight's technical difficulties.

"Party's over, huh?" Yusuf said as we watched the crowd of guests file themselves out of the park.

"You can say that again. Come on, let's go back to the condo."

"And face your parents?" Yusuf looked worried. "They still don't know I'm here! What about our plan? It got ruined by the power outage. I don't know, Cam. Maybe we should wait a little longer. Break it to them at a less chaotic time."

I sighed and dropped my shoulders. I had a bad feeling about hiding Yusuf any longer. We'd be better off coming clean now and dealing with everything at once. No more surprises. "Yusuf . . . ," I started.

"Please, CJ. Please," he begged.

People continued to maneuver around us rapidly as they fled the park. My thoughts started running faster and faster until I couldn't concentrate at all. I closed my eyes and covered my ears.

"Okay, fine. But no more delays after tonight. My

parents and Uncle Trey are going to be up talking about this all night in the condo, so you should stay at the Black Beat. There's a really cool hostel with comfy beds there. I'll come get you in the morning. Unless you'd rather camp under the stars in Future Trek?"

"With the tiger-revs roaming around?" Yusuf asked, his voice a little higher than usual. "No thanks. Take me to the Beat!"

I grabbed Yusuf's arm, and we rushed in the opposite direction to all the park guests, toward the Black Beat. Thankfully, it seemed like Mom's message had helped. People were still moving with urgency, but in a much calmer manner, without pushing or shoving. Through the controlled chaos, I noticed two people who stood out to me among the rest: the red-haired lady and her son.

Instead of rushing out of Futureland like everyone else, they stood calm but resolute amid the commotion. The lady helped usher people toward exits, pointing them this way and that. The son grabbed the hands of older patrons and escorted them to Jet-Blur pods. I raised my eyebrow. *How brave of them,* I thought as Yusuf and I set off. How helpful. How . . . strange.

Who were these people? And why weren't they scared?

UNKNOWN: Having fun yet, Cam?

You can't get rid of us. You can run, but you can't hide.

This will be much worse than Atlanta. Much, much worse. And there's nothing you can do. Nothing. I will have my revenge.

You thought it was over. But this is just the beginning.

You thought it was over. But this is just the beginning.

120

You thought it was over . . .

But this . . . is just the beginning.

FRIDAY, FEBRUARY 5, 2049 | 9:45 P.M.

EARL: Hey CJ. Wanna play Word Buddies?

It's a new game. You try to make as many words as you can from scrambled letters.

It's really fun.

121

10:00 P.M.

EARL: Hellooo? Anybody there?

If you don't want to play that's okay. You're probably having more fun in NYC anyway

10:15 P.M.

EARL: Hey CJ. Never mind. I'm going to go to Rich's and watch a movie.

Miss you, man. Wish you were here

122

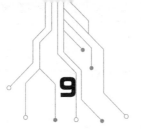

9

FAMILY BUSINESS

Saturday, February 6, 2049
9:00 a.m.

I don't think any of us got much sleep after the park closed early. Futureland was known for its opening weekend extravaganzas. When Iman Sheffield had gone missing in Atlanta, we kept running the park, hoping everything would work itself out.

My parents weren't that naïve anymore.

We closed Futureland down for the weekend and started a series of family meetings and individual tasks. We needed to investigate the power outage and solve the strange problems before they got too far out of hand.

"The cameras are shot," Uncle Trey called from the hallway as he exited the elevator and made his way into the living room.

He plopped down on the recliner and tipped it back. Several revs crowded the living room—Watchers, maintenance-revs, and others—there to take notes of our conversation. All these revs had been offline and in storage during the outage, so Mom felt like they were safe to use. I snuck a glance at my parents, trying to read their reactions to the bad news. All I saw was exhaustion.

I pulled my deerstalker down a little tighter on my head and brought my pajama-covered legs into my chest.

"But not the entire recording from the night," Uncle Trey continued. "Only the period of the outage and the glitchy stuff that happened after. Just like Cam said, his watch wasn't working while the power was out—it's like something sucked the power reserve out of the cameras *and* cut the power supply to everything else."

"But not the park itself?" Mom asked.

Uncle Trey shook his head. "Didn't drop an inch. Only the stuff inside. Me and my revs triple-checked everything. We've been hacked."

"Trey, let's not jump to conclusions," Dad said. "Isn't it possible that the Holo-pal chamber just required way more power than we accounted for on opening night? Maybe it caused a surge."

124

Uncle Trey frowned and looked directly at my dad. "No. No, that's not possible. The Holo-pal chamber takes a lot of juice, but I spent weeks getting that algorithm right. I didn't mess this up. Everything was perfect."

He crossed his arms and leaned back. An awkward tension crawled up my spine.

"Look, J.B." Uncle Trey let out a frustrated sigh. "I know nobody wants to hear it because we all wanted the nightmare to be over. We all *thought* it was. You think I want to go through this again? Seriously? Me, of all people?"

Dad stayed silent, averted his gaze.

"What does it mean, Trey?" Mom asked.

"It means that we probably can't figure out what caused the outage," he answered. "And if something somewhere is sucking juice out of our devices . . . then it could have been pulling other stuff out of them, too."

"Data?" I said.

"Bingo, kiddo," Uncle Trey said.

My mom sniffled. Dad pulled her closer into him with his hand around her shoulder. "So," she said, "we may have had even *more* private information stolen last night, and we have no way of knowing?"

Uncle Trey let out another big sigh. He drummed an anxious beat on his thighs. "We're gonna have to close the park," he said.

"Can't." Dad spoke up. "Taking a day or so off is fine, but we've got to open back up ASAP. The PR company and the legal fees leftover from Atlanta are still tallying. We're not in danger—yet. But we can't just stop making money. We have too many bills to pay to make sure things don't get even worse."

Uncle Trey put his face in his hands as a light bulb came on in my head.

"Uncle Trey, if so much power was directed into the Holo-pal chamber last night, maybe the opposite of what Dad is saying happened. Instead of the exhibit trying to take more power than was available, maybe it got so much power that it overloaded. Blacked out."

Uncle Trey rubbed his chin. "Nephew . . . it's possible. That could explain the outage. But it still doesn't account for why the power reserves or rechargeable devices would have been drained. Doesn't explain those revs moving in reverse, either."

"Maybe that's where the hacking comes in."

Uncle Trey shrugged, at a loss for words.

"I'm only asking because I met a really strange lady last night," I started. "She went into the Holo-pal chamber with her son, and the outage happened not too long after that."

"What was strange about her, Cam?" Mom asked.

"Um, well . . ." I paused for a moment. "I don't

know. She walked funny. And talked funny. She just looked out of place. And like I said—she wasn't even in the exhibit for ten minutes before the outage happened."

"Cam." Mom ironed out her expression, understanding but stern. "We can't blame people for things off just a hunch. And we have enough legal troubles without someone getting mad at us for accusing them."

"Your mom's right." Dad squeezed her shoulders.

My blood got hot. "I'm not blaming her," I said. "I'm just saying. She was odd but seemed nice. She even helped people find their way out of the park once the lights came back on. I think maybe if we can locate her, then we can ask her questions. I bet she'd be willing to help."

"There's probably better ways for us to spend our time," Mom said.

Without thinking, I balled up my fists. Why weren't they listening to me? First, they tried to keep secrets about the park from me. Now they wouldn't even listen to my ideas. I felt anger rising up in me like a volcano, but before it could reach the top, a wave of sadness cooled me all the way down.

My own parents didn't trust me. That was clearer than ever. I frowned, and the tension in the condo was thicker than Grandma Ava's cheddar cheese grits.

"I'll check the recordings from last night," Uncle Trey said, breaking the silence. "See what I can find. What did the lady look like, Cam?"

"She had red hair," I mumbled. "Bright red hair. And green eyes. And she had a son who looked just like her. They both walked really stiff. Like really proper."

"Got it. Sister, bro-in-law—we done here?" He pushed himself up and out of the recliner.

"Wait!" I said, my voice cracking. "There's one more thing."

"What is it, son?" Dad said.

I got up from my seat on the floor and rushed into my bedroom. I had debated with myself all night and all morning about sharing the messages with my parents—the weird, creepy messages that appeared from an unknown source around two in the morning.

If my parents weren't already terrified by this whole situation, this was sure to send them over the edge. I didn't want to tell Mom and Dad about the harassing messages on my Futurewatch. But it felt like the right thing to do. I grabbed the watch from my bed and noticed some messages from Earl asking to play a word game. I wished we were having fun together instead of dealing with Futureland drama. I missed my friends so much.

I came back from my room and set my Futurewatch

in my dad's palm. Mom quickly snatched it out of his hand and started going through it herself.

"Those messages came in late last night. I don't know who they're from, but I"—I exhaled deeply—"I feel like it might have been Southmore."

At the mention of Southmore's name, Uncle Trey sat up in his seat.

"Southmore's in prison, son," Dad said, leaning over to follow Mom's lightning-fast scrolling on my watch. "He can't do anything to you from in there."

"I know it sounds silly," I said. "But whoever sent those messages knows about Atlanta. They said they wanted revenge. It has to be him. He's the only one who wants to get me."

"You can't wear this anymore, Cam," Mom said. "We have to get this to the IT team and trace this message immediately." Tears started to form in her eyes, and her voice shook. She stood up, and my dad joined her. She shook her finger at me. "And you can't leave the park. You need to stay as close to us as possible. If you have to go somewhere, one of us will go with you. No revs. No holograms. Only humans."

I knew I shouldn't have told them about the messages. Why don't they believe me?

"But, Mom!" I whined.

"Stacy . . . ," Dad started.

"No!" Mom shouted. "We won't go through this again. I refuse. We have to keep Cam safe. We can't afford the risk. My heart can't take it. We need to have complete control."

"Well, what am I supposed to do without a Futurewatch?"

"Why don't you grab one of the old models from storage?" Dad suggested.

"Those don't work as well! And *all* my data is loaded up into that one. My whole life is in there. Those old Futurewatches can't even hold that much information."

"Why don't you grab one of the new Futurelink bands, nephew," Uncle Trey said. "It can transfer all of your data over. More than enough space. You can voice and text chat from it, too."

"Yeah?" said Dad. "Okay? Is that good enough? Temporary solution. We'll get your watch back as soon as we can, son, but it's way more important that we figure out where these messages came from right now. We'll figure this out, okay? Together. Family meeting adjourned."

My parents rushed out of the living room toward their bedroom, Dad still trying to comfort Mom. The revs went in different directions. Some back to the lab and some into the park.

My heart sank. Now I *knew* I couldn't count on my parents. They were too scared, too focused on the past to see the new mystery unfolding right in front of us. I felt so frustrated. Uncle Trey stood up and stretched, looked at me, and laughed the kind of laugh you go for when no words can communicate how you feel.

"Here we go again, nephew. This is wild, huh?" he asked.

"Uncle Trey." I lowered my voice to a whisper. "I need your help. Something you said reminded me of something else I noticed last night. But you can't tell Mom or Dad."

He looked over the top of my head to be sure that my parents had left the living space and then knelt down to face me, concern in his eyes. "What's going on?"

"Do you know if people's Futurelink bands worked last night during the outage?"

He put on a thinking face. "I'm not sure. I haven't checked the incident report database from last night to see what guests have complained about yet. Why do you ask?"

"Last night, when the outage happened and I noticed my Futurewatch got zapped, I was standing next to Yu—"

Oh, jeez. Nobody knows Yusuf is here. He's probably still snoring in the Black Beat. I can't blow our cover yet.

"I, um. I was standing next to *your* plants. The light-up ones. And some other people were standing next to me. One of their bands was glowing and beeping. I think it was a Haventech band and *not* a Futurelink band. But I'm not sure."

Uncle Trey scratched his chin. "I hear you, nephew, but I'm not sure I'm following. What do you need from me?"

"Do you think you could score a Haventech band for me? One we can break open and study?"

"Hmm. Tough one. Those things haven't even hit stores yet. They just keep popping up at those free giveaways all around the city."

"Please, Uncle Trey? Can you try? I'd do it myself, but Mom and Dad are going to be watching me like hawks. Maybe you'll find one and maybe you won't . . . but I've got a strange feeling about those bands. I just want to check it out."

Uncle Trey nodded and squeezed my shoulder. "I'll see what I can do."

"Thanks, Unc."

I walked back into my room and plopped down on the bed. Uncle Trey was headed to review more recordings from last night. The revs were hard at work. My parents needed time to cool down. Technically, my imprisonment had already started. But I had about an hour or two before any adult in Futureland would be paying enough attention to actually keep me there.

I needed to clear my head, and badly. This wasn't my first lockdown. I knew all the rules, especially the main one: don't leave Futureland.

So I did exactly what I had to do.

I pulled on my pants and sneakers as fast as I could and ran for the elevator, then took it up to the zero-gravity beam, only to float back down to the ground. Once my feet landed, I broke out into a run. I looked over my shoulder at Futureland but saw nothing. Invisible. I bounded across Central Park until I made it to Fifth Avenue and didn't turn back, not even once.

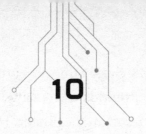

THE SMARTEST
TWELVE-YEAR-OLD IN NYC

Saturday, February 6, 2049
10:43 a.m.

As soon as I escaped Central Park, I ran into streets
lined with two things I knew would never leave
New York: cafés and construction. I started to walk uptown. I needed to calm down, clear my head. My little
unapproved escapes from Futureland had become my
go-to method for blowing off steam and getting away
from the commotion.

I kept walking and observing all the people zipping
in and out of shops with their steaming cups and tiny
paper bags. Others zoomed through traffic on bicycles
or cruised down the lanes in pedicabs, their drivers
pointing out landmarks and destinations. People of all
shapes, shades, and sizes in suits, sneakers, sunglasses,
and sweaters crossed the streets at red lights, dozens

and dozens at a time. That's one thing I always loved about New York—everyone there is so unique, so different. New York was like a glimpse of what life would be like if Futureland was the *actual* world and not just one tiny piece of it, floating high in the sky.

New York was the closest thing to making all our dreams real that I'd ever seen.

I came to a busy intersection and stopped in my tracks. My breath caught in my chest, and I froze at a sight in the distance. The red-haired lady! She wore a red trench coat and stood on the sidewalk across the street from me, waiting to cross. The crosswalk light changed, and I slipped through the crowd trying to get close to her. When we met, we made eye contact for a half second before she kept walking.

"Hey! Don't you remember me?" I asked.

"Huh?" she said, taking a long look at me. "Do you live at the shelter?"

"What? No, no. I met you in the park the other night. In Futureland. You came with your son." I turned back around to cross the street alongside her.

"Oh!" She dabbed at her eye with a handkerchief as people moved all around us. "My apologies. I volunteer at the shelter down the street. You remind me of one of the little boys there. Anyway—Futureland. That was some power outage, huh?"

"It sure was," I said. "My parents were talking about it this morning. We talked about you, too. I must have the best luck to see you here. We need your help."

"My help? What could I possibly do?" she asked.

"Well, first off, we wanted to thank you. I saw you helping people get out of Futureland when everyone started to scatter. That was very brave."

She blushed. "Oh, that's no problem. I believe we all have a duty to do what's right."

I nodded, continuing. "The outage happened not too long after you went into the Holo-pal chamber. My parents thought maybe you saw what caused it and would be willing to help."

She shook her head as we reached the other side of the street. "I'm sorry. I didn't see anything." She turned on her heel and started to walk away. I sighed and trotted after her.

"Well, at least come by so they can thank you in person. They'll probably even give you free Future Passes or something. Maybe you can tell them your idea about a spooky Futureland night. What's your name? I'll tell security to let us know when you arrive."

The woman paused to consider my offer. "That's very generous of you. I'm Ruthie. Ruthie Bowen. I'll come by tomorrow," she said. She turned again and shuffled off even more quickly than before.

136

"Thanks, Ms. Bowen," I said, even though she was out of earshot. *What a strange woman,* I thought. *But her heart seems like it's in the right place.* We could at least get Ruthie Bowen to Futureland and butter her up with some praise and free perks. Then maybe she would warm up to the idea of helping us figure out what happened in the minutes before the outage.

I crossed the street again and walked aimlessly, just letting thoughts tumble through my brain. I took some deep breaths to try to relax. The farther I walked up Fifth Avenue, the more I started to see shops and small businesses. Places to work. Places to eat. And of course, places to live—fancy-looking apartments in buildings that probably reached all the way up to Futureland. Maybe even higher.

Every few buildings, I would see one that stuck out. They were totally black with tinted windows. They looked eerie in the daytime—I'm sure they were creepy at night. One even had an intricate white skull spray-painted onto its side. I shuddered as I walked past.

I was so busy taking in all of the sights that I didn't notice the girl. But she noticed me.

"Ayo, what's good with you?"

"Huh?"

She was standing directly in front of me, in the middle of the sidewalk. The people who were walking

137

behind us parted to go around on either side, throwing us nasty looks and mumbling under their breath as they passed. The girl looked about my age, but I wasn't sure. Something about her looked a little older. She wore a black headwrap pulled tight around her hair and tied in a knot at the front. She had on what looked like a vintage sweater with the letters *NYU* across the chest. She had round cheeks and a plump shape, and the most perfect dark brown skin—like smooth earth. She stared at me with a raised eyebrow.

"I said what's good with you?" she repeated. "You acting mad weird. You been walking right behind me for, like, five, ten blocks, making every move I make. You following me or something?"

"Uh, no." I felt my cheeks warm. "I—I didn't realize. I'm—"

"You know me or something?" she went on. "From school? Nah, you don't look like no 527 kid. Where you from?"

I swallowed. "I'm from Atlanta." My palms got sweaty from nerves.

"You don't sound like you from Atlanta," she said.

"Yo, move out the way! You in the middle of the sidewalk!" someone shouted as they walked past us. The girl pulled my arm until we were tucked into the entry vestibule of a building, away from the street.

"So, you from Atlanta, huh?" the girl said, her voice a little softer now that she knew I hadn't been following her on purpose. "Are you okay? You lost or something? You need help?"

"No, no." I shook my head and laughed nervously. "I—I'm visiting here. I was just going for a walk. I'm sorry about following you. I wasn't paying attention. I didn't mean to scare you."

"Word. It's all good," she said. "Just had to make sure you wasn't no creep."

We both laughed.

"Are you from here?" I asked.

"I'm from Harlem," she said proudly. "But . . . I don't live there anymore. We're going back, though! My parents promised me we're going back. Just gotta be patient, you know?" She sighed.

"Yeah," I said. "I've moved a lot, too. I know what it's like to want to go back. I've never been to Harlem, but one of my favorite graphic novels is set there. *Watson and Holmes.*"

"Yeah, yeah, that detective joint! Not bad." She nodded. "I'm Inaya, by the way."

"Cameron. Nice to meet you."

"So, who you visitin' here, anyway? How long you stayin'?"

I took a deep breath. In Atlanta, I had been so

scared to reveal the truth about my life. But once the crew found out who I was, they actually wanted to be my friends. This time felt different. I could be honest, be myself. I had nothing to hide. Besides, every person who I could convince to have a good opinion of Futureland would help turn our reputation around.

"Well, I'm visiting for a while," I started. "My parents—they run this park. Like, a theme park. And it travels around, so—"

"Yo! Nawwww, you talkin' about Futureland?!" Inaya interrupted excitedly. "Are you kidding me? Your parents run Futureland? *The* Futureland?!"

I couldn't stop my smile from spreading. "So, you've heard of it?"

"Heard of it? That's, like, my parents' favorite place! They used to take me every time it came to New York back when we could—um, back in the day, you know? I only remember a little bit because I was so small, but yeah. That's cool."

"Do you want to come by?" I offered. "I could show you everything that's changed since last time you saw it. You could bring your parents, too."

"Nuh-uh," Inaya said, crossing her arms. "No thanks. I heard that place be buggin' out these days— no offense. Kids disappearing and robots crushing people and—"

"Nobody got crushed—"

"All types of spooky men and fake robot parents. It was wild in the news. Y'all got all that under control yet?" she asked.

I sighed. "We thought we did. But we might have more work to do."

Inaya put her hand on my shoulder. "Hey. *Patience,* remember? Y'all will figure it out. And then, maybe— *strong* maybe—I'll come by."

I laughed and nodded.

"I didn't even know y'all was back in New York, though," Inaya added. "I definitely gotta tell my parents."

"Yeah, well, we just opened up yesterday," I said. "And the mayor is making us keep the park invisible whenever it's not open to the public. For *aesthetics.*"

"Invisible?" Her eyes widened. "Y'all can do that? Wow. And, ugh, everything around here is about aesthetics these days. Not the first time I've heard something like that. That's how we ended up with all these haunted-looking black buildings. I hate it."

I shook my head. "I was wondering about that. Yeah. Well. I'm sorry to hold you up, Inaya. You probably have somewhere to be. I should probably head back to the park soon, too. I'm not even supposed to

be gone." I checked my watch for the time. "Nice to meet you. Hope I run into you again."

She smiled. "You might if you're lucky. Catch you later, Cameron. Have fun in New York. And don't walk so slow. You southern people always walkin' slow up here. Pick up your feet!"

I laughed and started to wave goodbye, but something caught my eye on the building next to us. I read the vinyl lettering on the glass door once, twice, rubbed my eyes, and then a third time. I couldn't believe it.

"Oh my god! No way!" I shouted. "No way, no way!"

Inaya raised an eyebrow at me. "Cameron, you good?"

"I—I—" I pointed at the glass door.

HAVENTECH, INC.
HOME OF THE LIFEBUDDY WRISTBAND
RETAIL LOCATION
OPENING SOON!

Inaya's face hardened. "You know about Haventech?" she asked.

I shook my head, but I couldn't take my eyes off the glass. "I don't know enough," I admitted. "But remember when you asked me about figuring out all those problems in the park? Well, let's just say I've got a hunch that the more I figure out about Haventech and these LifeBuddy wristbands, the closer I'll be to stopping all the craziness that's going on in Futureland." I glanced back at the door and tapped on the glass. "It may sound ridiculous, but I think they're causing trouble in the park somehow."

Inaya glared at the door and shook her head. "It doesn't sound ridiculous at all. And it wouldn't be the first time." She looked at me again. "Cameron, *this* is why we met today. It has to be fate. I know you said you had to get home, but do you have time for one more stop?"

I shrugged. "Not really. But whether I go home now or later, I'm still going to get in trouble."

"Perfect," she said. "Come with me. I have something to show you."

Inaya and I took the train to Harlem, 135th Street. When we left the station, things looked nice enough—restaurants, businesses, and places to stay. But after a few minutes of following Inaya through grassy areas and alleys, I started to notice run-down buildings with rusted fire escapes and faded apartments with

missing windows and graffiti tags. Those places didn't look nearly big enough to house the number of people standing outside them. So many buildings were crumbling, abandoned. And here, uptown, even more of those spanking new black buildings. Bringing a dark energy to the entire neighborhood.

"Don't worry," Inaya said. "I know it looks a little rough, but this is home. They know me around here. We'll be okay." I nodded. She gave me her hand and I took it. She walked me to the front of a tall building with a stonelike foundation and an umber hue. It stretched three, maybe four, levels up, with ornate carvings making up the architecture of the doorway, windows, and roof of the building. Even with most of the windows broken and boarded up and the stains on the stone, it was beautiful. I stood in silence next to Inaya, just taking it in.

"Bagayoko," she said.

"Huh? Bagayoko?"

"Bagayoko." She nodded. "It's my last name. My parents are West African. They've known each other since they were our age. They came to America together, just the two of them, to start a new life—to make something that they could be proud of. They wanted me to be proud to be a Bagayoko."

"What happened?" I asked.

"This brownstone." She pointed at the building. "It isn't ours, but we used to have one just like it. After my parents finished school at New York University they got good jobs. And they started to rent a beautiful home. They said it would be ours to own one day. But then my dad got laid off, my mom was sick for a while, and someone new took control of the property."

Her voice had lost its dreamy joy. "They raised the rent so high that my parents couldn't afford it anymore, so we had to move to the shelter. That's where I stay now. They say it's only for right now, and that what matters most is that we're together. But I miss our home."

I dropped my head. "I'm sorry, Inaya. I'm so sorry. I've lived in Futureland my whole life, and until a few months ago I never realized how stuff like this happens. But I know now. And I'm sorry it happened to you."

Inaya looked at me with a sad smile. "I appreciate you, Cameron. But that's not all. I want to show you what I really brought you here to see." She pointed into the distance, toward a tall metal gate enclosing some other metal structures. "You see that over there? That's where *our* brownstone used to be."

"What is it now?" I asked.

"Come on," she said. "Let's get closer."

We headed back toward the train station, skipping across the crosswalks and talking about life. Inaya introduced me to everybody in her old neighborhood. Older people asked about her parents and about how school was going. Her friends asked her when she was going to come back and hang out.

I learned that Inaya wanted to go to medical school at NYU. After that she wanted to become the kinda scientist that makes prosthetic limbs—like replacement arms and legs—for people. She knew *so* much about science and the human body. She was probably the smartest twelve-year-old in New York.

I told her all about Mrs. Espinoza's class, and she hung on every word. Even asked if I could bring her my notes. Felt like a fair trade for how much she had already helped me learn about Haventech.

Inaya spotted another one of her friends walking toward us from a distance. All I could make out of the girl from far away was her purple shoes and two big afro-puffs. My heart thumped as we got closer and closer to meeting her at the intersection, but when we finally saw her face . . . it wasn't Dooley.

And of course it wasn't. I'd just thought . . . I didn't know what I'd thought, honestly. I just missed my friend. It seemed like lately I could be perfectly fine, having a great day, not even remembering what had happened last year, but then all of a sudden, missing Dooley would hit me like a subway train. My heart would sink into my sneakers.

It hurt. A lot. And missing Dooley also made me miss the rest of the crew. I wondered what Rich, Earl, and Angel were doing back in Atlanta. I wished we could all be together.

"Yo, Cam, you good?" Inaya asked as we parted ways with her friend, just a few steps from the subway station. "My friend didn't scare you, did she? She's loud, but she's cool. You gonna have to get used to that, being a new New Yorker and all."

"Huh?" I said, snapping back to reality. "Oh, no, no. I'm sorry. I've got a lot on my mind."

"Word," Inaya said. "Well, we're about to get you home, don't worry. This train is always on time. I bet your mother and father don't even know you're g—"

Deet deet deet da-deet-deet da-deet!

Oh no.

I lifted up my wrist and remembered I didn't have my Futurewatch. Whoops. Other wrist. My Futurelink

projection band was blinking. I lifted it up and it displayed a hologram of Yusuf requesting an incoming video call.

"Oh! Hey, hold up," I told Inaya. "This is my friend Yusuf. I'm going to see what he wants. You know, y'all would actually get along."

I tapped the hologram to accept the call and Yusuf's face materialized into the projection. I didn't have to look at him for more than two seconds to know that something was wrong.

"Yusuf . . . what's the matter?"

He cleared his throat. "Ah-ha," he laughed nervously. "Um. Good afternoon, CJ. How are you?"

"What? I'm fine," I said impatiently. "Why are you acting weird? What's going on?"

"I overslept," he said.

"Okay?" I was so confused. "That's fine. Are you still in the Black Beat?"

"Well . . . not exactly."

"Stop talking in riddles!" I hollered. "Where are you?"

"He's with us," a voice called out through the projection.

Mom's voice.

Yusuf angled the transmitter to the left, then to the right. Mom, Dad, and Uncle Trey all stood behind him with their arms crossed, glaring through the hologram at me. My whole body got hot, and my heart scrambled all around my rib cage.

"Sorry, CJ," Yusuf said, defeated.

"Cameron J. Walker," Mom said, "you get yourself home—right NOW!"

I took a big breath of the last free air I'd probably get to breathe as a kid, exhaled, and closed my eyes. "Yes, ma'am."

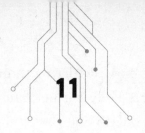

LONG STORY SHORT

Saturday, February 6, 2049
1:00 p.m.

What were you thinking, Cameron?" Mom's voice boomed off the walls of the condo, filling my ears. I winced.

"I—"

"How could you *possibly* have believed that *any* of the decisions you made in this situation were the right ones! I mean, seriously? Hiding Yusuf from us?"

"No, I—"

"Do you have any idea how dangerous this is?" she went on, apparently uninterested in my attempt to explain. "Do you understand how bad this could have been if something happened to him and we didn't even know he was here?"

"Mom, I—"

"No!" She cut me off again. "I don't want to hear it. You can't just do whatever you want, Cameron." She started to cry. "I *know* you miss your friends. You think I don't miss my mom? What's gotten into you?"

My chest felt tight, and I didn't want to look Mom in the eyes. She was getting more upset by the second.

"You have to stop this," she continued. "This thrill-seeking you've been doing. Leaving the park without telling us, running around New York City.

"You just stuck Yusuf into the park and thought everything would be okay? No, Cameron. No! Futureland is a dangerous place!"

She gasped, then put her hands over her face and cried some more. I think the words came out before she realized what she was saying. The room went silent as *Futureland* and *dangerous* in the same sentence crawled into our ears and dug into our brains. I had no idea how to respond.

Things had changed. She didn't mean the kind of danger that comes with any fast-paced ride or sky-high attraction. We couldn't control what happened in Futureland anymore. We couldn't be certain about anything.

And that made it a dangerous place, even for us.

Dad moved over to comfort Mom, but she waved him away and went into their bedroom, slamming the

door. Uncle Trey stood in the hallway near the elevator, arms crossed, not making eye contact with anybody. Yusuf and I sat next to each other on the couch. I felt so angry at him for getting caught before I found a way to tell my parents. If I would have told Mom and Dad when he first got here, we wouldn't have even been in this mess. Yusuf should have listened to me. I also felt angry at myself for not following my intuition.

"Cameron, your mother and I are very disappointed in you," Dad said.

"I know," I said. A guilty feeling in the pit of my stomach cut through the frustration.

"I don't think I have to explain how big a deal this is," he continued. "You need to stay put. No leaving Futureland unless it's with one of us. We've deployed a tracker and alarm to your Futurelink band so that anytime you go outside the park, we'll get a notification. When the IT team finishes up analyzing your Futurewatch, we'll put one in there, too."

"Okay," I said. I felt numb to everything. "Dad, is Yusuf going back to Atlanta?"

"No." Dad looked at me sternly, then at Yusuf. "Not yet. We called his parents and explained everything that happened. Yusuf is going to stay with us for a little bit longer until we can *personally* escort him back to Atlanta and his family. And *you* are going to make the apology of your life to his mother and father. Until then, both of you are on punishment."

"I understand," I said.

"Yes, sir," Yusuf said.

"And, Yusuf," Dad continued, "I know I'm not your father, but while you're staying with us, you'll have to follow the Walker Ways of Living. First things first, you need to . . ." He trailed off. "Is that . . . is that a Haventech wristband that you have there?" he asked.

Uncle Trey, still in the hallway, raised his head and looked in our direction.

"No, sir, I don't think so," Yusuf said.

"May I?" Dad asked, taking Yusuf's wrist in his hand. He turned Yusuf's arm over, looking at the wristband from every angle.

"Trey, you won't believe this," he said without looking up. "This looks like a Haventech prototype. No branding on it. Like an early model maybe. But the same tech we've seen on TV. And it certainly resembles the Futurelink design. Come take a look."

Uncle Trey stepped over and reviewed Yusuf's wristband just like Dad had. He widened his eyes and poked his lips out in surprise. "Well, well, well," he whispered.

"Yusuf, you mind if I grab this from you for a little while?" Uncle Trey asked. "We can get you a Future-watch or projection band in the meantime. Just want to take a closer look at it."

"Well, I don't know . . . ," Yusuf said, his face twisting in discomfort.

"I promise we won't mess it up," my uncle explained. "Just want to run some tests on it. Look at the design. Figure out how it works. That's all."

"Yeah, I get it, but I just—"

Uncle Trey, still holding Yusuf's wrist, gently moved to slide the band off as Yusuf protested. Yusuf flailed and snatched his arm back from Uncle Trey, hollering out.

"No!" Yusuf yelled. "No, you can't take it! It was a gift!"

We all froze. This was the second time I'd seen Yusuf act strange about that band. Something was definitely up with it. Before New York, I'd never even heard him raise his voice.

Uncle Trey put his palms out and tried to speak calmly. "Yusuf, hey, look. It's just me. It's Uncle Trey, okay? I'm sorry. I didn't mean to scare you. We won't take your band if you don't want us to." He turned to Dad. "J.B., walk with me? Let me holla at you."

They shuffled away, and Dad called out "No leaving

the park, Cameron!" over his shoulder. Yusuf and I rose and went into my room. I started grabbing shirts off the floor and halfway folding them up before stuffing them into drawers. I always did that when I wasn't sure what else to do with myself. I hadn't said a word directly to Yusuf since the hologram call. Something didn't feel right.

"Hey, Yusuf. You okay? You seemed pretty upset back there."

He sat cross-legged on the floor looking out the window, his left hand covering up his right wrist— where the band was. "It's *my* band. I don't have to give it to anybody. I don't have to *ever* take it off if I don't want to."

I stared at him. *Why is he acting like this?*

"Well, do you mind if I look at it? I won't mess around with it like Dad or Uncle Trey. Just wanna look."

He turned to face me. "Didn't you just hear what I said? I'm not taking it off. Not for you or your uncle or dad or anybody else. So quit asking." He stood up and pushed past me on his way out of the room, reminding me how much bigger and stronger than me he was.

I stared after him as my head started to thump. Yusuf was never irritable, and he never acted so angry and rude. Maybe it was just the stress of the

situation—we had all been on edge a bit lately. But I don't know. Something about him seemed . . . different.

I plopped down on the bed and hunched my shoulders, my hands folded in my lap. I threw myself backward onto the mattress in frustration, facing the ceiling. Tension squeezed into my temples, and I closed my eyes. *Not another headache.* How could so many bad things happen all in one day? I put my left hand over my forehead and massaged it gently. *Well, at least you met Inaya today. That's a good thing. Focus on the good things.*

Deet deet deet da-deet-deet da-deet!

"Ugh!" I snatched the projection band off my wrist and threw it against the wall, next to the closet. Jeez, all I wanted was some peace and quiet to focus. Just five minutes to relax and empty my mind. Was that too much to ask?

Deet deet deet da-deet-deet da-deet!

Deet deet deet da-deet-deet da-deet!

Apparently so.

I huffed and got up from the bed. It better not have been Yusuf calling me, after he stomped out of my room. And I loved Grandma Ava, but I wasn't in the mood for one of her long stories. Most of the other people who called me lived with me in Futureland, so who— Oh no.

Angel. Earl. Rich.

I picked up the Futurelink band and saw their holo-gram faces rotating around one another. They were re-questing a video call. At first, I didn't want to answer, but my band kept beeping. I might as well face the music.

"Hello?"

"CJ, ¡no me lo puedo creer! How could you?" Angel shouted.

Rich narrowed his eyes at me. "You really think that after we spent *all that time* helping you solve one of the biggest mysteries in Atlanta history, we don't have some investigation skills of our own? Huh? You think you're the only detective?"

Uh-oh.

"I mean, I'm just saying," Rich continued. "Who was there with you, in the trenches? You act like you forgot!"

"Ay, dios mío." Angel shook her head and frowned at me, the frustrated comments still coming, just lower under her breath now. I sighed and lifted my face to the ceiling.

"Guys, it's not like that—"

"CJ." Earl cut me off. "We went by Yusuf's house to check on him. His little brother Tahir told us he was in New York with you. Is that true?"

I nodded. "Yes." We were officially caught.

"Why didn't you tell us?" It was Angel this time. My headache thumped more with every word I tried to produce.

"I don't even know where to start," I said. "Everything happened so fast."

"No wonder you didn't respond when I asked you to play Word Buddies. Well, is Yusuf okay?" Earl asked. "That's most important."

"Yeah, he's fine. A little cranky, but fine. But we're grounded. I'm really sorry, y'all. Not one normal thing has happened since we got to New York. I have to bring y'all up to speed, but it's a long story."

"Well, hold that thought," Rich said. "Because we've got a story for you first, and things are about to get even less normal. You heard about all those people going into shock?"

"What? What do you mean shock?" I asked. "What people?"

"Angel, send the link."

Angel posted a link in our group chat, which automatically added another screen to the projection field. Now I could see Earl, Angel, and Rich, and beside them, a square hologram of the video Angel had sent that we could all watch together. The video preview showed a middle-aged Black man with a mix of gray and black in his low-cut hair, and I recognized the face.

Darren Dobbs, *National News*. More like national *bad* news. I'd never ever seen this guy talk about anything that wasn't scary or depressing. I took a breath and braced myself.

Good morning, citizens. This just in: reports from all over New York as dozens of simultaneous hospitalizations were brought on by a mysterious state of neurogenic shock. Between last night and this morning, over thirty people and counting were checked in to New York City hospitals after experiencing fainting and convulsions. After preliminary tests revealed no relevant underlying conditions for any *of the patients, interviews with each of them exposed a deeply troubling common bond: the last thing they all remember before going into shock was visiting Futureland. That's right, citizens— Futureland.*

Formerly considered the world's most technologically advanced amusement park, lately, Futureland has been looking more and more like the world's most dangerous place. While its owners, the Walker family, market a safe, family-friendly experience, a series of kidnappings and malfunctions associated with the park's visit to Atlanta last fall made many New Yorkers skeptical about its return to the Big Apple. Now our worst fears may be

confirmed as Futureland seems to be associated with this new danger in the city.

Some speculate that a massive power outage during Futureland's opening night could have had adverse health effects for everyone in attendance. Other, more radical thinkers believe that Futureland may be using some type of remote-control mechanism to force parkgoers to continue supporting them despite the apparent danger. There were indeed reports of several patients insisting that they heard voices during their states of shock—voices that told them to return to Futureland. . . .

I tried to keep focusing on the video, but a commotion started outside my bedroom window. I walked over toward the glass and looked out to find dozens and dozens of people marching in step with one another, coming in from the north entrance of Central Park toward the center. Close to where Futureland was hovering.

"CJ?" Angel said from the video chat. "CJ! You still there?"

I looked closer into the crowd. Something seemed off. In a rush, I left the window and scrambled underneath my bed for my trusty pair of Future-vision goggles to use as binoculars. I returned to the window, drowning out the sound of Earl, Angel, and

Rich calling my name from the hologram projection. I looked through my goggles to get a better look.

Something *was* off.

Each person marched in sync with one another. Other bystanders in Central Park pulled out their phones and recorded the group making their way down the path with perfectly timed steps. All together, like they made up one big instrument. As the marchers finally reached Futureland, they broke their formation to create a giant circle around the perimeter of the theme park. Their eyes opened—all at once—and they angled their heads up at the giant flying mountain range in the sky.

Even though they were awake, nobody looked *conscious*. They all had droopy eyes and slack mouths. Their expressions were empty, like they had no clue who they were or what they were doing. I used my Future-vision goggles to check out some of the other people in Central Park who weren't a part of the march. They, too, angled their heads up to the sky, but many of them seemed confused. They removed their sunglasses and strained their vision toward the sky. Some conversed with one another, pointing and shrugging.

"They can't see us," I said under my breath. "The park is on invisible mode. But these other people . . . they know exactly where we are. . . ."

My breath caught in my chest. Still in sync, each person in the zombie circle raised an arm and, with a single finger, pointed directly at Futureland.

"Uh-oh," I mumbled. My friends kept shouting over each other from my watch.

"CJ?!"

"What's happening!"

I opened my mouth to try and describe what I was seeing, but no words came out.

As soon as their arms were raised, all of the marchers' bodies stiffened. Their backs went straight and their knees locked, their eyes widening with fear. Their mouths opened and twisted up in horror, but no sound came out. No sound that I could hear, anyway. They all stood still, completely frozen.

Meanwhile, a frenzy started among the other park-goers. Some tried to pull the marchers away but couldn't budge them. Others made a run for it by themselves. But before anybody had a chance to get too far, all the marchers dropped to the ground. Their eyes rolled into the backs of their heads, and they started to writhe on the grass of Central Park's Great Lawn. My blood curdled as I watched the marchers sprawled out on the grass, convulsing. My heart beat like a drum as my eyes took in the horror, but I couldn't look away.

Screams rang out from below Futureland. People

164

dashed in all directions, and more and more parkgoers pulled out their phones—some to film, and some to probably call 911. But the marchers didn't get up. They continued to jolt on the ground with their twisted limbs and pained expressions. Almost like they were fighting against something.

"Guys . . . ," I finally managed to call out across the room to the hologram, my voice cracking. "I gotta call you back."

Z'S VIDEO STREAM CHANNEL

HOME   VIDEOS   MORE

Nemoree   Follow
XxGamerGirlxX   Follow
Peach_Tree   Follow
BakedBanolli   Follow

transcript ▼

Yo, what's up, this is Z. You already know what's good with my channel—all New York, all the time, the most important news coming straight at you from the five boroughs.

So, y'all know I like to keep it real actual factual on here, not bringing you no garbage stories, you feel me? But this one right here is wild, so stay with me.

As far as we can tell, there's some kinda mind-control conspiracy going on with Futureland. I mean, just think about it—this huge park using some kinda unidentified energy source comes to New York and then next thing we know, people buggin' out, passin' out, twitching all wild. And all they can remember is visiting the park and hearing voices that told them to go back.

Nobody knows if that park is really an alien spaceship. Like Mr. and Mrs. Walker, they look like nice people, right? But don't the aliens always look nice until they kersplat everybody on Earth? Haha! Nah, son, not me. I'm not trying to get kersplatted.

Anyway, check out my next video dropping next week. Imma go more into the history of Futureland and a bunch of weird stuff that happened there last year in Atlanta. Z, out!

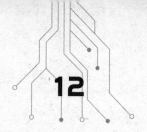

12

ROCK MOUNTAIN RACE

Tuesday, February 9, 2049
11:30 a.m.

My parents gave Yusuf and me a ton of busywork to do after school and on weekends. I think they figured it would keep us from watching the news, but staying away from bad news is easier said than done. Most of the time, we worked in near silence, still upset with each other over how he got caught. But when we did talk, we argued.

"You should have made a better plan to hide me!" he said.

My face twisted up, shocked at Yusuf's aggression. "Why are you blaming me?! We should have told my parents in the beginning, like I wanted!"

"You think you're always right, CJ. All you had to do was listen."

"That's not true! I tried my best and you didn't help at all!"

Yusuf calmed down after a day or so, but I was still worried about him. I had never seen him act like this before. I started to realize that maybe *this* was a part of making new friends, too. Fighting with them, seeing them angry and sad. Getting to know them in all different moods instead of just the one they bring to school every day. But still, it was no fun.

As for Yusuf's wristband, I didn't say anything else about it, but I noticed that he never took it off. Day or night, wet or dry, it stayed on his wrist.

Protests against Futureland started happening every day in Central Park, right underneath us. My nightmares got worse and worse, now featuring a group of zombie-looking marchers thudding to the ground and seizing. It did seem like bad press brought even more guests to the park, probably just so they could be nosy.

My parents and Uncle Trey argued long and hard about whether we should have opened back up. But we needed to keep the money flowing to pay the public relations bills and the growing mountain of legal expenses. So many New Yorkers were claiming Futureland had sent them into shock. Besides, most of the criticisms of Futureland were just silly speculations and theories. We weren't poisoning anybody with

169

radiation or sending them silent signals to pledge allegiance to the park. But how would we get everybody to realize that?

I had so little information. The Haventech wristbands; the weird, creepy playgrounds; and now the New Yorkers marching like zombies and going into shock. My intuition told me it was all related.

I just had to figure out how.

As much as I loved Yusuf, I doubted he would help me, and I couldn't trust him until I figured out what was going on with his wristband. So one morning I sent Inaya a text.

ME: Hey, Inaya. What's up?
Things are getting crazy here.
I still think something is up with the
Haventech bands. My friend has
one and he's been acting strange.
Idk what to do. Can I see you
again? I need help.

When I didn't get a response after a couple minutes, I decided to get started with the day. Mom and Dad had asked me to test out the Holo-pets from the Holo-pal exhibit and look for any ways to make them cooler, more fun. Uncle Trey had been putting in incredible work on the exhibit. Recently, he'd made it so guests could physically interact with the Holo-pals: slap hands, hug—that kind of thing. My mom couldn't figure out how her twin brother added a physical sensation response to a hologram projection yet, and Uncle Trey wasn't talking. He basked in every single moment of finally outsmarting his big sister, and he did it with a smile.

Uncle Trey had also updated the program so that guests didn't have to project both their Holo-pal and Holo-pet at the same time. They could do one or the other. That was Yusuf's idea, actually. He came up with it during family dinner one night while we chomped on Aurielle's signature lasagna.

"Some kids have enough siblings already," he'd said. "Like me. I love my brothers and sisters, but I wouldn't be able to keep up with any more of them. But if I had my very own pet, just for me, that would be cool."

As long as Futureland had the ability to create pets for people out of thin air, we might as well make them as amazing as possible. The only thing we had to worry about was how quickly we developed these new features. Uncle Trey, Yusuf, and I didn't have much time

171

to test the technology before making it available for guests. We barely ever closed the park, and revealing new details about attractions was the main way we got people excited to visit.

We had started running the park without following all of Futureland's usual safety guidelines of extensive testing. Out of necessity.

I walked out of my room and saw Yusuf waiting for me by the elevator. I hoped that some fun time in the park with Yusuf might put us back on good terms.

"Hey," I said.

"Hey."

"Know where we're headed?" I asked.

Yusuf nodded. He punched in my elevator code and directed us to the main platform. We could have just walked from the apartment, but Yusuf had been picking up a lot of Futureland habits since he'd come to stay with us. When we arrived, he called a two-seater Jet-Blur pod to take us directly to the Holo-pal exhibit. We wanted to mimic the full experience, taking all the same steps a guest would, since it was the best way to run a testing day.

I learned quickly to see Yusuf as more than just my friend from school who played basketball, the calm kid with the sweet smile. He was a really good helper. He had an incredible memory. He was clever and quick with connecting dots, and he wasn't too shabby with a wrench, either. Yusuf was the oldest of five siblings, so he learned to be responsible early.

He listened closely and took direction well, and usually thought about every piece of a problem before trying to solve it. I started to better understand him running away from home, stowing away in Futureland, his thirst for adventure. Yusuf just wanted to be a kid for a change. I couldn't blame him. Besides, it wasn't so long ago that I wanted a life that was the opposite of what I'd had.

The Jet-Blur pod zoomed into place right in front of us. Its exterior walls retracted, and we hopped into the bucket seats. The walls raised back up and enclosed us in the pod, then tinted themselves gradually, until the shiny gold designs etched into the sphere shone brightly. We lifted from the ground effortlessly and burst through the air toward the center of the park. I closed my eyes and let myself feel weightless—one of my favorite feelings in all of Futureland. One of my favorite feelings in all the world.

A few minutes later, we landed and made our way into the Holo-pal chamber. "Let's see if this works," I said, tapping my Futurelink band.

Slowly but surely, Sarafina appeared, yawning and snarling, her purple galaxy coat glistening. Yusuf

projected Ali, too, who immediately jumped over to him and propped himself on Yusuf's shoulder, snuggling into his neck.

"Ali gave Yusuf a warm welcome. No hug for me?" I asked Sarafina.

The caracal looked at me and huffed. Probably some kinda cat version of rolling her eyes.

"All right—what you got, Yusuf?"

"Me first? Cool. So, your parents and Uncle Trey gave us all these alteration codes to add new features to the Holo-pets, and I started thinking—what would I want to do with my pet if I had one? It was kinda hard to think about, since I never had a pet, but then it came to me: I would want it to fly."

I nodded, impressed.

"Okay, so, sugar gliders can't actually fly. But they can glide for about one hundred fifty feet," Yusuf continued. "As you can see here, Ali is about five inches long. And there's no specific code to make a Holo-pet fly."

Yusuf gave Ali some gentle scratches behind his little ears. "So I started thinking. You know how ants can carry stuff at least ten times their own body weight? That's a lot, but they're really small, so—"

"So it doesn't seem like very much to us," I finished for him.

"Right, yeah," he said, excited that I was following him. "But if ants were as big as humans . . ."

My eyes got big. "They would be way stronger than us!"

"Exactly," Yusuf said. "So, I ain't gonna lie, I didn't do all the math. But"—he tapped his wristband—"your parents *did* give us codes to make the pets larger or smaller. And if I make Ali big enough for me to ride . . . then those one hundred fifty feet stretch out. Far out."

Yusuf tapped on his wrist a few times, entering the one-touch codes Mom and Dad had provided for us to test a bunch of basic instant changes to the holograms. I looked closely and noticed that Yusuf still wasn't using a Futurewatch or a Futurelink band. He tapped the codes into his mysterious gift band, and Ali the sugar glider hopped to the ground and started to grow, larger and larger, until he was about five feet tall—chimpanzee size.

Ali's neon-blue fur with silver streaks looked even more brilliant on this bigger body. He immediately scurried back over to Yusuf and wrapped his legs in a hug. Yusuf laughed and looked across the room at me. "This little guy is strong!"

"Okay, okay, my turn!" I said, excited. "Ever since my uncle figured out how to let us touch the

holograms, I thought about all the ways that could be helpful. Let's say a kid falls and scrapes their knee. Their Holo-pal could pick them up and carry them to one of the medic-rev tents."

"Sounds useful for sure," Yusuf said.

"But!" I added. "Their Holo-pal can only pick them up if they're strong enough. I'm not sure Goggles is much stronger than me. So, if he needed to carry me, it might be a struggle. Unless . . . I could increase his strength from my wristband."

"Like you can do with revs!" Yusuf said. "When you go into their settings and stuff."

"Yes! The final piece of my master plan is similar to yours," I explained. "If we apply the changes to the Holo-pets, we can make them bigger, stronger, faster, or more helpful at a tap of the wrist. Which means . . ."

"Safari race!!!" Yusuf shouted.

We rushed out of the chamber, Ali scampering behind us and Sarafina plodding along at a leisurely pace. When the four-seater deluxe Jet-Blur pod arrived to take us to Future Trek, the park's best destiny for nature activities, Sarafina pushed in front of all of us. She curled up in the back seat like royalty, resting her head on her paws.

"That cat is into luxury," Yusuf said.

The rest of us squeezed into the pod and took off

through the Futureland skies. We soared above everything: the swinging, living bookshelves of the Word Locus, the spinning menagerie of Wonder Worlds—we even got high enough to sneak a peek at the glowing orbital bodies of Galactic Gallery. We zipped and flipped through the air until a cover of trees appeared below us. Rivers, streams, and grasslands came into view beyond the treetops. Wild rev animals roamed with their packs—playing, resting, or traveling to new ground. I couldn't wait to feel the thick, warm tropical air of Future Trek on my skin.

The pod landed deep in the jungle. We hopped out and surveyed the area. I grinned at Yusuf, and he grinned back.

"All right, so, first one to the big rock mountain wins," he said.

"That's pretty far. You sure Ali is going to be able to keep up once we make it out of the trees?" I teased.

"You're assuming Sarafina is going to even *make* it out of the trees," Yusuf shot back with a laugh.

I looked to my side and saw Sarafina lying on the jungle floor, licking her paw.

Yusuf had a point.

"Ah! One sec." I tapped my wristband and navigated to Sarafina's settings. I increased her speed to the max, as well as her power. Made her a little bigger, too, only one and a half times her original size. I rubbed her head a few times and pleaded with her.

"Come on, Sarafina. We have to win this. Goggles will be so proud of you."

Sarafina's long, tufted ears perked up. She hopped up off the jungle floor and came over to me, nuzzling into my leg. She eyed Yusuf and Ali and hissed. I smiled and nodded mischievously. She was ready for competition.

I got onto her back and wrapped my arms around her neck. Yusuf did the same with the supersized Ali. I clicked the timer on my Futurewatch.

Activity beginning in 3 . . . 2 . . . 1 . . .

Sarafina blasted forward so fast I almost fell off her back. It took all my strength to stay mounted as she blazed through the jungle, dashing through the foliage and bouncing from side to side to dodge obstacles. *I should have put on my Future-vision goggles!* She moved so fast that my eyes started to water. I could only open them every few seconds, and even then, everything around us looked like nothing more than a green blur.

Yusuf was done for. There was *no* way he and his king-sized sugar glider could keep up with this blazing fast cat.

Or could they?

A series of high-pitched yips—short, squealing

barks—sounded out above us. I angled my head up as best as I could without Sarafina's speed shaking the bones out of my neck.

And that was when I saw them.

Ali had crawled into the treetops and was jumping from branch to branch, high above us. He landed perfectly each time and didn't waste a second propelling himself back into the air. Each time he lifted into the air with Yusuf on his back, he let out a yip. "How's it going down there, slowpoke?" Yusuf yelled.

I blinked the moisture out of my eyes just in time to see Ali take one massively powerful jump into the air. And this time, he didn't come down.

"Wooooooo-hooooooo!" Yusuf screamed as he and Ali took to the skies, gliding higher and higher into the canopy and farther and farther into the distance. I blinked again and they were gone.

"All right, girl. Let's do it," I whispered into Sarafina's ear. "Come on, let's go!"

Like clockwork, she put on an extra burst of speed, kicking it up to the next level. Instead of dodging items in our path, she began to leap over them, landing with enough agility to never break stride. I could see the jungle's edge up ahead—if we could just get beyond the trees, then we'd probably be able to see Yusuf and Ali in the air, maybe even catch up before they made

it to the big mountain. I put my eyes forward again as we zipped through a clearing and caught sight of . . . something. It happened so fast I couldn't be sure, but the neon-blue blur *had* to be Ali.

I figured that maybe Ali and Yusuf had run into a branch or something. This was our chance! Sarafina and I exploded out of the jungle. The two-hundred-foot rock wall of Eagle Mountain stood tall ahead of us. Victory was ours.

Yip, yip-yip!

Oh no.

I looked overhead again and saw that Yusuf and Ali had recovered. They soared above us, heading for Eagle Mountain at the exact same speed. Ali cut through the air at a downward angle as we approached the rock wall, swooping lower, lower, lower . . .

Hissssss!

Ali swooped so low he almost cut in front of Sarafina. She snarled and jumped into the air to avoid him, but we collided instead. We tumbled through the air, then down to the ground, rolling over the soft savanna grass of Future Trek until my back landed up against the rock wall. Ouch.

I'm definitely gonna feel that one tomorrow. But whoa. Dooley would have loved this.

I groaned and looked over to Yusuf. His back was

up against the rock wall, too. He leaned over and massaged his knees. Ali and Sarafina stood in the grass a few feet away, stretching and grumbling. Yusuf's eyes met mine, and we remained deadlocked in a stare for a couple seconds before . . .

"We totally won!" I bellowed.

"No way!" Yusuf countered. "You tumbled to the rock, I touched it with my hand first!"

"Your flying bear cut Sarafina off!"

"He's not a bear! He's a marsupial, actually." Yusuf grinned. "And he didn't cut off your cat—she jumped into the air and made us all collide. We had the win in the bag. She cheated!"

"Nuh-uh!"

"Uh-huh!"

"Nuh-uh!"

Eventually, we burst out laughing and got to our feet. We shook hands for a race well run and decided to call it a tie.

"Let's get these pets down to their original size and head back to the chamber," I said.

"Good idea," Yusuf said. He paused for a second, contemplating something. "Uh, CJ?"

"Yeah? What's up?"

"I miss home. And my parents. And my siblings. I think I made a bad decision sneaking into Futureland.

I know you tried to help me, and I just wanted to say that I'm sorry."

I eyed the ground. "Yeah, I'm sorry, too. My dad told me once that sometimes you have to make the decision nobody is happy with now so that things can be better later. I thought being a good friend meant doing what you wanted. But really, it's making the decision that would keep you the safest. I know now."

"Yeah. Well, I promise not to sneak in again and put you in a predicament. Friends?"

"Real friends," I said, shaking his hand.

Suddenly, Yusuf felt his wrist and his eyes got as round as golf balls. He dropped to the ground and started scavenging frantically.

"What's the matter?" I asked.

"My wristband," he wailed. "It's gone. I can't. I just . . ."

Yusuf whimpered as he crawled around. He beat the ground with his fists. The stress of losing the band hit him so hard, he looked like he might cry.

I looked down and saw the dim glow of something lying in the grass. I bent down and grabbed it—Yusuf's band. I held it up. "Hey, Yusuf, I found—"

"Give it here!" Yusuf shot over to me and snatched the band out of my hand, yanking my arm as he grabbed it. I stood staring at him, shocked, as he struggled to get it onto his wrist as quickly as possible. Once it was in place, he closed his eyes, relaxed his shoulders, and exhaled deeply.

"I'm sorry, CJ," he said once he realized what he'd done. "I just—I need my band. I don't feel right without it. My head feels so fuzzy when I don't have it."

"Yeah," I said, barely above a whisper, still in shock.

"You ready to go?" he asked.

Deet deet deet da-deet-deet da-deet.

"Um, yeah," I said, looking at the incoming message on my band. "I'm just going to check this message and set Sarafina back to default. Go ahead. I'll catch up."

Yusuf shrank Ali back down to shoulder size and started to make his way back through the jungle. I reset Sarafina, and then navigated to my messages. Inaya had finally responded.

INAYA: Hey, Atlanta Cam. Started to think I had scared you away. I'm down to help. You think you can swipe that band without your friend noticing? I have a hunch.

ME: Thanks. It won't be easy, but I think so. Can you come to Futureland in the morning? As early as possible. I'll get you breakfast.

INAYA: Free food and a mystery? An offer I can't refuse.

It was official. I *knew* something was wrong with those bands and I was going to prove it, with Inaya's help. Maybe then we could get to the bottom of why Yusuf had started acting so strange. Everything was set. Now all I had to figure out was how to get his band without him freaking out on me. I proposed a new Walker Way of Living in my head, #11, inspired by Yusuf himself.

He had once told me that the basketball coach from Clark Atlanta University came to his practice to say he'd be interested in recruiting Yusuf to play there

one day. He had shared the school's motto and my approach to the next twenty-four hours:

Find a way. Or make one.

UNKNOWN: You think you're so smart, don't you?

You're not. You got lucky.

I thought I told you that you couldn't hide from me. No more watch? No problem. I'll find you wherever, however I need to. For the rest of your life.

I

See

Everything

Have your little fun while you can.
Playtime won't last much longer.

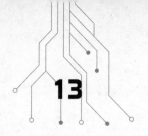

13

BRAIN WAVES

Wednesday, February 10, 2049
7:01 a.m.

I stood below invisible Futureland rubbing my hands together in the frosty dew of early morning Central Park. As Inaya approached the Great Lawn, I walked to meet her.

"Morning," I said. "Thanks for coming."

"No sweat. Let's make it quick, though. I've got to get to class after this."

"For sure," I replied. "In and out, before my parents start sniffing around."

We turned to walk back beneath the park. I wondered if Inaya would enjoy taking the antigravity beam up to the Guest Hub. Dooley used to love that. . . .

Ugh, no. Maybe the antigravity beam was too

much. I decided we'd use the extendo-stair, like reasonable people.

"Did you see that?" Inaya stopped cold.

"Huh?" I snapped out of my own thoughts. "See what?"

"Shhh. Over there. It looked like a kid . . . or a tiny ninja."

I turned my sight to where Inaya pointed. A shrub rustled, and out of it sprang a flash of black on two legs. The person sprinted, carrying something, until they found another bush to duck behind.

"Weird," I said.

"Let's check it out," Inaya said.

"Wait, but—"

Inaya was already gone.

I darted off behind her as we took the shrub the tiny ninja had hidden behind first. When they sprang out again from their new hiding place, we sprang, too, following.

"Hey!" Inaya shouted. "What you doing?!"

The ninja turned over their shoulder while running, startled at the sight and sound of us. They tripped while carrying a heavy black bag at their hip and tumbled over into a heap. Inaya and I caught up to them. They sat on their bottom, coughing into their

hands. The bag had spilled open and wrenches, screwdrivers, and other tools littered the ground.

"Whoa. Who are you? And what do you need all these tools for? You building something?"

The tiny ninja looked up at us and glowered but didn't speak. They were covered in black from head to toe, only their emerald-green eyes shining out from a mask that covered the rest of their face, like a balaclava. They quickly started stuffing the tools back into their bag. I noticed something glowing on their wrist.

"Inaya! Look! It's a wristband!" I pointed. Inaya gasped.

"You're from Haventech . . . ," she said.

At the mention of Haventech, the ninja's eyes grew wide. They jumped up, now with a full bag, and fidgeted nervously. Then we heard shouting in the distance.

"Hey, you! Stop right there!"

Inaya and I turned behind us to see two police officers sprinting toward us. We turned back to the ninja, but they were a dozen yards away now, leaving a trail of footprints in the frost. Inaya started to chase after them, but I grabbed her arm and shook my head. The police officers made it to us, panting.

"The kid . . . with the bag . . . which way did he go?" one asked.

I pointed in the direction the ninja had run, and the officers took off again. I could hear my heartbeat in my ears, and all the blaring alarms and flashing lights of my intuition had started to go off in my head. Inaya and I exchanged a silent nod. I took her hand and led her back to Futureland. We had work to do.

"So . . . this is it, huh?" Inaya walked with me through the halls after we got off the elevator. "The marvelous Futureland. Wow!" Every few steps, she paused to admire a piece of art or décor. I should have guessed she'd care about the feng shui of the place based on her outfits. After all, Inaya was a stylish girl.

"Well, not exactly," I said. "This is just the condo where we live. Most people are more amazed at, you know, the actual theme park."

Inaya smiled and shrugged. "Seen one park, seen 'em all. But the décor in this condo? One of a kind."

"Bonjour, mademoiselle," Aurielle greeted Inaya from behind the counter in the kitchen. "Enchantée. Monsieur Cam has prepared us for your arrival," Aurielle continued. "And very soon we will have a breakfast most délicieux for you."

"Cool!" Inaya smiled. "Could I have a glass of orange juice?" she asked hopefully.

"Certainly." Aurielle produced a glass of juice and handed off to Inaya, who looked at me with her mouth open in astonishment.

"Hey, I told you I would take care of you," I said. "I appreciate you coming over." I sighed, my mind still spinning with thoughts about the mysterious ninja. "Where do we start?"

Inaya sipped her orange juice. "Wow, that's good. You growing the oranges back there too, Ms. Chef?"

Aurielle smiled and curtsied.

Inaya took another sip, then returned her attention to me. "All right, so something funky is definitely up with those bands. You saw the same thing I saw—that ninja was wearing one."

"Yeah." I nodded. "And that bag of tools. If the ninja is really from Haventech, I bet they were building something. Maybe even another nightmare carnival, like the one by your old house."

Inaya's eyes got wide. "I didn't even think of that. Oh no, Cam. We have to stop it from happening. We have to."

"I think we can," I said. "But first we have to figure out the connection between Haventech and these bands. The *real* connection. I slipped my friend Yusuf's band off while he was sleeping last night. Kid snores like an ogre. We can use it for the testing before I sneak it back into his room."

"Lead the way, my guy."

"Might wanna hold on to my arm," I said.

"Huh?"

"I said, you *might* wanna hold on to my arm."

Inaya laughed. "Atlanta Cam, you're cute and all, but don't think this is some kinda date or something, you feel me? I'm here for the science. And I might come back for some of that orange juice, too, because—"

The secret tile in the middle of the kitchen depressed itself from the rest of the floor and started to lower us down to the lab space. Inaya shrieked, then covered her mouth with one hand, grabbing my arm for stability with the other. Once she realized what had happened, she gave me a sour look. I could barely keep my laughter tucked behind my lips.

"That wasn't funny."

"Alejandro," I whispered into my Futurewatch. "Can you bring our breakfast down when it's ready?"

"¡Claro, Señor Cameron!"

I walked over to Inaya with a wrinkle in my brow.

"You good, Cam?" Inaya asked.

I shook my head. "Yusuf just texted me. He said he's feeling sick and he needs his band. I lied and told him I hadn't seen it."

"Good thinking," she said. "I'm sure you didn't want to lie to your friend, but you just bought us a little more time. That could help us find a critical clue."

"I hope so," Inaya crunched down on her final piece of bacon and then licked her fingers before wiping both hands with a sani-pad and flicking out two big projections in front of us.

"Before I start," she said, "I just gotta say—your parents got a dope setup down here. Are they looking for an assistant or something? An intern? I work here for a few years and I'm *positive* NYU is gonna have to let me in."

"I'll see what I can do." I laughed. I'd never met a sixth grader so focused on college. But to be fair, I hadn't met very many sixth graders at all. "How did it go?"

"Aight, yo." She met my eyes. "This is an interesting little piece of tech you got here, Atlanta Cam." She flipped the band around between her fingers. "Based on these models of the Futurelink bands you showed me, this thing here is *definitely* a rip-off of what your parents created. A very advanced rip-off with some additional capabilities."

"Like what?"

"A lot," Inaya said. "There's a lot of data stored in this thing. Way more than what the Futurelink bands store. Your bands take *just* enough data from someone to create that holographic copy pal thing. But this thing . . . it takes triple that amount of information and stores it . . . behind a wall. I can't even tell what it's being used for."

I rubbed my chin.

"Oh!" she exclaimed, remembering. "And this hypnopedia thing. Very, very interesting."

"What's hypnopedia?" I asked.

"It's like . . . learning in your sleep," she said. "Some scientists a long time ago came up with this thing where if you play Mozart for babies while they nap, they'll become geniuses or something. Anyway, people use it in all kinds of funny ways, like learning different languages while they sleep or cramming for a test. But *this* thing—it's sending specific information to whoever wears it as soon as they fall asleep. All night, until right before they wake up."

"What kind of information?" This didn't sound good at all.

"Just like before, I can't really tell." Inaya frowned. "But what I *do* know is that it's collecting data from the wearer every single day. And it's sending a part of that data back to them as messages during the night."

"Like a loop?" I said. "So, let's say I had a bad day. If I couldn't take my mind off how stressed I was, the band could send back stressful vibes to me once I fell asleep?"

"Sure," Inaya said. "But! It could also be the opposite. Just depends."

I thought about Yusuf. *I need my band. I don't feel right without it.* Was the band talking to him in his sleep? Convincing him that he needed to wear it everywhere no matter what? Was he really sick this morning, or was it all in his mind?

"This is really good to know," I said. "Thank you."

"Wait! There's one more thing." Inaya flipped down the two projection screens before opening a totally new one. It showed a diagram of the Haventech band, pulsing gently every few seconds.

"You know anything about heart monitors?" Inaya asked me.

I nodded. "Yeah, a little. We talked about them last

198

week in Mrs. Espinoza's science and tech class. It's a little device, I guess. A little battery thing that goes into a person's chest to, like . . . watch their heartbeat. To make a record of how their heart beats. How fast, how strong."

"Very good, Atlanta Cam. Now—do you know what a *pacemaker* does?"

I shook my head.

"Okay, check it out," Inaya said. "Similar concept. Little device that goes into the chest. Only this one has its own electrical impulses that it can send directly to the heart. If your heart beats too slow or too softly, the pacemaker can step in and try to correct it."

"Wow," I said. "That's intense. So it can basically control your heart?"

"In a way," Inaya said. She flipped the projection away and held up Yusuf's band. "Your friend told you this was a regular fitness band, yeah? Tracking his sleep, heart rate, calories. *Tracking*, not controlling. Kinda like a heart monitor. But, Cam . . . every single second that somebody is wearing this thing . . . it's sending electrical impulses through their skin."

"Like a pacemaker."

She nodded. "And it looks like they're traveling . . ." Inaya drew a line with her finger from my wrist, up my arm, around my shoulder to the base of my neck,

then walked two fingers up to the top of my head and tapped it. "Right here."

"To the brain." My jaw dropped at the realization. "To *control* the brain."

We both went silent as the weight of the moment landed on us.

Mind control? Like, seriously? The thought was outrageous. But then again, it would explain a lot of things—the zombie-like hospital patients who walked into emergency rooms all over New York on the same day, the mesmerized marchers who started convulsing below Futureland last week. Some of Yusuf's strange behavior.

Maybe Haventech was *making* them do it. First, they stole my parents' tech, and now they wanted to ruin Futureland's good name, turn everyone against us, probably so they could steal even more.

It was like Atlanta all over again.

But why? And who? Southmore knew that he couldn't create Future City while Futureland still existed—it would have been too obvious where he was stealing the tech from. So he had to try to get rid of us. But Haventech . . . Haventech had already successfully stolen one of our designs and turned it into a product they could make money from.

Why keep going?

200

They must want more than money, I thought. But what else? A blur of memories played through my mind, frame by frame.

Convulsions. A creepy, abandoned park. Power outages. News reports. Angry Yusuf. A glowing wristband. A marching crowd. Those weird messages on my watch and tablet.

All of these things fit together. I know they do.

"Inaya," I started. "Are you sure this thing is capable of using electrical signals to control the brain?"

Inaya tilted her head and rubbed her chin. "There's only one way to find out for sure," she said. "Where's that friend of yours? You want to bring him down for a brain scan? We can look at his brain waves and check for irregular patterns."

I shook my head. "I can't put Yusuf through that. He's already suffering enough."

Inaya nodded. "Yeah, I understand. Besides, if our hypothesis is correct, maybe his brain waves have already changed. Not a good place to start the testing."

"Is there another option?"

"Hmm," she pondered. "It would be better if we could scan someone's brain *before* they wore the band, and then again after, to see if anything changes." She swirled the tiny silicone ring around on her finger and looked at me.

"Me?" I said, my eyes widening. "You want to scan *my* brain?"

"It's either you or your friend," Inaya said. "We can't just pull somebody random off the street. And we only got one band."

I sighed. What choice did I have?

Inaya fiddled around with one of my mom's rev scanners and then attached two little stickies to my head. She sat me down in a chair and tapped away at the screen projecting from her tablet. "Just relax, Atlanta Cam. You won't feel a thing. By the way, you got a notebook or something? I'm gonna keep a log of your tests. I like to write by hand. Helps me remember."

I closed my eyes as the tabs on my temples pulsed gently.

Here goes nothing.

Curious. Very curious.

Atlanta Cam has been wearing Yusuf's band for a few days, but I don't notice a difference in his brain waves yet. He doesn't feel any fatigue, no brain fog, and he definitely hasn't shown any signs of a quick temper like Yusuf.

Hmm.

I really thought I was onto something with that brain control band. But maybe there's a simpler explanation for all the weird stuff that has been going on. Who knows, I'm not the detective. Just a scientist.

Anyway, guess I better get ready to head back to Futureland for Cam's final scan. If this one doesn't show any signs of change in his brain waves, we'll have to go back to the drawing board. This time, Cam actually got permission from his mom for me to come over. I think she thinks we're . . . you know. Ew. Anyway, she said she has some pretty nail polish colors for us to try out. Cam says I should just go with it so she won't get suspicious. Sigh.

The sacrifices we make for the love of science.

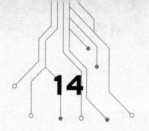

THE BOY IN BLACK

Inaya was a no-show. I called and texted, but I couldn't get ahold of her. I started to get a little worried, but what could I do? With my plan for the morning stalled, I turned my attention toward other ways to occupy myself.

"Where's Yusuf?" Mom asked, sadly stuffing nail polishes back into a cosmetic bag. I could tell she'd been really excited to meet Inaya. Where *was* that girl?

"He's still feeling sick," I said. "I went to check on him this morning, but he wouldn't let me in. I left some food at his door."

"Oh, this is breaking my heart," Mom said. "I'm so sorry he's not feeling well. I was sure J.B.'s famous chicken noodle soup would fix him right up last night. Should we call his parents?"

"Not yet," I said. "I'll check on him one more time and let you know."

"Okay, sweetheart. Hey," she added. "I saw your notes on the Holo-pets, too. They look good. I like your ideas. Me and Trey added the functionality so guests in the park can use it today. You want to go down a little early and make sure it's working? I know it's not much of a testing period, but it's all we got."

"Yeah, okay," I said.

"Thanks, Cam-Cam."

I hurried into the Holo-pal exhibit and turned on the chamber. I didn't have long before the park would open up for the day, and Mom was counting on me to make sure our new updates were functional and safe for guests.

The New York news outlets still weren't giving Futureland any room to breathe, linking us to the hospitalizations, replaying the bystander videos from the marching mob, and even broadcasting claims of other strange happenings people wanted to blame on

Futureland. One principal had even sent a video that said all her students skipped school because of us, saying they heard voices in their heads from Futureland telling them to play hooky.

Sometimes, the world is one big joke.

The park updates helped, though. Every week, Mom, Dad, and Uncle Trey figured out ways to tweak attractions or destinies to add a little something different. I'd never seen them work so hard. It wasn't enough to escape all the slander going around, but people on social media continued to spread bits of good news about fun times at Futureland. Thankfully, people kept lining up under the great big park in the sky.

"Detective Cam Walker," Itza said as the chamber reached full power. "Back again?"

"Hey, Itza," I answered. "Just testing things out before the park opens."

"Testing things out for yourself or for Yusuf?" she asked.

"Huh?" I looked up in confusion. "What do you mean?"

"I noticed you're not wearing your own device. The band you're wearing only has Yusuf's data uploaded into it."

"Oh, right," I said. "Well, could we download my data into this one?"

"One moment, please," Itza said. Her voice went quiet as the chamber started to whiz and whir.

"Error detected," she finally said. "This device is encrypted. I can access only a portion of the data already present on the band, and I am blocked from submitting additional data to its memory."

"What?" I said. I wrinkled my nose and thought for a moment. "Itza, is that how regular Futurelink bands work?"

"No, it is not," Itza said.

Strange. By now, the whole family knew that the Haventech mock bands—which we suspected Yusuf's band was—had ripped off Futureland tech to make their own design. Inaya had mentioned something similar about the hidden data when she analyzed the technology before. What did they have to hide?

"Fine, fine," I said to Itza. "Well, could I project Yusuf's Holo-pet from this band? Just as a test."

"I believe that is possible, Detective. Hold, please."

The giant column in the center of the room whirred and sparkled. The room lights darkened and came back up after a few moments, but I didn't see Ali. I looked around for the little neon-blue sugar glider, but I couldn't find him anywhere.

"Itza, are you sure it worked?"

"The process was initiated and completed," she

said. "Perhaps there was a glitch with wearer compatibility."

"Ugh," I grumbled. My ears got hot with frustration. *This would be so much easier if I had my band.*

I thought about going back up to my room to get my Futurelink band, but I heard Inaya's voice in my head, nagging me for messing up the variables in her experiment. If I took off the band before she came back, I would probably throw the brain-wave readings off.

I couldn't use Yusuf as a tester—he'd realize that I'd taken *his* band. In fact, I'd been hiding it from him under my long sleeves for days. His frustration about it going missing had eventually turned into sadness. He'd almost stopped talking altogether.

I'd have to go get Uncle Trey to run the test projection or something. Way more work than I planned for. I turned to exit the chamber and a rush of kids met me, screaming and shouting and pushing to the front for their chance to step into Itza's chamber.

"One at a time!" I hollered.

Jeez. Futureland was already open. I wouldn't have any time to test the Holo-pets' new functionality. A flash of guilt came over me. Mom was counting on me, and I'd failed. But everything had worked when Yusuf and I did the race in Future Trek, so it would probably be okay, right? I hoped so.

I left the chamber, stepped out into the bright lights of Futureland, and looked around. It was a light day. A few families moved around the park casually, kids sucking on lumi-pops and downing solar shakes all swirled together with chocolate, sparkling sprinkles, and cream. I maneuvered around a few people and their Holo-pals on my way to catch a Jet-Blur pod back up to the condo.

But then I saw Yusuf.

If I didn't know any better, I would have thought it wasn't Yusuf. Maybe a Yusuf-rev. Or an evil twin. But we met eyes as he strode across the park like a zombie. And even though his mind seemed somewhere far away, I knew it was him. And he wasn't acting sick anymore.

Yusuf stepped across the park in a slow, measured way, his hands clasped at his waist. He had an arch in his back that pinned his shoulders in perfect posture and lifted his head up high. Yusuf took one step at a time, flowing across the park in smooth strides like a ballroom dancer. His expression was blank as he stared straight ahead.

"Yusuf!" I called. He didn't turn. "Yusuf!" My heart began to race.

"Hey, mister!"

"Huh?"

A little kid with a neon tongue and bright candy stains all over their face tugged on the back of my jumpsuit.

"Hey, mister!" the kid repeated. "Our fake pets won't show up."

I glanced back to see where Yusuf was going. He moved steadily toward the main entrance terminal at the front of the park. My eyes darted quickly back and forth as I tried to listen to the park guest but not lose sight of Yusuf.

"I'm sorry, kid, I have to—"

"But they won't show up!" the kid whined. "You're supposed to help. Don't you work here? You got the suit on."

"Yes, yes, I work here," I admitted, irritated. "Look, did you go into the chamber? All you have to do is go in there and get a band—"

"But I did!" they said, holding up a projection band that matched the shade of their tongue. "I went into the spinny thing and told the lady what I wanted, but when I came out, my pet wouldn't show up."

I looked back toward the front of the park. Yusuf was gone.

Ugh! I faced the kid again.

"Hey, I'm sorry about your pet, okay?" I tried to tell the kid. "But I have to do something really important right now. I'll send somebody to help you. Can you be patient for, like, ten minutes?"

"Five minutes," they said.

"Ugh, okay. Five minutes." *Whatever.* "I'll be back, okay?" I turned and got ready to rush off in the direction I had seen Yusuf go.

"Okay," the kid agreed. "Just watch out for *that* thing."

"What thing?" I said.

The kid pointed over my shoulder. I looked behind me and saw nothing, then followed their pointer finger, up, up, up to Futureland's ceiling. I saw a small, fluttering object bouncing up and down on the glass. I pulled my Future-vision goggles out of my pocket and slid them onto my face, tapping the right lens twice to start the binocular setting.

The jittery, flittering thing on the ceiling was no object. It was an animal. And it wasn't even really on the ceiling. It was outside on the *roof.*

And after a split second, I realized it was *Ali* on the roof!

A neon-blue sugar glider flipping and zipping across the top of Futureland, *outside* the park. *How did he get all the way up there?*

"What in the world—"

A commotion started all around me. Park guests rushed to the side walls of Futureland to peer down to the ground below, cupping their hands on either side of their eyes to examine Central Park's Great Lawn beneath us. I used my goggles to look down.

Dozens of Holo-pets, maybe even a hundred of them, were all outside the park. An array of spectacularly colored hybrid beasts that the outside world had never, ever seen before. Some of them tried to graze on the grass. Others scampered off or flew away. A few of them even trotted behind joggers, who picked up the pace as soon as they noticed the strange creatures pursuing them.

"Hey! My pet's outside!" a guest yelled. Frustrated chatter started up from the other guests, too.

This has to be a glitch. These pets can't leave the park. And even if they could . . . can they interact with the outside world?

I looked back toward the entrance of the park. No Yusuf. I started to panic. I could chase after him, but I had no clue where he had gone. And this Holo-pet situation was quickly turning into an emergency. I needed to find Mom and Uncle Trey. ASAP.

I sprinted back to the main terminal, using the elevator to get down to the condo. I dashed through the open doors into the hallway leading to our living room hollering out, "Mom! Uncle Trey!! The park! Everything is—" Then I froze in my tracks.

"Inaya?"

Inaya stood in the kitchen, wiping tears and trying to steady her heavy breathing in between sips from a tall glass of orange juice. Mom sat next to her on one of the breakfast bar stools, rubbing her back.

"Inaya had a little scare, Cam-Cam," Mom said. "But she's here now. She's safe."

I stepped closer and could see stains from tears running down Inaya's cheeks. "Are you okay?" I asked.

She nodded, sipping from the glass again.

"I'll leave you two to it," Mom said. "I've got a call on hold." She rushed around the corner.

"Wait, Mom, the Holo-pets—" I tried to explain, but she was already gone.

Inaya took another deep breath, then one more gulp of juice before speaking.

"Sorry I'm late." She wiped her eyes and reached into her bag. "I'm *never* late. But I had to take a detour. He was following me, Cam. It was so creepy." Inaya shivered. She pulled the brain scan stickies out of the bag and pushed them onto my temples before booting up some program on her tablet.

"He?" For a moment, I forgot all about the Holo-pets gone wild in the park. "Following you?"

She nodded again, continuing to fidget with the tablet. "The ninja. Dressed in all black. From the other morning. He was standing across the street when I left the shelter to come to Futureland. I even took the long route, but he followed me the whole way. I got scared, hopped in a taxi, and rode around until I could make it back here. Whoever it is knows where I live. He watched me walk out of the shelter. I called my parents, but I'm scared to go home."

"You can stay here for a little while," I said, my heart racing at the idea of the creepy masked boy following Inaya around the city. "We will figure it out."

"Thanks, Atlanta Cam." She removed the stickies from my face. "Well, I'm sure you knew this already, but your brain looks fine. I'm guessing you haven't been feeling strange or hearing any secret commands in your sleep? Your scans are almost identical to the ones we took three days ago, aside from some current elevated stress levels. I'm sorry. Maybe we were wrong about the band." She paused, studying my face. "You good?"

"I guess," I said uneasily, before I suddenly remembered. "Shoot, the park! Yusuf! I have to find my uncle Trey. Come with me?"

"Never a dull moment with you, huh?"

Inaya and I rushed to the elevators to get back upstairs to the park terminal. I called Uncle Trey from my band on the way.

"Yusuf?" he answered.

"Huh?" I said, confused. "No, it's me, Cam."

"Oh, hey, nephew," he said. "Why are you calling from Yusuf's band?"

I put my palm to my forehead. "Uh, uh, where to start? Look—Uncle Trey, something is wrong with the Holo-pets—"

"I'm already on it," he cut me off. "To be honest, I don't have the first idea about how these things glitched their way out of the park, but I've got some maintenance-revs down there capturing them and bringing them back in now. We're going to shut down the Holo-pal exhibit for the day until we figure it out. You okay, kid? You sound stressed."

I paused to listen to myself panting heavily. Inaya and I stepped out of the elevator only to see Uncle Trey from behind, manipulating several projections screens. He turned and noticed us, and we ended our transmissions.

"Yeah, yeah, I'm good," I answered, even though my heart still felt like it was trying to pump out of my chest. "I was just worried about the pets. So, wait. Everything is good, then?"

"Everything is under controoooool," Uncle Trey said coolly, still flipping through screens and entering commands for his maintenance-rev army. "You know, when you work in Futureland maintenance for as long as I have, you learn to expect the unexpected. Anything can go wrong on any given day. But we've got guests to please. And your parents still ain't hearing nothing about closing this place down while we work out the kinks, so . . . we gotta be ready to solve problems on the fly." He looked to Inaya behind me and cocked his head. "Oh, hello," he said. "Name's Trey. I'm Cam's uncle. With whom do I have the pleasure?"

"Inaya Bagayoko, Harlem's own," she said, and they exchanged smiles.

"Now that's what I call a name!" Uncle Trey remarked. "And ooo-wee. Harlem." The dazzle of memory danced in his eyes. "Boy, I used to have some good times out there. Used to go down to Sylvia's all the time."

"That's my block!" Inaya said with pride.

"Right on, right on." Uncle Trey high-fived Inaya. "Harlem's own, huh? You all right with me."

"Uncle Trey, we've got to find Yusuf," I interrupted, my nervousness still clawing at me.

"Where'd he go? Sure be easier to find him if he had his own band on." Uncle Trey laughed.

"This is serious!" I said, jumping up and down anxiously. "I saw him in the park before the Holopets glitched. He was walking toward the exit. Getting ready to leave."

"Whoa, whoa. All right, I get it. Calm down for a second." Uncle Trey looked over all the security screens. "I'll check the surveillance feeds for the park and see what I can see. In the meantime, can you two go down to the ground and make an announcement? I know the Holo-pets spooked the people in Central Park. Just make a quick apology and summarize what happened. Local news is down there." He rolled his eyes. "They'll love that."

"Okay," I said, sighing with relief. "Thank you. And no problem. We'll head down."

Inaya and I lowered ourselves off the terminal and into the green zero-gravity beam. We floated through the air, all the way down to the ground, while the people below clapped and took pictures. Once we landed, I straightened up my clothes and used the microphone on Yusuf's band to speak to the crowd.

"Hi, everyone," I started. "Sorry about the mishap. Looks like we added a little extra nature to the park today." People around chuckled. "What you saw were—"

"Cam," Inaya whispered, tugging at my sleeve. *"Cam!"*

"Huh?" I lowered the band for a moment so the microphone wouldn't pick up our voices. "What is it?"

"That's him." Her voice quivered. "That's the boy who was following me."

Inaya pointed into the crowd, where I saw a figure

dressed in all black. A ski mask covered his entire face except for the eyes. He stepped forward through the crowd. Realizing people were still watching me, I raised the microphone again while trying to keep my eyes on the boy at the same time.

"What you saw were some of our newest attractions," I said. "Holographic pets. Looks like even pretend pets can be mischievous enough to get out of their kennels. We're sorry for the scare, but if you're interested in getting your own Holo-pet, come visit Futureland sometime!"

People laughed and clapped again before starting to disperse. The boy in black pushed through the crowd, going against the tide of everyone departing. Inaya slid behind me, ducking behind my shoulder, and held on to me tight. When he finally made it to us, his chest heaved and made a rattling sound as he struggled to steady his breath. His eyes were green, and poking out from beneath his mask was one tiny tuft of red hair.

"Do I know you?" I asked.

The boy didn't speak. Instead, he reached into his pocket and pulled out a folded slip of paper. He placed it into my hand gently, then turned and bounded away. I unfolded the paper and read it to myself.

"What does it say?" asked Inaya. "Cam . . ."

"We've got to go back to the park," I said, my heart

dropping into my stomach. "We've got to find Yusuf. And then we've got to get outta here."

don't wear the bands
get rid of all the holograms
Leave New York while you still can
THE ARCHITECTS ARE COMING

ANGEL: I feel a little bad for making a chat without CJ and Yusuf

EARL: Yeah, me 2

RICH: they never respond anyways

RICH: they are having their own adventure in NYC. we need to plan our research trip so we don't fail social studies. it's in less than 2 weeks

ANGEL: I know. You're right. It just still doesn't feel right.

RICH: yeah

EARL: 😥

222

Hey . . . anybody wanna play Word Buddies? I made nine words from the letters E-A-T the other day.

Helloooo? Anybody?

Smh y'all are no fun

15

THE ARCHITECTS

Saturday, February 13, 2049
8:03 p.m.

oom. Boom. Boom.

B My heart thudded in my ears as I pounded my fist against the door of Yusuf's hotel room in the Black Beat. Uncle Trey hadn't seen him on the surveillance footage, and after the park closed, he didn't come to the Guest Hub to help with cleaning and closing. Alejandro and Aurielle usually delivered all of Yusuf's meals and cleared his empty plates. So as soon as I stepped into the hallway and saw the full tray on the floor, my palms started to sweat.

Knock, knock, knock. "Yusuf?"

No answer. I held my Futureland ID up to the door and heard the lock click. I pushed the door open slowly, sticking my head in.

"Yusuf?" I looked all around the room and its connected bathroom. I poked my head into corners and even looked under the bed.

No Yusuf.

My breath shortened. The last time I had seen Yusuf, he was kinda . . . gliding through the park—in a trance, moving just like those people from the news broadcast. Just like the marchers who fainted beneath the park that day. He was headed toward the exit of Futureland.

What if he's gone? My stomach somersaulted with guilt. I watched him leave and didn't go after him. Instead of worrying about the Holo-pets, I should have made sure Yusuf was okay. Especially since he hadn't been acting like himself lately.

My body felt numb, except for some slight tingling in my fingertips. I grabbed ahold of the sink in Yusuf's room to steady myself. I splashed some cold water on my face and took a deep breath. *I have to tell Mom and Dad.*

I rushed back to the condo and burst through the door, sprinting into the living room.

"Mom! Dad! Yusuf is—"

"They're still out. Meeting on meetings," Uncle Trey said, sitting in the reclining chair with a huge bowl of cereal in his lap. He spooned crunchy flakes

225

into his mouth and smacked loudly. "But they wanted me to tell you that the IT people are almost finished with your Futurewatch. Bad news, though—they say it's corrupted. They're trying to trace the source and save your data, but you'll probably need a new watch," he said through a crunchy mouthful.

I shook my head and plopped down on the sofa. "Great. Just great."

"Sorry, kid," he said. "They were almost done with it, but some more of those creepy messages came in, so they wanted to do another round of tests. They think it's a bot, though."

"It wasn't a bot," I murmured. "Whoever sent me those messages *knew* things."

"Bots know things." Uncle Trey wiped his mouth with his sleeve and slurped the milk out of his bowl. "Now, what's this about Yusuf? I thought you found him."

"No! I went to Yusuf's room and—"

"Oh, wait. Hold on, Cam," he said, pointing to the entertainment projection filling up the living room. The nightly news had just started. "News came out and did an interview today. I think I'm gonna be on TV."

I huffed, rolled my eyes, and turned to the screen.

The news appeared on the screen to deliver the local story. We hadn't missed a local story since Futureland's second day in New York. And they hadn't missed covering us since then, either. The news was our best way to know what *other* people were thinking about Futureland. But I also hoped that one day a clue might fall right in my lap from the broadcast.

Thanks, Jessica, the news anchor said. *Well, folks, here's a little something funny for our feel-good section. You know there's always a new craze with the kids these days. Who knows what it will be next month? But this month . . . it's gliding!*

The broadcast flipped to homemade videos of people walking down the street. Daytime, nighttime, through the park, near the subway. They all walked the same—hands clasped at their waists, back stiff and arched, taking calculated steps in long strides.

It's not the wildest trend we've ever seen in the Big Apple, but it has certainly taken the city by storm. Our social media is blowing up with videos of New Yorkers "gliding" all over the place. I can't decide if these folks look like runway models or pretend figure skaters. Haha!! Jessica, you think you can do this one? Yeah, this feels like one even us old folks can get involved in. Not too hard on the knees or back. . . .

"That's exactly how Yusuf was walking," I said, my mouth dropping open as I watched. "And everybody else who's been acting strange around New York."

Anxiety started filling me up like water to the rim of a glass.

"Is it?" Uncle Trey said. "Hey, where is Yusuf, anyway?"

"That's what I've been trying to tell you!" I shouted. "He's not in his room!"

Uncle Trey stood up and set his cereal aside. "And you haven't seen him since earlier? Why didn't you say anything?"

"I tried!"

"Here, take my ID and go to Galactic Gallery," he said, moving frantically around the room. "Check the screens and see if you can catch something I missed earlier. I'll hop in a pod and see if I can find him in the park. Feel free to invite your little girlfriend back over, too. We could use the help."

"Okay." I breathed a little easier. "I can do that. And Inaya is not my girlfriend!" I insisted.

"Whatever you say."

I headed toward the elevator. Finally, I would get a chance to look at Futureland's surveillance footage for myself.

Whenever I looked at the Haventech case details I had gathered so far, one thing always seemed to stick out as extra strange: the power outage. Uncle Trey had said that he'd review the park footage from opening night to see if the red-haired lady had done anything suspicious. But he never came back with any good intel. Now I'd have a chance to look for Yusuf *and* find out exactly what Ruthie Bowen had been doing around the time of the outage. She never returned to Futureland to help us like she said she would.

And I was starting to believe there was a good reason.

I had made a copy of that note from the boy in black for Inaya so we could both look into this "Architects" thing, but I hadn't done much research yet. I was having trouble focusing. My headaches had returned, this time in the top of my head, under all my locs. A throbbing, piercing pain that came and went.

I took a Jet-Blur pod to Galactic Gallery. I had forgotten how chilly it gets when the pod bursts out of the atmosphere of the park and enters the cool, dark expanse of Futureland's space-themed destiny. My pod floated between glittering, swirling planets and bright lights made to look like stars. When the pod finished its weaving routine through the constellations, it landed on the moon—the location of one of Futureland's command control centers.

I hopped out of the pod and moon-bounced to the space station, a metallic building that looked like it stood on stilts. I made it to the door and used Uncle

Trey's ID to key my way in. The warmth of the station welcomed me as all the lights on the control boards and operational switches blinked and flashed. I sat in front of the dozens of wall-o-grams depicting every area of the park. I started programming them to show me the last twenty-four hours. I crossed my fingers, hoping for a glimpse of Yusuf.

As my eyes darted between the wall-o-grams projecting the camera records, the headache I dreaded so much forced itself back into my skull. It felt like someone started drilling into the top of my head, trying to make a hole just big enough to peep through. I closed my eyes and put my hands over my face. Flashes of heat enveloped my entire body.

Deet deet deet da-deet-deet da-deet.

I peeked at my band through my fingers and saw Inaya's face requesting a video chat. I accepted the call.

"What do you want?" I said.

"Huh?" Inaya said. "Ayo . . . why you answer the call like that?"

The pain in my head started to fade, slowly. I took my hands away from my face and looked at Inaya's projection, my cheeks warm with embarrassment.

"I don't know," I admitted. "I'm sorry. I think I'm just stressed."

"Word," Inaya said. "You better do some yoga or

something. I thought southern people were supposed to be polite. Anyway, got a sec?"

I looked back to the wall-o-grams in front of me. "Yeah, for sure. I'm just looking through some park security footage."

"Trouble in paradise?"

"I still can't find Yusuf." To say it out loud made me feel even more freaked out. I had to find him.

"Yikes," she said. "Well, I'll make this quick, then. You found any info about the whole 'Architects' thing yet?"

"No." The pain from the headache had faded, but not disappeared. "I've been a little busy. What you got for me?"

"All right, so I had to try mad different libraries," she explained. "The one at school, NYPL . . . wasn't coming up with anything. I'm searching *architect* and mainly getting a lotta hits about construction and real estate, like, ugh! But then . . . I went with my father to the main NYU library. Jackpot."

"NYU, really?" She had my attention. "What was in there?"

"I found some old school newspapers that mentioned an 'Architects' business club way, way back at NYU," Inaya continued. "Like a student group. Then I found pictures of the club in some of the old yearbooks,

231

too. It hasn't existed for a long time. But it sounds like it may have been the beginning of a lot of problems in New York City."

She took a deep breath and launched right into it.

"Way back in the eighteen hundreds, a few students started the Architects Business Club. Their parents were the wealthiest elite of the world. Most clubs are for fun things, you know, like playing chess or cooking or whatever. But not these kids. They wanted to change New York with their power and money—to make it their playground."

"Change it how?" I asked, my eyes still darting between the projections of Futureland park footage. Still no sign of Yusuf. Or maybe I'd missed a quick glimpse of him because of the drilling feeling in my head. It was coming back again, tingling my nerves down to the bottom of my neck.

"Well, the articles I found didn't exactly say," she said. "But most of the families built their fortunes in stuff like manufacturing, real estate. Lot of politicians. The club kept growing under the radar for a while—new generations of the same families attending NYU. But they ended up getting in trouble."

"What kind of trouble?"

"They got caught in a scandal, and the school made

them shut down," Inaya explained. "Something about bribing the local government in New York. Like, yo, *students* were paying the mayor, and the city council, and other people to do what they wanted them to do. Some of them went to prison, but not all of them. It doesn't seem like anybody could really tell how many people were involved. And once the trials ended and NYU shut down the club, they got real hush about it, just tried to move on like it never happened."

"Those families probably still own businesses and buildings in New York," I said, thinking out loud. "If this club has anything to do with the Architects from that note, maybe we can find out who was in the club and trace them to someone who's alive today."

"You're so smart, Atlanta Cam," Inaya said with a laugh. "But not as smart as me. Because I already thought of that. And *this* part is really going to blow your mind. You want to hear the names of the original club members? Most of them are from the same families who were on campus when the club got shut down."

0:10

0:20

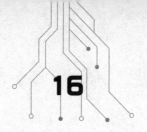

16

THE CREW

Saturday, February 13, 2049
11:12 p.m.

I paced back and forth in my room with my hands together, rolling my thumbs over one another. The drumbeat in my head hadn't stopped for twenty minutes. Every time I tried hard to focus, the pain got even sharper. I needed Uncle Trey to get here, and fast.

"Cam!" Uncle Trey poked his head into my bedroom, his hands stained with oil and his jumpsuit all wrinkled up. "I came as quick as I could. What's up?"

"Where have you been?" I yelled. "I called you forever ago. What took you so long?"

Uncle Trey angled his head at me and squinted. "You feelin' okay?" he asked.

"I'm fine!" I tried to calm my breathing as I continued

to pace. "I'm just— My head hurts really bad. So many things are happening, and I need your help."

Uncle Trey came into the room, sat me down on the bed, and sat down next to me. He massaged the nape of my neck with his oily hand. "Hey, everything's all right. I'm here now. What do you need?"

I took a deep breath as the pain in my skull got a little duller.

"Are Mom and Dad here?" I asked.

He shook his head. "They've been on the ground all day. Meetings. But they should be back soon."

"I need your help," I finally admitted. "Bad. It's something big. And we can't tell Mom and Dad until we can't afford not to tell them."

"Slow down." Uncle Trey looked serious now. "What's going on?"

"It's Southmore," I told him. "He *was* sending the messages to my watch. Just like I told you. He's back, *I knew it,* he's back and—"

My uncle cut me off. "Wait, wait, Southmore? He's in prison."

"No!" I said. "He's back, and he's still hacked into Futureland. I don't know how, but I know it's true. His grandfather went to NYU, and he was in this 'Architect' club and they've been controlling everything, the whole time, for centuries."

Silence as my uncle absorbed my words.

"And Whitebourne!" I added, remembering. "Whitebourne was in it with him. The same Whitebourne who sent us the letter about making Futureland invisible. Whoever that is. They're *still* in control. They're *still* running things. But nobody knows. They think it's over, and Ruthie Bowen never came to the park, and—"

"Cameron." Uncle Trey grabbed my shoulders and turned me toward him. "This is a lot to take in. But I believe you, okay? What do you want me to do *right now*?"

I inhaled deeply, trying to calm my nerves.

"I need you to help me get my friends," I told him. "Angel, Rich, and Earl. I need them here. Yusuf is missing and we need to solve this mystery, but I need their help. I need them here in New York as soon as possible."

I reflected on everything the crew and I had been through since we met. I knew that bringing them to New York would put them in harm's way. But they cared about Yusuf just as much as I did. If we had any chance of saving him, they wouldn't miss it for the world.

"My friends . . . they've got my back no matter what," I said. "When I'm in trouble, they're the first people I think to call. I know they'll help me. I know we can figure this out together. I need them."

"Sounds like you've got some great pals, kiddo. I probably wouldn't be here in front of you if it wasn't for y'all teaming up back in Atlanta. I'll see what I can do." Uncle Trey squeezed my shoulder and stood up.

"Don't do anything dangerous. Keep an eye out for Yusuf. Maybe we'll get lucky and he'll show up. It's a big park—he could be anywhere."

Uncle Trey turned and moved briskly toward the door.

"Wait!" I called after him. "You're not taking me with you?"

He turned and smiled. "Somebody's got to run the park. I'll let you know when I'm back. *Please* be careful. And keep your band on in case I need to reach you."

Uncle Trey disappeared from the room, and I stayed on the bed, collecting my thoughts. I projected the crew's group chat from my band and sent a few messages.

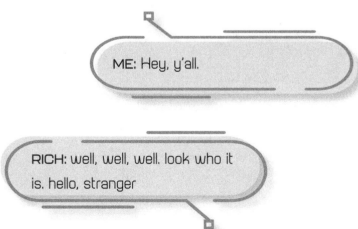

ME: Hey, y'all.

RICH: well, well, well. look who it is. hello, stranger

EARL: CJ! Where you been, man? We missed you.

ANGEL: CJ . . . is everything okay?

ME: I came up with an idea for our research project. Anybody else ever been to New York?

EARL: you can't be serious right now. Are you serious?! The City of Dreams!

ANGEL: I've always wanted to go!

RICH: what's the catch?

ME: Just send me your addresses and your parents' numbers. My uncle Trey will call them and explain . . . and he'll be there to pick you up soon, so start packing!

ANGEL: pick us up soon?

EARL: seriously?!

RICH: there goes my weekend

I closed the chat and stood up. *Okay, okay, okay. Think, Cameron. Think. How does this all fit together?*

I grabbed my deerstalker hat off the shelf and pulled it onto my head, continued pacing around my room. After a few moments, I threw up some blank projection screens and grabbed a phantom pen to write my thoughts onto the holograms. I took a deep breath and tried to focus on making sense of the case details, mumbling under my breath as I jotted furiously.

Still, my guilt about Yusuf crowded my thoughts.

"Southmore . . . owned a business . . . hacked Futureland data . . . wanted to steal revs . . . create a copycat city."

I stood back to look over what I'd written so far, biting my lip before continuing.

"Haventech . . . also stole Futureland data . . . causing glitches in the park? . . . selling bands . . . controlling minds . . . knocks down homes to build parks instead . . ."

I needed to get absolutely everything out there before I could start to connect any dots. What else? I thought about all of the discoveries Inaya had shared.

"Architects . . . have controlled New York behind the scenes for ages . . . Southmore and Whitebourne both connected through their families . . ."

I remembered the notice we'd received about Futureland's ability to go into invisible mode.

"Whitebourne . . . works in the government in New York . . . what do they want? . . . who was the boy that gave me and Inaya the note? . . . what's the connection?"

I lowered the phantom pen and stared at my notes. I could feel the throbbing in my head coming back. I had to figure this out, decide on my next step, before the pain became unbearable.

A few things were clear: the Architects Business Club never really died; it just transformed into something larger—something more evil and hidden. The Southmores and Whitebournes had been controlling cities and businesses from behind the scenes for hundreds of years. But it wasn't just in New York anymore—maybe they had even expanded worldwide.

Southmore stole data, and Haventech used the same data to create those LifeBuddy bands. Southmore's company, ADRC, along with Haventech, were both using the same tricks to try to take down Futureland: cause glitches in the park, ruin our good name, and build something new and terrible by stealing my parents' original ideas. I wouldn't be surprised if Southmore owned Haventech, too, and was controlling them from prison as a way of getting revenge on us.

But there was one thing I *didn't* know: Who was Whitebourne?

When the city served us the invisibility notice, it was signed by somebody named C. Whitebourne. If Whitebourne was a part of the Architects, too, then maybe Southmore had given *them* the data to continue his terrible mission after we defeated him. It made sense, especially if their families had been friendly for hundreds of years.

I chewed on the end of my pen. That's what had to come next. I needed to figure out more about this Whitebourne person. How did they fit in with Haventech? With the bands? With the glitches? And with Southmore? Whitebourne was the last piece of a puzzle that I had almost completed. Once Earl, Angel, and Rich arrived, we'd be able to plan and cover more ground way faster. But I already knew where to start.

The boy in black. He knew something.

I saved my projections and notes and flicked them back into my band for storage. My head was clear. Now I needed to go look for Yusuf. I wouldn't have been so sure he flew away on Ali's back if I hadn't seen it with my own eyes. But since I had, I knew he could be anywhere in New York City. I could start in the park and look around, get Goggles and Sarafina to help me. I hoped that Uncle Trey was right and we'd get lucky. But it didn't look good.

I gathered up my stuff and rushed to the door. "Here I come, Yusuf," I said under my breath.

Cameron . . .

I stopped short and whipped around. Had someone called my name?

Don't look for Yusuf.

"Hello?" I called out, confused. "Who's there? Who's talking!"

Don't look for Yusuf. Yusuf is fine. He doesn't need your help.

My head suddenly got cloudy, and a piercing pain shot right through the top. I fell to my knees near the door of my bedroom, fighting to stay upright. I tried to lift my body, but I couldn't move.

"What's . . . happening to me . . . ?" It was getting more difficult to talk by the second. "Who are you?"

Get some rest, Cameron. It's time to go to sleep. Sleep, sleep, sleep.

"Sleep, sleep, sleep," I repeated, in monotone.

Very good. Yusuf is fine. He doesn't need your help.

"Yusuf is fine," I agreed. "He doesn't need my help."

Sleep . . .

"Sleep . . ."

I collapsed onto my stomach on the floor. My eyelids fluttered as I lost consciousness, the world around me getting darker, and darker, and darker. The last thing I remembered was Yusuf's projection band, on my wrist, vibrating and blinking.

I closed my eyes and fell into nowhere.

Little shock waves shot into my wrist every three seconds.

Buzz . . . buzz . . . buzz

I opened my eyes. My face felt numb.

How long have I been here? Did I fall?

I pushed myself up off the floor, my entire body aching. I stretched out and looked around the room. What had I been doing? *That's right,* I remembered slowly. *I was looking for Yusuf. But . . . Yusuf is fine. He doesn't need my help.*

The band on my wrist kept buzzing. I finally looked down at it to see a call coming from Uncle Trey, and I answered.

"Kiddo!" he said. "Where you at? Everything all right?"

"Yeah, I'm good." I stared at the spot on the floor that I'd woken up on, still feeling confused. "Just a little tired. What's going on? Where are you?"

"I'm pulling into the main terminal now," he said. "Come up and meet me. I've got a surprise for you."

I walked out of the condo and up the stairs to the main entrance terminal. All the lights in Futureland were off, the park long closed.

It must be pretty late. How long was I out? I wonder if my parents are back yet.

The automatic doors separated, and I entered the Guest Hub terminal—a big open space where Futureland guests would gather and wait for the doors to open. It was like an airplane hangar, with photos of amazing Futureland moments on the walls and banners celebrating our success. But in the middle of the room was something I had never seen before.

It looked like a Jet-Blur pod—but humongous! The big sphere shone with a metallic glow, just like our regular pods, but it had two giant wings protruding from its sides. As I approached, the wings folded and collapsed into the walls of the super-pod. Then, just like a normal Jet-Blur pod, the walls retracted to reveal the passengers.

"CJ!"

Angel was the first out of the pod, sprinting over to me, both hands pressing down on her backward baseball cap to keep it from flying off of her thick, puffy hair.

"¡Te extrañé!" Angel wrapped me up in a tight hug. She smelled like peaches and sunshine.

"I missed you, too," I said, my voice muffled against her hair. Earl and Rich ran up and glued themselves to me and Angel, making one huge group hug.

"What's up, CJ!"

"Good to see you again, bruh."

When we separated, my friends all beamed with excitement. Rich's curly hair looked like he hadn't combed it before rolling out of bed that morning. Earl had on a black jogging suit, and for some reason, pink house slippers with bunny faces on the front of them.

I'd ask later. For now, I was just happy to see them.

"I'm so glad y'all are here," I said.

"We would have been here faster," Rich said, throwing a side-eyed glance to Earl. "But you know Mr. Hungry here, had to stop for some cheesecake."

Earl shrugged. "I heard New York has the best cheesecake. You've got to take advantage of these opportunities, you know? Seize the meal. *Carpe eatem*."

Angel cocked her head. "That's . . . not the saying."

"It's close enough." Earl winked at her.

Uncle Trey finally made it over to us after shutting down the giant pod.

"Nephew!" he greeted me. "How'd I do? Got you reunited with your friends, just like you asked. By the

250

way, how do you like my new toy?" He pointed his elbow toward the super-pod.

"It's amazing," I said. "What is it? A huge Jet-Blur pod?"

"Well, it's a little more like a Jet-Blur *jet*," he answered. "Fastest private vehicle in the skies. Only a couple hours to Atlanta and back. That time I spent in the Air Force comes in handy every now and then. I just never liked waking up early. Anyway, I'm thinking of calling it the Mammoth."

Nobody said anything.

"Aw, come on! Y'all don't like the Mammoth?"

"Maybe keep working on that one, Uncle Trey," Angel said. "CJ"—she turned back to me—"you said it was an emergency. What's up? We're ready. And where's Yusuf? Uncle Trey said he was here with you."

Yusuf . . .

I tried to remember where Yusuf was, but nothing came to mind. I couldn't remember the last time I'd seen him. I stood still, searching my brain for the latest memory of Yusuf, and said the only thing that came up.

"Yusuf is fine."

"Really?" Uncle Trey said. "That's great news! I knew he'd turn up. All right, let's get you kids downstairs to the condo. I programmed some revs to make up the guest rooms."

He lowered his voice so that only I could hear him.

"And I convinced J.B. and Stacy to spend a night away from the park. Y'all have got until the morning to come up with a plan before we have to tell them everything. Good luck."

I smiled. "Thanks, Uncle Trey."

Me and the crew rushed up to my room, laughing and tripping over each other every step of the way. Rich had to pull Earl away from the kitchen when we made it to the condo. We made our way into my bedroom and closed the door behind us.

"CJ, I almost forgot how nice your place is," Angel said, tapping my framed Futureland posters on the way.

"My room is cooler," Rich said.

"Not everything is about you, Christopher," Angel spat.

Rich growled. "I told you not to call me that!"

I smiled. Oh, how I had missed them.

"Rich's room *is* pretty cool," I agreed with a laugh.

"CJ . . ." All of us stopped and looked at Earl. "Where is Yusuf? I thought you said he was here."

The fog came over my brain again. I scanned all the memories in my mind for answers, but I couldn't find any. A bead of sweat formed on my head as my friends waited for me to explain.

Yusuf is fine. We'll see him later.

"Yusuf is fine. We'll see him later," I said.

Rich stood in the corner, fiddling with one of Uncle Trey's prototypes. Earl stared at me without blinking. Angel narrowed her eyes.

"Well, you had some big emergency, CJ," she said. "Don't you think it's about time you told us what's going on?"

"Right," I said. "Umm, okay. Here!"

I projected my investigation notes onto my wall-o-gram and dimmed the lights. After about fifteen minutes, I had explained the entire conspiracy of Haventech and Southmore. I'd explained the Holo-pal, the weird, gliding zombies around New York City, and the original Architects Business Club. It was a *lot,* but luckily, they picked up on everything quickly.

"I'm famished," Earl said. "That was so much info. Time for a snack break?"

"Hold on, Earl," Angel said, staring at my outstretched arm as I stored away my holograms back into my band. "CJ. That's not a Futurewatch on your wrist. We all used to have matching ones. What's that?"

"Oh. This?" I glanced down at the band. "It's, uh . . ."

This is one of the new Futurelink bands my mom designed.

"This is one of the new Futurelink bands my mom designed," I said.

"Oh, cool," Angel said, leaning closer. "Can I see?"

"Well, I don't really—"

Angel gently grabbed my wrist before I could finish and lifted it up to get a closer look at the band. I panicked and snatched my arm away from her. She screeched and lost her balance, falling backward. In a flash, Earl rose and caught her before she hit the floor. Rich rushed to her side from the corner of the room.

"CJ!" Earl cried out. "What's wrong with you, man?"

"Yeah, why you actin' so violent, bruh?" Rich's eyebrows furrowed as he and Earl helped steady Angel.

I scrambled for words, but it was no use. My mouth hung open and my shoulders slacked. Moisture made Angel's eyes glisten. My stomach dropped.

"I'm sorry, Angel," I said, my voice near a whisper. "I don't know what got into me."

"CJ," she answered. "Are you *sure* you're feeling okay? You've been acting a little strange since we got here, and I just want to know if—"

"Knock, knock!" We all faced the bedroom door. Inaya poked her head in, her headwrap a burst of color in the room.

"Ayo, Cam, sorry I'm late. I got your message from earlier. Oh—" she said, looking at my friends. "Who are these kids?"

254

"Who are we?" Rich answered, astonished. "Who are *you*?"

"Y'all, this is Inaya," I said.

"Bagayoko," she added. "Harlem's own."

I motioned for Inaya to come in. "She's been help-ing me with the case. I sent you a message?" I asked her, confused.

"Uh, yeah," Inaya said. "Right after the park closed. Said it was urgent. You don't remember?"

Earl slapped his palm to his forehead. "Man, what? CJ! You only been gone a few weeks and you already replaced us? You already making a new crew?"

"It's not a crew!" I said. "It's just Inaya. She's cool."

"I didn't even know you had a crew, Atlanta Cam," Inaya said with a raised brow. "I thought it was just you and Yusuf."

"Atlanta Cam?" Rich laughed. "Nah nah, that's CJ. And yeah, he *has* a crew already. Me, Earl, Angel, and . . . yeah, wait—for the millionth time, where is Yusuf?!"

"Everybody just calm down!" I yelled, a little louder than I had intended, the mention of Yusuf's name making my head feel all warm and weird again. The room got quiet. "Look, Inaya is smart. Like, a genius. She's been the one helping me figure all of this out. She's going to be rolling with us until we figure out where Southmore is and how to take down Haventech."

Earl rolled his eyes. "Fine."

"Man, whatever," Rich said.

Angel stepped forward to Inaya and shook her hand. "If you're as smart as Cam says you are, then we're definitely going to need your help. This is one complicated case. And by the way, I like your headwrap."

"Thanks, girl," Inaya said. "I like your hair."

"Thank you," Angel returned. Rich and Earl made gross, mushy, mocking faces behind them.

"Well." Inaya crossed her arms. "It looks like I crashed this party at just the right time. I do love just a li'l *pinch* of drama, you feel me? But, Cam, boy, do I have a story for you. I know exactly where we need to go next with the investigation."

"The boy in black," I said.

"Huh?" Inaya's eyes widened in shock. "Wait, how did you know? Have you been back to the creepy carnival in Harlem?"

"Carnival?" Earl said. "Like . . . funnel cake carnival?"

"No, I haven't been back," I told Inaya. "What's going on? What about the carnival?"

"Y'all might want to sit down for this one," Inaya said, turning to close the door behind her. "It's about to get mad wild."

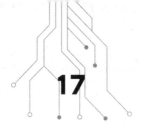

JORDAN

Sunday, February 14, 2049
2:30 a.m.

I called Alejandro and Aurielle in for the night shift to make us some Astromilk and star-cookies. Then me and the crew mixed Cosmic Cocoa powder into the milk and swirled in a few marshmallows. If we were about to have a weird night, the least we could do was make it delicious.

"So," Inaya said in between crunches on a star-cookie, "remember that spooky Haven Properties carnival I showed you?"

I blew some steam off the top of my mug and nodded. "Yep. And I told the crew about it, too."

"Ah yes. The carnival. Part of the web of deception," Earl said.

"The what?" Inaya asked, the corner of her mouth turning up in a half grin.

"The web of deception," Earl repeated. "That's what we're calling this whole thing. I just made it up, just now."

"Hush up, Earl." Angel rolled her eyes. "Keep going, Inaya."

Inaya took another bite of her cookie. "Aight, so don't tell my parents, but, uh . . . sometimes I sneak out of the shelter and go back to Harlem late at night. Real late. Like, four in the morning."

"What do you do there?" I asked.

"Mostly I just think," she said, chewing. "Breathe. Close my eyes and remember. Especially if I was having nightmares that night. It helps me clear my mind. My neighborhood. My friends. My brownstone. Sometimes I just go back to my block and pretend like none of this ever happened." She shrugged. "Anyway, I went back last night, late—after my parents fell asleep. And you'll never guess who I saw."

"The boy in black?" Earl guessed.

"Spoiler alert," Rich said.

"Slow down, fam." Inaya laughed. "Yes, but no. Before I saw him, I saw *them*."

"Who?!" Angel said.

"The zombies. The Gliders."

I looked at Inaya in surprise. "Really? In Harlem? How many of them?"

"Dozens," she said with a shiver. "They just kept

258

comin'. I watched 'em from behind the bodega across the street. They opened up the carnival gate and walked right in. And then they started fixing stuff. Testing it out. Building on it, almost like they were—"

"Finishing the project," I said.

"Word," confirmed Inaya.

"Did they talk?" The idea of those zombie Gliders working on that creepy carnival was enough to make my skin crawl. "Did anybody say *anything*?"

"Not a word," Inaya said with a frown. "They kept at it for a while, makin' that thing all shiny and new. But then they stopped, all of 'em—at the exact same time. They left through the gate, and who appeared to close up after them but our little ninja friend."

My mouth dropped. "No way. That explains why we saw him with that bag of tools on the Great Lawn that morning. He's leading them. He's helping them build," I said.

"So we got that kid linked to the Architects Business Club and now to Haven Properties," Angel said. "You think he might know something about Whitebourne?"

"He's our best shot," Inaya said. "He's the only connection we have between the Architects, all of the Haven companies, and the bands."

"Rich," I started, "can you hack into the NYU

library archives remotely and find out anything else there is to know about Whitebourne?"

"I'll get on it," he said. "But, Inaya—what do the bands have to do with this?"

"Huh?" Inaya scrunched up her face. "The note he gave us. It only had three instructions and a warning." Inaya pulled her copy of the note out of her pocket. "Not to wear the bands, not to use the holograms, and to get out of New York because the Architects were coming. Plus, he was wearing one when we saw him in Central Park."

Angel grabbed the paper from Inaya and examined it. Rich and Earl peered over Angel's shoulders to read too. "CJ," Angel said. "You didn't tell us the boy in black's note said anything about the bands."

I scrambled for a response, but the one that came out didn't feel like my own. Almost like someone else put the idea in my mind, and my mouth turned it into words before I had a chance to stop it.

I didn't? I thought I did.

"I didn't? I thought I did."

"No . . . you didn't," Angel said, eyeing me suspiciously. "Didn't you say Yusuf had one of those bands?"

The word *Yusuf* made my brain start straining all over again. What was happening? My thoughts felt like scrambled eggs. Soft, mushy, and mixed all around.

"Ayo!" Inaya interjected. "Maybe we should scan your brain again, Cam. Maybe you're experiencing some delayed effects!"

"Scan his brain? For what?" Earl asked.

"Well, we had stopped. But we *were* scanning his brain every few days to check its activity because he's been wearing—"

"STOP!" I shouted, rising to my feet. "Just stop. We're not scanning my brain! Yusuf is fine! There's nothing wrong with my band. Now, everybody get ready. We're going to Harlem. We've got to see if we can talk to this boy in black. Hurry up! We're leaving in ten."

I stood in the middle of my bedroom, my shoulders rising and falling with every breath. The pain in the top of my head returned, slowly trickling down my neck and into my spine.

A heavy quiet fell over the room. Rich and Earl shot glances back and forth between each other. Angel stared at me. Inaya raised her eyebrow.

"Y'all heard Detective Cam," Angel said slowly. "Let's get ready to roll. Bathroom break for me first. Inaya, come with?"

"For sure, girl, let's go," Inaya said. They both made their way out of the bedroom.

"Girls," Rich said, rolling his eyes.

"Look at 'em," Angel said, peeking out from behind the bodega. "They look so creepy."

"I think they look graceful," Earl said. "Like swans."

"Both of y'all shut it before they hear us," scolded Rich.

Me, Angel, Earl, Rich, and Inaya crouched in the shadows behind the bodega across the street from the Haven carnival. By the time we caught a train uptown and made our way into Harlem, the Gliders had already started their nightly work. Some of them carried materials in through the gate, while others carried debris from the park out. A few of them tested the rides with blank expressions, going around and around on the carousel of nightmarish beasts and never cracking a smile.

We staked out the carnival waiting for the boy in black for so long that I started to get sleepy. The ache in my head wouldn't let up. Inaya went into the bodega and got snacks and juice for all of us. As we were finishing them up, all of the Gliders froze, turned toward the exit, and started leaving the park. Just like Inaya had described before.

"Come on, y'all," I said, motioning for everyone to take their stations. "It's time."

As the last Glider made their way out of the gate and around the corner, the boy in black appeared. I almost missed him, the way his clothes blended in with the night. His hands worked quickly on the lock to the gate, securing it after a night's work completed.

"Now!" I whispered to Earl and Inaya.

We rushed out from behind the bodega. The boy in black noticed us coming but couldn't finish locking the gate fast enough before we stopped in front of him. As soon as we made it to him, he turned and tried to run the other way, but Angel and Rich had crept around the block and sealed him off from the other side. He had nowhere to go.

"You need to leave," he said. His voice sounded familiar, a raspy, wheezing quality to it.

"Is that a threat?" Inaya asked.

"You have no idea what you've gotten yourselves into," he said. "You need to stop digging. Stop right here, because if you go any deeper . . . you won't be able to dig yourself out."

"What do you know about the Architects?" Angel asked.

The boy turned toward her, his black winter mask covering everything but his eyes.

"What do *you* know about the Architects?" he asked her back.

"Ayo, you some kinda parrot?" Inaya barked. "We asked you a question. We already know all about the business club at NYU, the government scandals, and the property—"

"Ha!" The boy laughed, doubled over, holding his stomach. "Haha haha!" It didn't take long for his laughs to turn into a mini coughing fit.

"What's so funny?" I asked, unamused.

"You think this is about some club at a college?" he managed to wheeze out. "We're way past that now. Everything that's coming is way worse. You may not want to believe this . . . but I gave you that note to *help* you, okay? I made it very clear what you need to do. If you don't want to take my advice, then that's on you."

"What makes you think we have a reason to trust you? To believe anything you say would help us?" Earl asked.

"You want trust?" the boy said. "Fine." He reached to the neckline of his mask and pulled it upward, over his head, removing it from his face. Tufts of messy red hair flopped out. It was the boy from opening night, the one with the red-haired lady. Just like I'd suspected.

"You're Ruthie Bowen's son," I said.

"No, I'm not. I'm Jordan," he said, coughing into his elbow. "I don't know any Ruthie Bowen."

"Then whose son are you?" I questioned.

"None of your business," he said.

I shook my head. "Well, I'm Cam. And this is the crew. Earl, Rich, Angel, and—actually, I'll let her do it." I turned to Inaya.

"Inaya Bagayoko. Harlem's Own."

"Charmed," Jordan said. "So, is that enough? You know who I am now. Cam, you've even seen me in your parents' park. Now please, everybody, do yourselves a favor and just get outta here."

"We need to—" I tried to start speaking, but the pain came on like a thunderbolt in my skull. I clutched my head and bent over. "Arrgh!"

"Cam, are you okay?" Inaya rushed to my side. "What's wrong with you?"

"Probably the same thing that's wrong with me and all the others," Jordan said, eyeing me. "That band." He pointed to my wrist as my hand rested on my head. "That's Haventech?"

I shook my head. "No way. This is . . . this is a new Futureland model."

Jordan smirked and shook his head. "You can't fool me." He flashed the band on his own wrist, almost identical to the one I was wearing. "Looks like it's starting. You must have been wearing it for a while."

"What's starting? What others? What are you talking about?" Angel shouted.

"Has he been having mood swings?" Jordan asked

my friends. "He won't be the Cam you know for much longer if you don't get him out of here and away from that wristband. Everyone thinks they'll overcome it, but they never do. I'm the only one that ever did. And even my day is coming."

I dropped to my knees and propped myself up with one hand on the ground, the other still trying to contain the volcano erupting inside my head. I saw flashes of memories. Woody chasing us. Dooley fighting. My dad powering her down for the final time. My friends crowded around me, struggling to pull me to my feet and back toward the train station. Jordan put his mask back on and turned to leave, but not before Rich called out.

"What do you know about Whitebourne?!"

Jordan froze. He turned to face us, the dim glow of the streetlights bouncing off a twinkle in his green eyes.

"The whole world is just a playground," he said. "Have as much fun as you can."

And like the wind, he was gone in the darkness.

My vision went blurry, and all the feeling drained from my limbs. My body threatened to collapse to the ground, but my friends grabbed me and held me up. The last thing I remember is all of the lights going out— the lights on the bodega, the streetlights, and even the blinking dials on the Haven Properties carnival. My friends were rushing me through the night as fast as they could when everything went black.

SUNDAY, FEBRUARY 14, 2049 | 4:44 A.M.

UNKNOWN: You should have left while you had the chance.

No cell can hold me.

I'm coming for you, Cameron. You and your whole family. I'm going to destroy everything you love.

Just like I destroyed Dooley.

Time's up. See you soon.

267

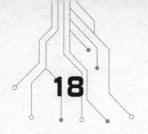

18

A SETUP

I ran as fast as I could through Futureland, trying to get to the center of the park so that I could hit the reset button and restore all the revs to their original settings. I needed to regain control over them from Southmore. I ran into Dooley and we started to tussle, but before either of us could get an advantage, Southmore appeared.

His pale skin and sniveling sneer sent chills down my spine. He commanded his army of corrupted revs to attack me and Dooley. They descended on us, trying to smother us and take us offline—for good. I struggled under a pile of revs, fighting to breathe, reaching out for Dooley. I opened my mouth to scream, but I couldn't make a sound. The revs pinning me down spoke in hushed tones to one another.

Turn him over!

Grab his left arm. . . . No, his other left arm. You get his leg.

Shhh, shhh!

Be careful, be quiet—you'll wake him up.

Hmm . . . weird. The revs looked like revs. But they *sounded* like Earl, Angel, and Rich. I tried to shake my body and fight them off, but they were strong.

He's kicking! Hold him!

Get his wrist! We've got to get that band!

"Huh?"

I woke up from my nightmare to see all my friends leaning over me in my bedroom. Earl and Rich had my legs pinned down, and Angel had my right arm. Inaya was working on the left, trying to snatch Yusuf's band off my wrist.

Don't let them take it, my brain commanded.

"No!" I shouted. "Wait! Please!"

"He's up!" Angel yelled over me. "Do it! Do it now!"

"Ugh," Rich grunted. "For a skinny kid, he's really strong."

I kicked my leg out, knocking Earl to the ground. I ripped my arm away from Angel and used it to try to pry myself from Inaya's grasp. We struggled, scratching each other's hands. I had almost completely removed her grasp on me when Rich belly flopped onto me from the bed frame and landed directly on my stomach, knocking the wind out of me.

"Oof!" I wheezed and fell back on the pillow. Inaya yanked off the band as I lay flat, trying to catch my breath.

A few moments after they removed the band, a sense of calm came over me. The tension melted out of my body and my head felt lighter than it had felt in days. I felt weak, but free—normal. Like a heavy weight had been lifted off me.

"They don't call me Cannonball Rich for nothing," Rich said.

"Nobody calls you that," Angel said.

Inaya pulled two brain sensor stickies out of her pocket and attached them to my temples. She got on a tablet and started flipping through screens.

"What's happening?" I asked.

"We're saving you," Angel replied. "During our little girls' trip to the bathroom last night, Inaya told me the parts of the story you left out—wearing Yusuf's wristband, how we have no clue where he is, and the secret mind control theory. She figured if you'd been acting weird, it would be because of the band."

Memories slowly started to flood back in. "Yeah. Yeah, Yusuf didn't want to take it off, either. The band . . . it talks to you. Late at night, when no one else is around. It asks you to do things, and then it *makes* you do them. When I finally got that band away from Yusuf, he got so sick."

"Well, you're gonna feel better in no time," Inaya chimed in. "You only wore that joint for a little while. Nothing happens the first few days. Probably so you don't get suspicious while you're still in control of your own mind, you know?

"But after that . . . the change comes rapidly." Inaya pointed to my latest brain scan projections. "The time you wore Yusuf's band is enough for me to notice a difference in your brain waves, but I bet it won't stick with you long-term. But Yusuf . . ." She winced. "You said he'd been wearing that thing since December?"

I nodded.

"Then it probably became easier to control his mind the longer he wore it," she said.

I shook the dizziness out of my head, the mystery of the Haventech bands finally clicking in my mind. "By the time I had snuck the band away from him, the voices in his head were already too loud. That's probably why he left. They called to him."

"There's something else," Angel said.

"Huh?"

"We all got those bands. Me, Rich, and Earl."

My skin began to crawl. "What do you mean? How?"

"Well, one showed up in my mailbox in December, in an unmarked container. But my foster parents didn't trust it, so they threw it away," Earl said.

"Yeah, it was one of my many, many Christmas presents," Rich said. "It's probably still in the house somewhere, honestly. I'm taking my time working through everything my mom and dad bought me."

"And mine came from my tía," Angel said. "She works in the same office as Yusuf's mom. She said her manager gave one to her. Some kind of holiday giveaway. My tía sold it and we split the extra cash, so I never wore it."

"For all we know, Southmore probably owns the company that your tía and Yusuf's mom work at," Inaya said. "That's how they knew exactly where to find you all."

"Somebody targeted all of you. To get to me," I said, hanging my head. "It was a setup. Yusuf never wanted to leave his family and follow me to New York to solve mysteries. He was just the only one who got tricked. They've been controlling his mind much longer than we thought."

My eyes stung and I sniffled, turning my face away from my friends. The gravity of the guilt pulled my heart down into my stomach. I had put my friends in so much danger. "This is all my fault. I knew something was off with him and I didn't help. I didn't save him."

"It's not your fault, CJ," Earl said, coming over and patting my back. "You tried your best. But we're here now. And we've *got* to find Yusuf."

"And fast," Inaya said. "Judging by your scans, Cam, Yusuf's symptoms would be ten times more advanced—mood swings, headaches, and hearing voices. All things that the Gliders checking into hospitals are experiencing. All things that could be a part of the Haventech mind control."

"How do we find him?" I asked. "Where would he be?"

Inaya shrugged. "It all depends on who's giving the orders. It's been a while since you saw him—he could be on Broadway or all the way to Bridgeport by now." She sighed. "I wish that redheaded boy hadn't spoken in riddles all night. Maybe then we could have gotten a clue on where to start."

"We'll figure it out," I said. I sat up in the bed and looked around the room. "Thank you—all of you—for saving me."

"No problem, CJ," Angel said.

"We got your back, bro," Earl said.

"Facts," Inaya said.

"Aren't we *always* saving you?" Rich added. "But yeah, you're welcome anyway."

"Cameron! Cameron!" We all turned toward the

voice yelling my name from the hallway. Uncle Trey burst into the room and doubled over with his hands on his knees, panting hard. He looked at all of us, then did a double take at me on the bed, Inaya's sticky sensors still on my head.

"Do I want to know what's going on here?" he asked.

"Probably not," said Inaya.

"Cool. Won't ask. But I have news." He stood upright as he finished catching his breath. "First, your parents are on their way back. I stalled them with a fancy breakfast, but they know something is up."

"Thanks, Unc," I said. "We can take it from here." I stood up and pulled the sensors off my head, tossing them back on the bed. "We've got our story straight. Is there something else?"

"Yeah, this." He reached into his pocket and pulled out my Futurewatch, passing it to Rich, who tossed it to me.

I turned the watch over in my hands until the face of the device lit up, revealing a stream of messages that had been sent at 4:44 a.m. Messages that threatened me and my family. Messages that taunted me about Dooley.

Southmore. I knew it had to be him, could feel it in my bones.

"I told you it was busted—nothing IT could do with

it—so I had them give it back," Uncle Trey explained. "I had it last night when these messages came in. I'm sorry I didn't believe you, nephew. It really looks like this Southmore dude is making his way back after all. I don't know how, but that doesn't matter anymore. We've got to stop him."

"This is getting complicated," Rich said. "Where do we even start?"

Rich wasn't wrong. Between the creepy carnival, Jordan and his weird warnings, and having the mind control device wrestled off me, things had only gotten wilder. At least Uncle Trey was in on it now. If we were going to solve this mystery, we'd need every little bit of extra help we could get.

"We should split up," Earl said. "Like they do in those old mystery shows."

"Does that really work?" Inaya asked. "Shouldn't we all stick together?"

"I think splitting up is a good idea, actually," Uncle Trey said. He scratched his chin. "I don't want you kids tangling with this Southmore dude anymore. He's dangerous—I know from experience. I'll focus on figuring out what's up with him. If we can get some details on where Southmore is supposed to be, then we can check and see if he's there, make sure it's him and not a rev."

"Then *we'll* focus on finding Yusuf," I said. Locating

him was our top priority. Thinking about how the Haventech band had mind-controlled me into forgetting about my missing friend caused a lump to form in my throat.

"You still don't know where he is?!" Uncle Trey gasped.

I shook my head. "It's a long story. But we're back on track now. Between the five of us, we should be able to cover a lot of ground. And once we find him, we'll have a lot more information about all this weird stuff that's been going on."

"Goodness gracious." My uncle pinched the bridge of his nose. "All right. I'll get Yusuf's parents on the phone, too, let them know we're working on it. And I'll leave a pilot-rev in the Mammoth—er, I mean, in the Jet-Blur jet—in case y'all need to get really far, really fast."

"Yusuf left on his Holo-pet, right?" Angel asked. "CJ, is there some way you can track where the flying monkey—"

"Sugar glider," Earl corrected her. Angel shot him a death stare.

"As I was saying," she continued, her voice daring Earl to cut her off again. "Is there any way you can track where the flying monkey is now? That may lead us right to Yusuf."

"That's a good idea, Angel," I agreed. "Inaya, can you pull the Holo-pet data and track Ali?"

"Sure thing."

"Uncle Trey, get started making those calls." I gave him a nod. "Let us know what you find. I'm going to keep my old Futurewatch with me, just in case any more creepy messages come in."

"Ten-four," he said. "Need anything else?"

I paused before I answered, memories rushing into my mind. My eyes started getting watery all over again.

"I don't think so. I just wish Dooley was here."

Uncle Trey's face softened. "Me too, Cam. But she's with you." He tapped his heart. "In here. Real friendships never die. Never forget that."

I nodded. "Angel, Earl, Rich—I need your help finding Jordan."

"Again?" Rich said. "That dude didn't help us at all. He barely gave us any information."

"That's true, but I think he knows more. About the wristbands, about the mind control, and about this whole Architects business. Most importantly, about Whitebourne. They're the key to this. Did you see his eyes when we asked about them? We have to make him talk. If we can figure out this Whitebourne thing, I know we can find Yusuf and bring him home."

"Yeah, but how you gonna find Jordan, Cam?" Earl said. "He's like a middle school ninja."

"And if he's smart," Angel added, "he won't be popping up at that eerie carnival for a while, now that he knows we were watching him. We'd need some kinda miracle to get some good intel."

"No. Not a miracle," Inaya said, smiling. "Just a little parental guidance. Come with me."

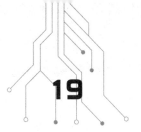

19

WHITEBOURNE

Sunday, February 14, 2049
2:00 p.m.

We shuffled behind Inaya up to the Metropolitan Museum of Art. All five of us walked up the steps to the wide, bone-colored building with three arches sandwiched between massive columns. Inaya pushed open the glass door and we all made our way into the cool, quiet air of the museum. A security guard smiled and tipped his cap to Inaya.

"The youngest Bagayoko. I see you've got some friends with you today. What's up?" he asked.

Inaya gave him a fist bump. "Not much, Geoffrey. Looking for my parents. Are they here?"

"You know it. Second floor."

We rode the elevator to the second floor and

walked down the hall to the Egyptian art collection. The room we entered was broad and mostly granite, with a huge wall of windows on one side and a rectangular reflection pool near the back of the terrace. People sat along the ledge of the pool chatting quietly and taking pictures. In the front of the pool sat two humongous pharaohs carved in dark stone, and behind them, across from the pool, a magnificent temple.

The temple looked so authentically Egyptian I couldn't believe my eyes. Pink stone material formed an archway, and behind it, a four-walled temple big enough to hold multiple rooms. "Whoa," I said aloud. My eyes grew wide in amazement.

Inaya's parents greeted us with smiles as we approached them. They stood quietly in uniform beside the windows, holding hands. Earl kept thrusting his phone into my face, showing me the newest high score on Word Buddies. I jabbed him in his ribs to make him put the game away in front of Inaya's parents.

"Mom, Dad, are you on break? I need help," Inaya said once we reached them. "Oh, and these are my friends. Too many names, too little time. Everyone, meet my mom and dad."

"Looks like we are not on break anymore." Inaya's dad, a tall man with smooth dark skin and tightly coiled hair, laughed. "Inaya, what kind of adventure have you adopted this time?"

Inaya smiled coyly. "Come on, Dad, please!"

"Hello, everyone. I am Amadou," he said to us.

"And I am Mariam," her mom said, an adult-sized Inaya with a voice like velvet. "What do you need, my love?" she asked.

"These are my new friends. And this is Cam. His parents run Futureland."

"Are you kidding?!" Amadou said, his eyes lighting up. "We love your park. One of our first dates was there." Mariam smiled warmly at the memory.

Inaya continued. "Cam is looking for information on somebody named Whitebourne who works in the government. The park depends on it. I thought you could help." Amadou and Mariam shuddered at the sound of the name.

"Clare Whitebourne. The woman who stole our home," Mariam said, seething.

"Whitebourne is a woman?" Angel said. "We tried to look up the name and couldn't find anything specific about her. No photos, no birthday. Nothing."

"Yes. She's very powerful," Amadou said. "You will have trouble finding pictures of her online. After New York passed the Digital Anonymity Act years ago, it made it hard to research most local government

281

officials. They thought the law would keep public officers safe, but it has allowed many of them to do bad things under a cover of secrecy."

"Before she worked for the government, she ran that awful property company that destroyed our home and built that monstrous park," Mariam said. "We did not see her often. Once, maybe twice. But each time it sent a shiver up my spine."

"She was a strange woman," Amadou said. "I have known her since college at NYU. We even took some business classes together. A strange one, indeed. Involved in a lot of frightening activities—scary movies, Halloween costumes, making spooky art on campus. She got in trouble once for trying to paint her dorm building solid black."

The black buildings around New York!

"She seemed so nice at first, before she took our home," Amadou continued. "All the questions she asked about our neighborhood, about our struggles. We thought she would be on our side. But some people only make it look that way. So they can get what they want." Amadou shook his head.

"When our community came together to protest her demolishing our homes, it was clear she didn't see us as people. Just obstacles. She has a bizarre opinion of how the world should be and enough power to make it reality. And she won't take no for an answer," Mariam said.

"How can we find her?" I asked.

"Why would you want to do that?" Mariam asked.

"Somebody we care about needs our help. And we think Whitebourne has some answers."

"I would not usually advise children on how to go looking for trouble," Mariam said, hesitant. "But I've learned they'll find it anyway." She smiled. "We've seen the news about strange things happening in Futureland. Finding answers is probably for the best."

Mariam turned and pointed out the window. "You're in luck. She works in the building next door, seven days a week. I see her car parked every day. Bright red. Fancy."

"I found it!" Amadou exclaimed, holding up his phone. "I knew I had saved one picture of her from our town hall meeting. It's not very recent, but it's the best I have."

He flipped the phone around for us to see, and my mouth fell open. The palms of my hands went clammy. I recognized the face.

"Are you sure this is Whitebourne?" I asked.

"Positively certain," Amadou said.

"I—I know this woman," I stammered. "I met her.

She was in the park on opening night. When we had the power outage she stayed to help people evacuate safely."

"Ah. So she has tricked *you* with her performance of genuineness as well," he said.

"She told me her name was Ruthie Bowen."

"No, this is Clare Whitebourne. I'm sure of it," Mariam said.

"They're the same person," Earl said. We all turned to look at him as he tapped away on his phone. He looked up and noticed us waiting for him to explain.

"Oh. Here, see?" This time, he held up his phone. Word Buddies, the spelling game, filled his screen. "Ruthie Bowen. Whitebourne. Eleven letters and they're all the same. She gave you a fake name, CJ. It's an anagram. It's been her the whole time."

My brain started to spin, and a fiery temper bubbled up inside me. Of course! How did I not think of that? I always knew there was something suspicious about the red-haired lady, and now I knew what. She'd pretended to be kind inside Futureland. She'd pretended like she wanted to come help with the investigation. But she had probably been gathering information about my family and the park the entire time. The person who forced Futureland to be invisible was the same person who had duplicated our wristband

284

technology to manipulate people's minds and throw the blame back on us.

"We have to get next door. We have to find her!" I said.

"Inaya, be home for dinner," Amadou said. "And please—be safe."

"Yes, Dad," she said, giving both her parents a hug. "And thank you."

"Rich, did you put the tracker in place?" I said through my Futurewatch. He and Inaya had gone to the parking lot of the building next to the Met to bug White-bourne's car. Me, Angel, and Earl stood watch from the street, waiting to see if we could catch a glimpse of Whitebourne.

"I think so. It's the only fancy red car over here."

"There she is!" Earl said, pointing.

We watched her walk out of the building. She wore an oversized red suede jacket, with a matching hat and a shiny black belt cinched around her waist. Emerald earrings dangled from her ears, and the red of her eye shadow and blush against her pale skin made her look like a carnival clown. She did her signature stiff walk

down the steps with her hands clasped together, smiling from ear to ear as she chattered away.

"Rich, she's on the phone. Can we get audio through the tracker?"

"Duh, CJ. What kind of cheap trackers do you think I brought?"

"Hush and turn on the audio," I said.

"Okay. She's getting into the car," Rich replied.

"Yes, master. It has been my honor to serve you as the Chief Officer of Beautification and Aesthetics for City. Though this was only a side mission, I know it brought great advancements to our overall goal.

"Thank you for allowing me to step down from the position now that phase one of the plan is complete. As you know, I have a sickly son, and I want to spend as much time as I can making this world better for him. Making it *exactly* what we want it to be."

Hold up. She was quitting? My mind clawed at the memory of when I'd first seen this woman. I thought about how she'd acted, how she'd asked questions about the park. I thought about Jordan coughing up a storm as he laughed at us back at the carnival in Harlem.

"I have greatly enjoyed serving you," Whitebourne continued. "I will use my new free time to glide

286

through life, pursuing business dreams that I've always wanted to chase."

New path? Lifelong business dreams? My eyebrows rose at her words.

"I will *always* love this city, but the whole world is just one big playground. And it's time for me to have as much fun as I can."

Rich's voice came through my Futurewatch.

"She's headed out of the city, CJ. We can track her as far as we need to, but if we don't want to lose her, we better start following."

"Copy that," I said. I turned to Earl and Angel and nodded. We started making our way to the parking lot of the government building to meet up with Inaya and Rich.

"Hey, Inaya?" I said.

"What's good?"

"Remember how you said you wished Jordan had given us a clue?"

"Yeah?"

"I think he just did."

287

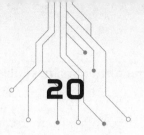

20

THE CASTLE

Sunday, February 14, 2049
4:00 p.m.

What could I say? Sometimes Rich annoyed me more than anybody else in the crew. But when he was good, he was *really* good. His quick research on Whitebourne confirmed everything Inaya's dad had told us about her. Every year young Whitebourne spent at NYU, she got involved in something creepy: writing horror stories for the school magazine, turning the cafeteria into a haunted house on Halloween, even wearing a werewolf costume to class sometimes. It was clear that she had always loved the horror genre, for whatever reason.

Rich's tracker bug stayed with Whitebourne all the way until she stopped moving, somewhere on Long

Island. Once we had the address, Rich and Earl stayed in Futureland while me, Inaya, and Angel left Manhattan and made the journey.

Each of us placed Futureland surveillance logo pins on our shirts. The pins were only about the size of a button but could send back a live audio and video feed to Rich and Earl in case we got into trouble. When we arrived at 301 Crystal Turtle Way, I froze, astounded.

As we watched Jordan through the window, I remembered his mom's words from the phone call: *I have a sickly son, and I want to spend as much time as I can making this world better for him.*

"I pop the windows at the shelter all the time when I'm sneaking in and out," Inaya said. "Step aside, southerner." Like magic, she pulled a tiny blade from her pocket and ran it along the window sash until it cracked. She jerked on the window until it popped open, and we climbed into the room.

Jordan remained still, the soft beeping of machines the only noise in the room. I remembered Angel and her distraction—we had to do this fast. I gently shook Jordan's shoulder until he awoke with a start, his eyes popping open. He scrambled up in bed and scooted away from us, scowling.

"What are you doing here?" he wheezed.

"Shhhh!" I whispered. "Please. We need answers. We didn't come to hurt you."

Jordan started removing tubes and pulling wires off himself. He swung his legs over the side of the mattress and leaned forward, resting his elbows on his thighs as he massaged his temples. "You can't hurt

292

me any more than she has. She's going to know you're here, you know? There are cameras everywhere."

"We'll worry about that later," I said. "Look, we know Clare Whitebourne is your mom. She's the same person that forced my parents to make Futureland invisible during off-hours, and your family has been a part of the Architects forever. But we need to know what she's trying to do. We need to know how to get my friend Yusuf back."

Jordan sighed and shook his head. "You'll never get your friend back," he said. "My mom, she's . . . she's not right. She's not good, and she's gone too far to stop now. Nothing can change her mind." Jordan coughed a few times and cleared his throat.

"What is she trying to do?" Inaya asked.

"You wouldn't believe me if I told you. My mom has been running the Haven brands for years," Jordan rasped. "Haventech, Haven Properties, everything. She's got this . . . *obsession* with theme parks. Carnivals. Scary ones, too." Jordan sighed.

"She's using her companies and all her money to make her dream come true." He shuddered. "She wants to turn all of New York into a theme park. Thinks it'll make people happy. And once her mind is made up, there's no changing it." He stared blankly ahead. "She's always been like that."

My mouth dropped open. I didn't know what I had been expecting, but it certainly wasn't this. Of all the things you could do with money and power, why waste it on something so . . . silly?

"That explains the playground in Harlem," Inaya said. "But why? Why carnivals?"

Jordan shook his head. "Who knows? But when she talks about it, she gets this look in her eyes. Like she'll do it no matter the cost, no matter what happens to people who get in her way. She's spent millions of dollars building tiny versions of her dream, like the one in Harlem. And even more money experimenting on people. Experimenting on . . . me."

Inaya let out a soft gasp. My stomach sank.

"What kinda experiments?" I asked quietly. "What is she doing to you?"

"My mom tried to get people to help with this carnival thing so many times," Jordan explained. "They all laughed at her. So she decided to force them. She says sometimes people don't know what they really want, so you have to make them see.

"That's why she made the wristbands control everyone. She thinks if she can get enough people under her command, she can transform New York faster. And then everybody else will see what she's seen all along. And they'll all be thankful for her."

294

"Ayo, that's messed up," Inaya said. I had to agree.

"Cam." Jordan had to clear his throat before going on. "As soon as she heard about what was going on in Atlanta with your family's park, she felt like it was a sign. She knew your family had the type of tech that could control robots, so she just needed to tweak it a little to control humans."

I gulped. It was all so horrible. "And what about you? About this?" I pointed at this wires and tubes. "Did she do this to you?"

Jordan nodded, coughed quietly. "I was the first one she ever tested the bands on. She needed a guinea pig to make sure the mind control worked, but she didn't know what she was doing. I get sicker every day. My brain . . . my nerves . . . they're all messed up."

"We can fix you," Inaya said. "We can reverse it. Cam's parents—"

Jordan shook his head. "Everything hurts. My mom says my sacrifice will be worth it. That I'll be a hero in the world she creates and that nobody will ever forget my name. That's why she needs your friend—to replace me when I'm gone. She likes him. He's tall, strong, athletic. His body won't give up like mine did."

His eyes welled up with tears. I clenched my fists at my sides.

"We're not going to let that happen to you," I

295

promised. "And we're not going to let her hurt anybody else, either. Do you know where we can find Yusuf?"

"You've seen the carnival in Harlem," Jordan said, "but there's another. The big one. The one she says will be the start of everything. All the Gliders are meeting there tonight to finish building it. I can't lead them anymore—I'm too sick. Yusuf had to take my shift, so he'll be there. But *she'll* be there, too."

Tonight. Possibly our last chance to save Yusuf.

"We're not scared of her," Inaya said.

"You should be," Jordan warned. We heard a door close in another room and footsteps in the hallway. I leaned in close to Jordan and whispered in a rush.

"Where is this other carnival?" I asked. "The big one. Where will they be tonight?"

"Right under your nose," Jordan said, looking nervously at the door. "Down the rabbit hole. Where *everyone* is mad. It's close to Futureland, but you'll have to go late. Very late. When everything is dark—at the start of the nightmare hour."

"That's a pretty unbelievable story, CJ," Rich said, projecting as a hologram from my Futurewatch as me,

Inaya, and Angel finally made it back to Central Park. We approached the zero-gravity beam that would bring us up to Futureland.

"What reason does he have to lie?" I asked.

"Umm, I don't know," Rich answered me sarcastically. "Maybe the fact that his *mom* is a liar and a villain? Maybe because he wants to send you into a trap, or worse, send you on a wild-goose chase while Yusuf is in some kind of real danger?"

"He did seem pretty genuine to me," Inaya said. "Just saying."

"It's the only information we've got, Rich," Angel added. "We have to follow the lead."

"Lead? What lead?!" Rich exclaimed. "A bunch of nonsense. Humans can't even fit in rabbit holes. I still say it's a setup."

Angel, Inaya, and I floated up, landed on the main entrance terminal, and walked through the automatic double doors. We ran right into my parents, standing with their arms crossed, glaring at us.

"Oh yeah," Rich's projection said. "My bad, CJ. I forgot to tell you that your parents made it home, and, uh, you're in trouble."

"Thanks a lot, Rich." I exited the call.

"Cameron . . . ," Mom started dangerously.

"Mom, look, you have to understand!" I tried.

"There's no explaining your way out of this one, Big Man," Dad said. "You and Trey . . . I swear, I think *he's* the twelve-year-old sometimes. You already have one friend in danger. How could you bring all your other friends here, into the same situation?"

"I need their help to find Yusuf!" I said. "We're working together." My fists clenched, and I felt myself trembling from frustration.

"Not anymore you're not," Mom said. "The police are looking for Yusuf. We didn't want to get them involved, but Yusuf's parents are worried sick, and they asked us to make a report. The officers said they spotted him about twelve hours ago on one of the traffic cameras in the city. They're doing a full search of Manhattan right now. We have to get out of their way and let them work, Cam."

"But it's more than just Yusuf!" I explained. "It's Clare Whitebourne and Haventech. The bands! They're controlling people and Southmore's coming back, and—"

"Trey already gave us the full rundown," Dad interrupted. "Southmore used his connections on the outside to get access to your devices. There are still plenty of people who fear and respect him. But he *is* in prison. Our main concern is getting Yusuf back safely. As soon as we have him, your uncle is going to take that abomination of a machine he built and fly all your friends home."

"The Mammoth?" Angel asked.

"Whatever he calls it," Mom said, rolling her eyes. "Cam-Cam, I know you wanted to help. But this can't be our battle. It's too big. The police are confident they can track Yusuf down in a few hours. This is too dangerous for you and your friends. You're only kids."

I tensed up. Embarrassment prickled my skin. I cleared my throat. "We weren't *only kids* when we defeated Southmore and saved the park before. We solve mysteries, Mom. *I* solve mysteries. And I can solve this one, if you only give me a chance. If you just believe in me."

My mom covered her face and turned away. My dad rubbed her back and gave a heavy sigh.

"Maybe you're right, son," he said. "You did an amazing thing, and we both believe that you'll do many more. But you shouldn't have to do this. A kid shouldn't have to save the world. Go upstairs and spend some time with your friends, Big Man. Don't go to our lab and don't leave the park. Lights out by 9:00 p.m. This will all be over soon."

We all stood around for a second, unsure of what to do. That was that. Mom and Dad sent us upstairs to rejoin Rich and Earl. They had heard everything that

happened at the Whitebourne mansion through our Futureland logo spy pins.

"If Momma Whitebourne is really planning what Jordan says she is, there's no way the police are going to find Yusuf before tonight," Earl said. "She needs him to control the other Gliders until they finish whatever evil project she's working on. She's probably got him hidden away somewhere nobody can find."

"For all we know, Whitebourne could be controlling the police," Rich added. "Didn't she work for the government? They probably know all about what's going on and won't try to stop it anyway."

"Either way it goes," Angel started, "we know when and where all of this is supposed to go down. The least we can do is show up and check it out. Cam, do you think we're going to be able to get out of here after everyone goes to sleep?"

"I don't know," I said, dejected. "Now that my parents are back, they're going to lock this place down and keep an eye on my locator. I do still have Uncle Trey's ID card, though. That could help us get to the ground, but we've got to make our way out of Futureland first. I can't think of a way we're going to be able to get out without being noticed."

Earl sighed. "Man, this stinks. I wish Yusuf was here. He'd know exactly what to do."

I hung my head. Thoughts flooded in from all angles like rivers meeting the ocean. I remembered Yusuf's smile on my first day at Eastside Middle School. He was the first kid to talk to me, the first in the crew to start helping me investigate Southmore. Why is it that the person most willing to help often has to make the biggest sacrifice?

If you had told me months ago that I'd be in the middle of such a big mess—that I would've lost my best friend and would be about to lose another—I never would have believed it. Truthfully, I was still amazed sometimes that I had made such good friends at all.

I looked around the room at everyone—Rich, Earl, Angel, Inaya—my crew. My friends. All their solemn but determined faces. I refused to lose them. If the shoe was on the other foot, Yusuf would never leave me out to dry. No, I wasn't going to let it go down like this.

We had one more chance to save Yusuf and I wasn't going to waste it. Not after all he'd done for me. I pondered Earl's comment again—he was right. Yusuf *would* know exactly what to do.

An idea came to me. "Earl, you're a genius."

"I am?"

"Yes!" I nodded excitedly. "Yusuf did know exactly what to do. And he already showed me. I have an idea,

but we have to start preparing for it right now. Can you fit under my bed?"

"I think so," Earl said, raising an eyebrow.

"Good. Everybody, put on your shoes. We have to make a stop. I'll tell you the plan on the way."

The crew gathered their things and we left my bedroom, headed upstairs to the park. We only had a few hours to set up our escape before bedtime. After that, we'd need to make it to the secret location Jordan shared with us if we wanted any chance of saving Yusuf and stopping the next stage of Clare Whitebourne's plan.

If we didn't . . . we might never get him back.

HAVENTECH LIFEBUDDY.
YOUR BUDDY FOR LIFE.
DOES IT ALL! YOU'LL NEVER NEED ANOTHER DEVICE.
HAVENTECH
LIFEBUDDY WRISTBANDS
FINALLY AVAILABLE WORLDWIDE. ORDER ONLINE OR VISIT YOUR LOCAL TECH RETAILER.

21

UNDER WONDERLAND

Sunday, February 14, 2049
9:00 p.m.

"All right, kids." Mom stepped into the doorway of my bedroom with her arms crossed, her beehive of locs almost higher than the top of the doorframe. "It's time for bed. Tomorrow, J.B. and I will be able to help you with your research trip project. Take you around New York."

We sat around in our pajamas with more pillows than anyone could need. Angel and Inaya shared my bed for the night, while Rich took the futon, and I crashed on the floor.

"Any word on Yusuf?" I asked.

"Um, well." My dad popped out from behind my mom and adjusted his glasses before speaking. "We just got off the phone with the NYPD. They haven't been able to locate him yet, but they assure us they have every unit they can spare on the case. We know you're worried about your friend—we're worried about him, too. But remember, this is what his parents want. We have to respect their wishes."

"Everybody understand?" Mom said. "No leaving Futureland tonight. No leaving *this room* tonight. If you need something, call Alejandro or Aurielle. They'll be up all night to bring you things. All right, I see Angel—hey, sweetie. The lovely Inaya. My one and only son. Christopher—"

"Rich, Mrs. Dr. Walker," he cut in. "It's Rich!"

"Oh, yes, yes." Mom nodded through a little smile. "Sorry. Rich. And . . . where's little Earl at?"

"Earl is sleeping already," I said. "In the closet."

My mom raised her eyebrow. "Say what?"

"He gets shy sleeping around other kids," Rich added. "Every time we had sleepovers in elementary school, he would always go home early." He changed his voice to a whisper. "But he's a little sensitive about it, so we try not to mention it."

My mom gave Rich a skeptical look. "You know what, Rich, I'm so sure that's true. But Cameron has mentioned, more than one time, your, erm—*talent* for storytelling. Let me just take a peek in this closet to see with my own eyes."

Rich shot me a worried glance, and then we all watched and waited, tense as my mom approached the closet. She turned the doorknob and gently opened the door.

"Earl?"

A buzzing roar of Earl's snores erupted from the closet and into our room, louder than any kind of mythical beast you could imagine. My mom tried to take a step farther into the closet, but Earl's snoring got even louder. Mom backed out of the closet and stared at Dad, surprised.

"That little boy is *exactly* where he needs to be. These kids wouldn't even be able to sleep if we hadn't soundproofed most of these doors," she said. "All right, y'all. Time for bed. Good night."

My parents switched the lights off and left the room. Angel started the timer, and we waited in the dark for hours until we knew my parents wouldn't come back by to check on us.

"Angel," I whispered, from under my blanket. "You up?"

"You know it. It's time."

We all shook off our covers and walked to the closet. When we opened the door, the loud, snarling snores of Earl made their way out. I tapped a button on my Futurewatch and paused the sounds. Rich stepped into the closet and snatched the blanket off the sleeping body.

"You know, he really does look like Earl," he said.

"I know, right?" Angel said.

"I was worried Cam's mom was gonna walk in and notice the skin pattern," Inaya said. "Never seen a boy with cheetah-print skin before."

We all laughed. We had created Earl's Holo-pal in just enough time to make it back to my bedroom before nightfall, so my parents didn't suspect anything. I recorded some sounds of Earl pretending to snore and implanted them into his double to play them on a loop. Kind of like Yusuf had done with my mom's voice when he first tricked his own parents and snuck into Futureland.

"Any chance your parents left the door unlocked?" Inaya asked.

"No way," I said.

Rich made his way over to the door and turned the knob. "It's unlocked!"

We all froze. "Wait, really?!" I said.

"Naw, I'm just playing. Call Earl."

I rolled my eyes and tapped my Futurewatch. Rich played too much. Time for plan A.

"Skyboy to Little Bite, Skyboy to Little Bite—do you read me?"

"Little Bite to Skyboy, I read you. Did you really have Yusuf living in this detective-office room before he disappeared? There's no snacks in here. No fridge, no—"

"Stay focused, Little Bite," I said. "Are you ready for the next part of the plan? Tap the door four times when you're outside."

"Ten-four," Earl said.

We waited a few minutes that felt like forever, and then we heard them: four light raps on the door. I took Uncle Trey's ID out of my pocket and slid it under. Seconds later, Earl quietly opened the door and we all tiptoed out, one by one. As we made our way through the hall to the staircase, I noticed Aurielle and Alejandro slumped on the couch, their eyes dim and their necks leaning enough for their heads to rest on one another.

Offline.

I looked at Earl and he winked. "Snuck up on them from behind and pressed their shut-down buttons," he whispered.

Our plan had worked like a charm.

We made our way through the halls, stopping quickly to grab one of my dad's newest designs from the storage closet—stealth black Futureland jogging suits and matching winter hats. I pulled on my deerstalker instead of a regular beanie, of course. Me, Earl,

308

and Rich got dressed in the hall, while the girls got dressed in the closet. Once everybody was changed, we continued our escape from Futureland.

"All right, where's this infamous rabbit hole?" Rich asked once we'd made it to the ground. We all studied the holographic map rising out of Angel's watch, trying to determine the next step toward our destination.

"Umm . . . ," Angel said. She squinted at the hologram, turning it in different directions.

Rich shook his head. He mocked Jordan with a weak, raspy voice. "Down the rabbit hole, where everyone is mad. Blah! I told you that place doesn't exist."

"Yes, it does!" Earl said. "It's from *Alice in Wonderland*."

"Earl, you're a genius," Inaya said.

"I am?"

"Yes! There's an Alice in Wonderland statue in this park. I've seen it plenty times before. I'm not sure how to get there in the dark, though."

"Found it!" said Angel, pointing to a spot on the hologram. "It's southeast of here."

"Which way is southeast?!" Rich said.

"It's right, then left," Earl chimed.

"My right or your right?" Inaya asked.

"Shhh!" I raised a finger to my lips. "Everybody! Come on, follow me."

We hustled through the park, scuttling over the sidewalks and disappearing into the bushes like shadows. We needed to get to the famous Alice in Wonderland statue in Central Park—that was the location Jordan had hinted at. He promised that Yusuf would be there, leading all the Gliders as they constructed Clare Whitebourne's most evil project yet.

The one we had to stop in order to free Yusuf and the Gliders from her mind control.

"You know," Rich whispered, looking at a photo on his phone, "I still don't buy that Jordan kid's story. We're talking about an eleven-foot-tall bronze statue— you really think it's just going to lift up and have some whole secret underground workshop beneath it?"

"Stranger things have happened," Inaya said.

"Oh yeah? Like what?"

"Like sometimes, people in Times Square for New Year's Eve wear diapers since it's too hard to find a bathroom," Inaya said. "Or that we have a windowless skyscraper on Thomas Street that can withstand nuclear fallout for up to fourteen days. Or that one time, in 1884, they put twenty-one elephants on the Brooklyn Bridge to—"

"Okay, okay." Rich rolled his eyes. "Sheesh. Weird stuff happens in New York all the time. Point taken."

"There it is," Angel said. "Up ahead."

We approached the huge bronze statue and looked up at it. Alice sat on a flat-top mushroom, playing with a tiny animal. The white rabbit stood beside her in his fancy jacket and waistcoat, trying to hand her a clock. On the other side, the Mad Hatter sat smiling, looking intrigued by a little mouse.

"So, do we just . . . move it?" Earl said.

"It's too heavy for us to push," Inaya said.

"What did Jordan say?" Angel asked.

I thought back to when Jordan was talking to me and Inaya in his bedroom. "He didn't really say anything," I recalled with a frown. "He just said they'd be here."

"Oh, great," Rich said. "The little ninja boy isn't reliable. I wonder who saw *that* coming."

"He told us to be here," I insisted. "He said it would happen."

"It's twelve thirty-seven," Earl said. "Maybe we missed them and they're already underground."

"No, no, no," I gumbled. "We can't be too late. We can't!"

I had already lost Dooley, which broke my heart in half. If I lost Yusuf, too, what was left of it would shatter into a million little pieces.

"Ayo . . . y'all hear that?" asked Inaya.

I listened in at the rhythm of a steady beat on pavement. "Sounds like footsteps," I said. "Marching."

"They're getting closer. Quick! Let's hide in the bushes," Angel suggested.

We dove into the brush just in time to watch the crowd of Gliders emerge from the darkness, stepping toward the statue in unison. People of all colors, shapes, and sizes. They kept the same posture as always, straight and stiff, as they made a neat circle around the bronze monument. Each raised their right arm toward it in perfect synchronization.

"What is that thing?" Earl whispered in shock, looking to the sky with wide eyes. "It's huge!"

I followed his gaze, and my heart skipped a beat. "That's Yusuf," I said. "He's here!"

Yusuf looked like a shadow cutting across the moon as he floated through the sky on Ali's back. Ali turned over in the air acrobatically. He dove hard and then spun, tumbling to the ground and making a grand entrance. Yusuf delicately dismounted the oversized sugar glider and petted his head.

The color of Ali's fur had changed from neon blue with sliver streaks to jet black. His beautiful crystal eyes had turned red. He looked like a vampire-bat version of his old self.

Yusuf walked around the outside of the circle of people under Whitebourne's control, examining each one. His expression was empty and emotionless as he inspected all the Glider minions. I noticed a sparkly new Haventech band on his left wrist.

"He's got a new band," I whispered. "We've got to get it off him."

"We need to get into that bunker first!" Rich said. "Look, he's opening it."

Yusuf grabbed the tail on the White Rabbit and slowly began to crank it around and around. As he cranked, the entire bronze statue lifted slowly off the ground like a platform. One by one, the Gliders stepped to the widening gap and made their way down below, into whatever existed beneath the bronze. Once Yusuf cranked the statue platform to a tall enough height, Gliders started descending more rapidly, in twos and threes.

"We've got to go now!" Inaya said. "We should blend with the crowd!"

Angel seemed unsure. "That's too dangerous. What if they see us?"

"It's going to close soon. We need to make a decision," Rich stressed. "Earl, what do you—Earl?"

Through the darkness of the underground bunker, I saw a haunted house, its entrance shaped like the face of a clown with its skin peeling off. The clown had yellow, chipped teeth and a menacing stare. There were several swings and carousels, all loud and rusted as they turned jerkily, grinding and clinking with each revolution. Carnival workers glided from tent to tent, setting up their attractions.

One tested out a balloon pop game with a dart, and when the latex erupted, a dark red ooze splashed everywhere. The Glider carefully clapped their hands, showing no emotion, before clasping them back at their waist and walking away. In the distance, beyond it all, I saw the tallest Ferris wheel I had ever seen. As one car reached the top, hundreds of feet above the muddy floor, it disconnected from the link and fell disastrously into the sludge, shattering into hundreds of pieces and splashing everyone nearby with mud. All the Gliders watching cheered.

Inaya let out the beginning of a shriek, but Angel quickly covered her mouth.

"Cam, what do we do?" Rich asked.

I searched around until I located Yusuf again. He

stood on a platform in the middle of the construction site. Every few moments, a group of Gliders would approach him. He'd say something I couldn't hear, then tap his Haventech band, and they would all leave.

"He's giving them instructions," I said. "Whitebourne is controlling through him the band, and then he's controlling the Gliders."

"So we gotta get the band from him," Inaya said as she watched.

"How are we going to do that?" Earl said.

"Earl, you're pretty good at that whole gliding thing," I said. "You think you can pretend again?"

"For sure," he said.

"Rich, think you got another one of those cannonball moves in you?"

Rich chuckled and rubbed his hands together. "I'd belly flop on each one of y'all for free, three times a day, if I could."

"Great," I said. "I've got a plan. Inaya, Angel—go right, over there by that pile of wood. Rich, you come with me. Earl, listen up. Your part is the most important. This is for everything. We only get one shot."

ONE SHOT

Monday, February 15, 2049
1:25 a.m.

Rich and I crouched behind Yusuf, barely able to peek over the platform where he stood.

"Is it time yet?" Rich whispered.

"No."

I looked to the left and to the right. In the shadows, Angel and Inaya had taken their stations.

"Now?" Rich whispered, leaning in close to my ear. I swatted him away.

Finally, the crowd approached—a fresh set of Gliders coming to secure their next assignment from Yusuf. The waking zombie workforce moved efficiently.

"How about now?"

I sighed. "Rich, will you—"

Yusuf turned in our direction, and we both ducked

our heads below the platform. *Sorry,* Rich mouthed. I hoped that Yusuf hadn't heard us over the sounds of banging metal and construction all around. I slowly peeked over the lip of the platform again and saw Yusuf walk to the front of it, ready to address his new workers. Nestled in the middle of the crowd, I saw Earl, blending in as a Glider—just as planned. Yusuf spoke to his minions, commanding their next duties.

"All of you over there, get to work on the Ferris wheel. Reconstruct the car that fell, and then reattach it to the wheel. Loosen up another one and let's watch it drop. You guys, fill up some more balloons. We need as many as possible."

When he finished giving instructions, everyone dispersed from the crowd except Earl. He stood there perfectly still, all emotion wiped from his face.

Yusuf shouted at Earl while tapping his wristband. "Hey, you. Get to work. Everybody has their assignments." Earl didn't move. Yusuf finally looked up from the band and stepped closer to the edge of the platform.

"What in the—" He peered at Earl. "Hey, don't I know you?"

Yusuf jumped off the platform and slowly walked up to Earl. Earl remained as still as he could, but I

could see him starting to crack. As Glider Yusuf towered over him, Earl closed his eyes.

"What are you doing here?" Yusuf asked.

"Rich," I said. "Now!"

"Huh? Like *right* now?" he said.

"YES!" I nearly bellowed.

I pulled Rich up onto the platform with me. Right as Yusuf yanked Earl up by the collar, I dove into him, tackling him from behind. Earl let out a high-pitched yelp and rolled away from Yusuf's grip. I wrapped my arms tightly around Yusuf's legs as he wriggled. He flipped over from his stomach onto his back and looked at me, sneering.

"Cameron," he hissed. He reached for me, but Inaya and Angel came right on time.

"Not so fast, basketball boy," Inaya said.

"Grab that arm!! I've got this one!" Angel called. They each held down one of Yusuf's arms, pinning him down to the ground with all of their body weight. I scooted my way up Yusuf's body, sitting on his legs to keep them pinned. It took all we had to try to keep him still.

"Hand me his arm, Inaya!" I yelled.

"I'm trying!" She thrusted Yusuf's arm toward me, and I scraped at his Haventech band, trying to remove it. Yusuf struggled, jerking his arm back and forth. Veins throbbed in his forearm as he grunted and growled.

"No! Noooo!" he barked, muffled under the weight of us all.

I almost had the band. I had pulled it over the heel of his hand and almost over his thumb, but Angel couldn't hold him any longer. Yusuf broke one arm free and pushed me off him. He did a backward somersault, twisted his way out of Inaya's grasp, and rolled to his feet. Me, Angel, and Inaya lay crumpled in a pile of defeat.

"Cameron," Yusuf said. "You brought your friends to stop me, huh? How sweet. Teamwork makes the dream work. As you can see, we're big on teamwork around here. And you will be, too—once you join my Glider army and help me finish my life's dream." Yusuf sneered with narrow eyes and a venomous grin. I shuddered. This wasn't the Yusuf I knew. Whitebourne had him deep under her control. He had no idea what he was doing.

"I know you're in there, Whitebourne!" I shouted as Glider Yusuf approached us. "Stop using my friend! Leave him alone!"

"I don't think I will," Glider Yusuf said. He grabbed the collar of my jogging jacket with two hands and lifted me up. He bared his teeth in anger.

"Geronimoooooooo!!!!"

Still clutched in Glider Yusuf's grasp, I watched his eyes grow wide with fear. He threw me to the side, but not in time to dodge Rich's infamous belly flop. They both toppled over from the force of Rich's weight. He had timed the jump perfectly. Rich was big and graceful, like a beautiful, chubby gazelle.

Inaya, Angel, Earl, and I scrambled back toward a dazed Yusuf and pinned his limbs down once again. I yanked the band off his wrist. As soon as we freed Yusuf from the Haventech device, he closed his eyes, took in a deep breath, and exhaled slowly.

"Cam? Angel?" Yusuf croaked. "You're here. You came to save me." I put my hand in his, pulling him up off his back and wrapping him in a quick hug.

"You know we would never leave you behind," I said.

Yusuf smiled weakly. "Real friends."

"Real friends," Angel, Rich, Earl, and I said at the same time.

"Oh, word? Y'all got catchphrases?" Inaya said. "That's cute."

We started to pull Yusuf up to his feet. He leaned on us as his legs wobbled. Despite all the commotion, none of the Gliders had stopped their tasks. They continued building Whitebourne's theme park of doom undisturbed.

"Let's go, Yusuf," I said. "We've got to get you out of here. Get you some help."

Yusuf paused and shook his head. Sorrow grew in his eyes and his expression pleaded for us to wait.

"What's the matter?" Angel asked.

"We can't leave these people down here," he said. Yusuf coughed and took a sad glance at the Gliders. "If we don't help them get out of here, there's no telling what she'll do to them. And all they'll remember is that Futureland was the beginning of the end of their lives."

"Yusuf, we can't possibly take all these people out of here!" Rich said. "There's hundreds of them! We have to get out while we can."

Yusuf shook his head. "We can't leave them."

"Can we take off their bands, somehow?" asked Inaya. "Like we did with Yusuf. Then they'll start to recover, and we can lead them out."

"It might work," I said, "but it'll take hours to remove everyone's band. And I'm not sure how many more belly flops Rich has up his sleeves."

"Ugh!" Yusuf said, rubbing his temples in frustration. "It's hard for me to think. My brain feels so fuzzy."

"Don't think too hard, my darling," came a voice from behind us. "You'll hurt yourself."

We whipped around and saw her. She was standing on the platform where Yusuf once stood, in her red jacket, matching hat, and high heels that made her look ten feet tall.

Whitebourne.

She smiled without showing her teeth, glaring at us with menacing eyes. She unclasped her hands from their resting place at her waist and put them on her hips.

"Welcome to my little playground," she said. "Leaving so soon? The fun is just starting."

Whitebourne let out a hideous cackle. Me and the crew scrambled to turn and go back toward the staircase that would lead us up to the Alice in Wonderland statue. But we couldn't go anywhere.

In a matter of seconds, all the Gliders had ceased their work and encircled us. No matter which direction we turned, a wall of mind-controlled zombie minions stood facing us, blocking our path. I looked back up at Whitebourne on the platform just in time for her to flash us a snarling grin.

"You'll never leave," she spat. "You're all mine. Forever."

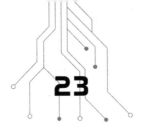

THE NIGHTMARE HOUR

Monday, February 15, 2049
2:22 a.m.

"Y ou kids don't understand, just like everybody else," Whitebourne said, pacing the platform as the Gliders kept us enclosed in the construction space. "Generation after generation of hard work has made my family one of the wealthiest and most powerful in the world. So much blood, sweat, and tears to make it to the top of the food chain."

My friends and I looked at each other in panic. Nobody knew what to do next.

"But we sacrificed so much," she continued. "All of us. Working all the time. Nobody has any *fun* anymore! When I was a little girl, I wanted ever so badly to go to the playground with my friends from school. Pull the heads off my dolls. Play spooky dress-up."

She snarled, baring her teeth. "But no! I always had to *study*, I always had to *work*, I always had to *prepare* to be the next great Whitebourne. My entire life has been all about work."

My eyes popped listening to her talk. Whitebourne wanted to . . . play? She was willing to ruin the lives of others just for a little enjoyment?

Jordan had been right—she was pure evil.

"You did all this . . . for fun?" I said.

"Fun is the most important thing in life," she said. "I would hope that you, as a kid, could understand, but even kids these days are too obsessed with school and growing up. I have to *make* people remember how to have fun. When I turn this entire city into the first ever Haven Horrors park, the world will see," she finished.

"Do you think you're treating Jordan any better than your parents treated you?" Inaya shouted. "You think he's having fun wasting away in that hospital bedroom? You're not changing anything at all. You're just causing the same kind of damage all the Whitebournes before you did!"

Whitebourne glowered at her. "Jordan is a hero. A martyr. He understands that giving his life for something this important is the greatest sacrifice of all. I'm proud of my son. There will be Jordan Whitebourne statues at every Haven Horrors park worldwide, in his honor!"

"He doesn't want statues!" I cried out. "He wants to live! You have all the money and power you need to change the world in a positive way, but you'd rather force people to do what you want? There's no honor in that!"

"That's what nobody understands!" Whitebourne stamped her feet in anger. "Ugh! *This* is why the world needs Haven Horrors. They need someone like me to show them how good something different could be. They'll be able to eat, sleep, and play at Haven Horrors, and never miss a moment! The fun won't ever end!

"You know," she said to me, "I actually did enjoy my trip to Futureland. It's an amazing park, quite honestly. Your parents are brilliant. I admire them. They've made something so *fun*. But it's not enough! It could use a little *edge*. A pinch of horror always makes things better. That's why I borrowed your wristband technology from my good friend Southmore."

Southmore. I knew he was involved with this in some way. I gritted my teeth, a fire sparking in my belly.

"Besides, with the amount of trouble you all have been getting into, it won't be long before the park shuts down forever." She grinned widely—madly—and winked.

"It's been you all along," Angel said.

"It was rather easy. I traded access to Cameron's personal devices for some of the data Southmore stole last year. But it wasn't until I noticed the prototype for Futureland's projection band that I discovered an easy way to gradually control people. It's worked quite well, if I do say so myself."

And I had thought that Southmore was as big and bad as they got. How wrong I was.

"You demolished my family's home!" screamed Inaya. She pointed right at Whitebourne. "Our brownstone in Harlem! Just to build one of those creepy parks!"

"I've knocked down hundreds of buildings on the way to my dream, darling," Whitebourne said, examining her bright red nails. "Sacrifice is necessary. Now, enough chitchat. The grand opening of the first Haven Horrors is almost here. Let's get to work!"

Whitebourne tapped on her own wristband, and the circle of Gliders around us started closing in. They grabbed at us and pulled on our clothes. Yusuf hiptossed and sweep-kicked a few of them. Earl scurried on his hands and knees between their legs until they ran into each other. Inaya and Angel fought back-to-back, kicking and pushing any of the Gliders that got too close.

Rich ran around the construction site, pushing materials down in the path of any Gliders that tried to follow him. I tried to make my way toward Whitebourne on the platform, but I could never get more than a couple steps closer to her before a Glider would pull me back into the circle. I yanked one Glider's shirt over their head and pushed them backward into a group of others, knocking them down like bowling pins.

There were too many Gliders. No matter how hard we fought, they kept closing in. One picked Earl up and pinned him up against the wall of the cavernous dungeon. Two others restrained Inaya's and Angel's arms behind their backs. Rich finally ran out of space to move as Gliders cornered him. Only Yusuf remained free, ducking under the reach of two Gliders and leaping onto the carousel as they collided. I barreled through a group of them and jumped on the carousel with him, riding around and around on the same beast, holding him for stability.

"Yusuf!" I called out. "Make them stop!"

Yusuf pulled the wristband out of his pocket and paused. He eyed it in the palm of his hand. "I can't, CJ," he said. "Whitebourne is commanding them. I can't control them anymore." He paused for a second. "But I think I can stop them."

"How?" I shouted.

"This wristband still has data for all of these people stored inside it—that's how I controlled them—and all of them have been to Futureland. They have Holo-pals. If I can project them down here, they'll be able to help us fight back."

"Will that work?" I asked, breathless. We were running out of time.

"I think so. Whitebourne has been tinkering with the Futureland tech a lot," Yusuf said. "She made it so that Ali could project outside Futureland and fly me to her. If it works for the other Holo-pals and Holo-pets, they should be able to get down here."

We didn't have another choice. "Let's give it a shot!" I said.

We continued to go around and around on the carousel. Gliders climbed up onto the platform and chased us, reaching out to try to pull us down. I looked over my shoulder and saw their arms outstretched, getting closer.

"Yusuf!" I cried. "Do it now! Do it now!"

Yusuf did a combination of taps on the wristband in his left hand. I felt someone tugging at my leg and turned to see a little girl with pigtails, not older than eight or nine, pulling at me with all her strength. She looked up with glazed eyes and gave me a close-lipped smile.

"Now!" I yelled.

A flash of light. The grip on my pants leg disappeared. I blinked the shine out of my eyes and looked over my shoulder again. This time, there was a brilliant sight to behold.

Dozens of Holo-pals stood on the platform of the carousel as Yusuf and I continued to go around, making a barricade that kept everyone away from us. Beyond them, hundreds more projections made their way into the crowd of Gliders, each one shined in their own unique way, copies of their people with aquamarine, electric-green, or hot-pink skin.

Relief washed over me. I tapped my own Future-watch, projecting Goggles and Sarafina into the space. The caracal growled and jumped into the crowd, scaring the Gliders away from my friends. Goggles winked at me, then pulled his shades down over his eyes. He leaped over a tall mound of concrete blocks, pushing a few Gliders down on his way.

Yusuf kept tapping commands into his band, and the Holo-pals began to fight back against the Gliders. They wrestled with them, tugging and pulling them all over the construction zone. Yusuf and I noticed that the brawl had allowed Angel, Rich, Earl, and Inaya to break free. We jumped down from the carousel and ran over to them.

"This is amazing!" Inaya said.

"Good thinking, Yusuf!" I agreed, giving him a high five.

"Thanks. But we're not done yet," he responded. "We've got to stop Whitebourne."

"But how do we—"

"*Ahhhhh!*"

Yusuf screamed as an enormous Holo-pet hawk swooped down and clutched him in its talons. The hawk was firecracker red with black streaks. It let out a shrill screech as it carried Yusuf through the air and over to the platform where Whitebourne stood.

"Yusuf!" we all yelled.

The Gliders and Holo-pals continued to battle around us as we raced to the platform. The hawk dropped Yusuf onto the platform, and Whitebourne snatched him up only to put him in a headlock from behind, choking him with her arm.

"You didn't think I'd miss the chance to make my *own* Futureland Holo-pet, did you?" she shrieked, her eyes mad. "They're oh so much fun. Good job, my little sweetie-kins," she cooed to the bird. The hawk screeched again and soared away.

Whitebourne ripped Yusuf's Haventech band out

of his hand and kept him clutched under her other arm. He clawed at her, kicking and struggling, but he couldn't escape her grasp.

"You're not going anywhere," she snarled into Yusuf's ear. "I told you, you're mine forever. You will finish what Jordan started. You will be my new son."

"Not if I can help it!" I yelled at her. "He doesn't belong to you!"

She threw Yusuf to the ground, hard. We tried to rush the platform, but several Gliders grabbed us and held us still. Two more Gliders jumped up and restrained Yusuf, offering his wrist to Whitebourne for her to place the band on him one final time. She smiled down at us as she stretched out the band over Yusuf's fingers. Yusuf struggled, but there was nothing he could do. She jammed the wristband down over his hand and onto his wrist.

We all tried to scream, but the Gliders covered our mouths. Whitebourne threw her head back, cackling. I thought the sound of her evil triumph would never end, but then I heard a voice.

Jordan jumped down from the construction pile and huddled with us. He was okay!

"Incredible timing," I said, smiling. "What is that thing?"

"It's a power-surge reverser," Jordan said. "Takes all the energy and data out of a power source, flips it around, then returns it. It's connected to my mom's wristband right now. It's what she used to tap into the Futureland bands and alter the projections when we visited on opening night. She had it connected to the Holo-pal chamber then."

"That's pretty handy," I said.

"You learn a thing or two growing up the son of an evil genius." Jordan returned my smile.

Boom!

Another small earthquake, another blackout.

The lights came back up in a flash. Slowly, the Holo-pals and Holo-pets started to dissipate, fading away pixel by pixel. Goggles knelt beside me, cradling Sarafina. He moved his goggles back up to his forehead and gave me a wink. Sarafina purred and licked my face. Goggles shot me a peace sign and smiled.

"See you later, dude," he said. "Had a lot of fun."

338

The others disappeared, too, stretching, waving, and saluting their way into invisibility. As they disappeared, the Gliders began to stir as well. They put their palms to their heads and rubbed their eyes. It wasn't long before the crowd came alive with a din of confusion.

Where are we?

What's going on?

How did we get down here?

Me and the crew hugged one another, jumping up and down at our success. Thanks to Jordan's help, we could collect all the Haventech bands, destroy them, and return everyone to safety. We still had hundreds, maybe thousands, of other bands out in the world to worry about, but we had stopped Whitebourne.

That was enough for now.

"Wait . . . where's Whitebourne?" Inaya said.

"I'm right here," Jordan said.

"Not you, silly. Your mom."

All of us spun around, searching for the woman in the bright red coat. We spread out around the bunker, but we couldn't find any trace of her.

"There must be some kind of secret exit in here only she knows about," I said after we ended the search.

"Villains *always* got the secret exit." Earl shook his head.

"She got away." Jordan coughed and dropped his head. He wiped the wetness out of his eyes and kicked at the sludge below us. "I let her get away. I'm sorry."

"Hey, don't do that," I said. My heart filled with admiration looking at Jordan.

"You saved us," I said. "Without you, we never could have stopped her from completing this place. We never could have freed all these people. I don't care what your mom tried to make you think you were. You chose to not keep hurting people. To us, you're a hero."

"A hero!" Earl and Rich agreed.

"¡El Valiente!" Angel said.

"Facts," Inaya said.

We embraced Jordan and he laughed. First time I'd seen him do that, I think.

The crowd of former Gliders got louder. Many had started to recognize and reunite with their friends and families. They asked each other questions, trying to piece together the story of their capture from broken details. Some of them roamed around the bunker, trying to find a way out. Inaya, Earl, and Jordan moved into the crowd, trying to corral people and guide them toward a safer path out of the dungeon.

"You're up, CJ," Angel said.

"Yeah, do your thing, Detective Cam," Rich added, handing me his Futurewatch.

I blushed.

"Hey, everybody!" I spoke into the Futurewatch using the megaphone setting. "Excuse me, everyone. My name is Cam Walker and these are my friends. Don't be afraid—you can trust us. I know you're probably wondering what happened to you and how you got down here. We can explain it all. And we will. But first, let's get you outta here. It's time to go home."

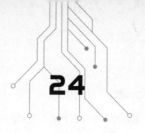

24

A BRIGHTER MORNING

Monday, February 15, 2049
4:43 a.m.

Yusuf didn't remember how to get us out of the bunker, but Jordan did. Unlike most of the Gliders, Jordan didn't need to wear a band to fall under his mother's control. Her experimentation on him had produced long-term effects in his brain. He could hear her commands and feel himself compelled to follow them with no technology at all.

His Glider memories attached to his regular memories with almost no separation. Whitebourne had escaped for now, but Jordan knew it was only a matter of time until she tried to bring him back to her—to put him to work again.

The crew and I guided the hundreds of Gliders up

the staircase. Jordan pulled the secret internal lever and the platform of the bronze Alice in Wonderland statue lifted up above us. The seven of us exited last to make sure no one got left behind.

As soon as we popped our heads out, roaring crowds began to cheer. There were enough people in Central Park surrounding the statue to make it look like opening night at Futureland! I surveyed the crowd and saw smiling faces, tearful mothers hugging their recovering Glider children, news cameras doing breaking reports. Even though it was loud, I couldn't hear much. It felt like I was there, but not really, like watching everything happen in a movie. I just wished Dooley had been by my side.

To see me. To be proud of me.

The police scurried out of the crowd from all angles, putting yellow tape around the perimeter of the statue. A few of them pushed past us to get to the bunker entrance and started to climb down.

"Hey, you guys are right on time," Rich said sarcastically. "Thanks for your all your help."

"Rich! Hush," Angel said. Rich shrugged.

"Just sayin'."

Mom, Dad, and Uncle Trey burst through the crowd, wrapping me up in the tightest hug they'd ever

given me. They hugged all my friends, too, wiped the sludge off our faces and asked us if were okay only about a thousand times.

"How did y'all know we were here?" I asked.

"All those loud booms. You could hear them from miles away. Everybody started gravitating this way," Uncle Trey said. "Those power outages blacked out half of Manhattan for a second, there. It was scary, nephew. When we couldn't find you kids, me and your parents figured you were down there. We just held hands and hoped for the best."

My parents squeezed me in an inescapable hug again.

"We're so sorry, Cameron," Dad said. "We should have listened. We should have trusted you."

"I thought if I just kept you away from everything dangerous," Mom said, "then it would make life seem a little more normal. I don't know. A little less scary. I'm sorry." She kissed me on the forehead.

I scrunched up my nose and wiped the kiss away with the sleeve of my jacket, but I had to smile. I hugged my mom again as she wiped the continuous flow of tears from her eyes and tried to keep herself together, with Dad holding her tightly.

"You don't gotta worry about me so much, you know, Mom? You and Dad always taught me that we have to face the things that make us scared. They're not going away. And neither are we. Isn't that right, y'all?" I turned to the crew.

"A hundred percent," Yusuf said.

"Ya tú sabes," Angel said.

"Never," Rich said.

"You know it," Inaya said.

"Earl? Earl?" I craned my neck to see Earl, twenty feet away, trying to exchange some of his pocket change for a hot dog from a vendor who had set up inside the park. I shook my head, and we all laughed. If I knew one thing, it was that Earl would always find a way to eat, *especially* after working hard on solving a mystery.

"CJ, can I talk to you for a second?" Yusuf asked. We stepped away from the crowd for some privacy.

"What's up, Yusuf?"

"I wanted to say thank you," he said. "And I'm sorry."

"Sorry? For what?"

"When I snuck into Futureland, I thought I knew best. Like I could just step into your world without a problem. I missed my family. Like, a lot. Missed the basketball team. And most of all, I put you in a really bad situation, hiding me from your parents and all. I apologize."

I patted Yusuf's shoulder. "It wasn't all your fault, Yusuf. Who knows how long that band was creeping into your thoughts, convincing you to follow me." I took a deep breath. "I'm sorry, too. I felt like something was off with you, but I was scared to believe my own intuition and that made it hard for me to help you. You're the first real friend I ever made, and you take on a lot of risk for my sake. I thought if I didn't do what you wanted then I would lose you. But this whole thing has taught me something very important."

"What's that?" Yusuf said.

"That friends may end up in bad situations together, but that doesn't mean they have to stay there. Even if we disagree, there's always a way to compromise."

"That's really smart, CJ," Yusuf said. "So, we cool? Still friends?" He raised an eyebrow.

"Forever," I said, slapping hands for our secret crew shake.

"Cam, Inaya . . . ?" I turned to see Jordan wobbling, his legs giving way beneath him. "I don't feel so good." He toppled over, and Uncle Trey caught him before he hit the pavement. The crowd gasped and a few people rushed over to encircle Jordan, looking down at him.

"Nephew, what's wrong with him?" Uncle Trey asked. "What do we do?"

"He's sick!" I said. "We've got to get him to a hospital."

Me and the crew made a hole through the crowd as my family rushed Jordan out of Central Park. Angel barked out commands until people moved out of the way. I held Jordan's hand as Uncle Trey carried him all the way to the street. Jordan came in and out of consciousness until we got to the taxi, and when Uncle Trey slid him in the back seat, he blinked twice and smiled weakly.

"We did it, Cam," he said. "We saved New York."

"We sure did, Jordan." I smiled back. "We sure did."

25

HUMAN INNOVATION

Monday, March 15, 2049
8:02 a.m.

It had been about a month since we stopped Clare
Whitebourne from unleashing Haven Horrors on the
world. My parents had Futureland running smoothly
again, for the most part. The news of Whitebourne's
plans helped convince everyone that we had been
innocent and that the city had been unfair to us. We
fought hard to get the restrictions on the park removed. Futureland could now be visible within Central Park twenty-four hours a day, seven days a week.
It even became somewhat of a local landmark after
people heard about how we saved hundreds of New
Yorkers from the Glider crisis.

We were selling more Future Passes than we had in
years.

What can I say? Any press is good press. But *real* good press goes a long way.

Deet deet deet da-deet-deet da-deet!

I took a break from screwing some bolts into the new light column in the Holo-pal exhibit. Itza was a big hit with New Yorkers, so Uncle Trey had decided to give her a bigger platform and transfer her artificial intelligence into a rev body so that she could guide guests, like a real park attendant. I looked at my Futurewatch face and grinned with excitement.

Deet deet deet da-deet-deet da-deet!

My parents had suggested I get rid of the watch and start using a new one, but I don't know—I felt attached to it. We had been through so much. Besides, if Southmore or Whitebourne or anybody else tried to make contact again, we'd be ready.

We'd collected and analyzed enough Haventech bands to know everything about them. We even put a special monitor at the Futureland entrance that would detect them if anybody tried to sneak one in. I doubted Haventech could be very successful with Whitebourne on the run, but we needed to prepare, just in case. The FBI had remotely deprogrammed all the bands so that none of them would work. They even started a special return program for ones that had been sold in stores so that people could get rid of the dangerous tech at their local law enforcement station.

Deet deet deet da-deet-deet da-deet!

Oh yeah, of course. I wouldn't want to keep Inaya Bagayoko, Harlem's Own, waiting.

"Hi, Inaya," I said.

"Ayo! Atlanta Cam, what's good with you?"

"Not too much, just fixing on some things here and there. What are you up to?"

"The same thing," she said. "I've got to be honest with you, your parents are really outdoing themselves with the new brownstone. Me and my parents come by to look at it every day, even though it's not finished. It looks almost exactly like our old one. I can't wait to move out of this hotel."

"At this rate, y'all are probably there more than the construction guys."

We laughed together.

"We're just so excited to have a home again," she said. "*Our* home. Can't thank you enough. Plus, it's way easier to work now that the city has demolished that miniature Haven Horrors nonsense next door."

"Good riddance," I said. "My parents were happy to help, by the way. We couldn't have stopped White-bourne without you. Besides, my mom still kinda thinks you and I are going to be a thing, so she'll do anything if I tell her it's for you."

"So I should wait until after our brownstone is finished to tell her that's not happening, huh?" Inaya said. "Got it." We laughed again.

"Have you heard from Jordan?" I asked, a bit tense. Sometimes it's scary asking for updates. My heart wanted to know, but my stomach wasn't sure it can handle the answer.

"Yeah, he's good." I could hear Inaya smile through the phone. "He has my family's old room at the shelter. It's nothing like that mansion he used to live in, but it's a lot of space for one person. And everybody there is very nice. He's said he wants to start at my school when the doctor clears him."

"That's the best news I've heard all day," I said with a sigh, the tense feelings melting away. "Do you really think he can go back to school?"

"We'll see, Cam." She didn't sound sure. "You know, I wouldn't want to hurt your brain with all this detailed science stuff, but Whitebourne's experiments hurt Jordan. Badly. His body and brain are slowly repairing themselves, but it's a process. For now, he's just happy to be feeling better and not coughing so much. Speaking of feeling better, how's Yusuf?"

"Well," I said, "Angel told me on his first day back in Atlanta that he still ran sprints faster and made more shots than all the other boys at practice, so I think he's recovering well. That kid, he's like Superman or something."

"Yeah, right," she quipped. "I bet I can take him in ball."

"You wouldn't be Inaya Bagayoko if you didn't feel that way," I said through a grin.

"Harlem's own!" she added. "All right, Atlanta Cam. I was just calling to say thanks again. Don't be a stranger. You're welcome in Harlem anytime. Just ask for Inaya."

"You bet I will," I said.

I ended the transmission and finished up with my tools. When I made it back to the condo, I took a shower and changed into some jeans and a vintage Futureland T-shirt from 2035. I was rubbing the last bit of water out of my hair with a towel when I felt eyes on me from behind. I whipped around and saw Uncle Trey peeking at me through my cracked bedroom door. He grinned mischievously.

"Ew! Creep!" I cried out with a laugh.

"Hey, nephew," he said in a singsong voice that I knew meant he was up to something. "What color were those sneakers Dooley used to wear?"

I narrowed my eyes at him. "Purple. Why?"

He smiled. "And your parents gave her a birthmark design, right? One to match yours? Which side was it on? Oh, wait. The left side. I can see it from here."

"Uncle Trey! What's going on?" I asked.

"Oh, nothiiiing," he said. "Have a good class." He shut the door and was gone.

Oh, jeez! I almost forgot about class!

Mrs. Espinoza was at her wit's end with me. I had missed a lot of virtual school during the Glider fiasco and hadn't done much better catching up in the last month. Even though there was no more danger, I spent most of my time trying to help my parents and Uncle Trey make the park as good as possible for New Yorkers. We'd had a rocky start, but people loved us here.

I scrambled to get my tablet and set up my wall-o-gram for class, which had started two minutes ago. I flung the projection onto my wall and found myself stuck in the virtual waiting room. Yusuf had once said that Mrs. Espinoza treated the waiting room as if a kid had shown up to class after the bell, keeping them stuck outside looking in.

"Yoo-hoo!" Mom and Dad cracked my door and poked their heads in.

"Mom! Dad! Why does no one knock around here?!"

"Hey there, superstar," Mom started. "You may

solve the mysteries, but we pay the bills. Don't get too smart at the mouth. Besides, we came with news!"

"Good news *and* bad news," Dad clarified.

"Really? What's the news?" I asked. I checked the wall-o-gram. Still stuck in the virtual abyss.

"Bad news first," Dad said. "Certainly, we all thought that our visit to New York would be different than Atlanta, but . . . luck wasn't on our side this time. We had a sit-down with the mayor earlier. We're not in trouble or anything—technically. But after the advice from Mrs. Mayor, our lawyers, and the public relations company—"

"We're moving again, aren't we?" I interrupted.

Dad gave an empathetic frown. "Sorry, Big Man."

I cycled my thumbs over one another. Moving was stressful. I mean, jeez, I just got here! I would miss Inaya. I would worry about Jordan, too. Seems like lately, as soon as one adventure got started, it was time to move to another.

I frowned. I missed when our lives were simple. Just me, Dooley, Uncle Trey, and my parents, safe inside the park. Nothing could shake us or knock us off course. But those days were over.

"Hey, hey, hey, pick your chin up, Cam-Cam," Mom said. "We've still got the good news! It doesn't make much sense for us to keep trying American cities with all the drama going on in the media. So . . . we're going abroad!"

I jumped back, caught off guard by the news. "Wait, really? Out of the country? Where?"

"That's the best part," Mom said. "It's up to you! Any ideas?"

Thoughts zoomed through my brain. I remembered us visiting Brazil and Australia and England. Those were some of the most fun times I'd ever had. Maybe this *was* a good idea—a way to hit the reset button and get back to good times at Futureland. But where to?

The swirling symbol on the virtual waiting room disappeared and I was placed into class. My view of the classroom populated on the wall-o-gram and I could see Mrs. Espinoza and the entire class staring back at me, Mom, and Dad.

"Mom! Dad!" I hollered. "Go! I've got school!"

"We tell the kid to pick his own destination any-where in the world and he's wrapped in a bundle about school," Dad said. "I'll never understand the new gen-eration."

"Oh, hush up, J.B. Our Cam-Cam is a little scholar." Mom backed out of the room, and Dad slipped be-hind her. "Just keep thinking about it. Come up with some options—a list! We'll look it over and decide as a family."

I blushed with embarrassment. I noticed Yusuf on the screen, shaking his head while holding his laugh in. My classmates chuckled as Mom blew me a kiss and shut the door gently.

"Well, well, *Cam-Cam*," Mrs. Espinoza said, grinning. I heard a chorus of giggles from my classmates in the background. "How nice of you to rejoin us. You've been absent from class for quite a while."

"I know. I'm sorry. I'll get those assignments in as soon as I can."

"Oh! I'm sure you will," she said. "While you're in the sky, everyone here is abuzz with talk about your research trip project you completed with your friends. They're saying it's one of the best Eastside has ever seen. I should be *positive* I can expect work of the same quality for your Human Innovation presentation, right?"

"Uhh, yes, for sure. When is that due again?" I asked. I had no clue what she was talking about. A bead of sweat formed at my hairline.

Mrs. Espinoza grinned. "We're sharing our presentations today. Even though you haven't been here, I just know you've been following along in the syllabus and are ready to talk to the class about your project, right?"

My ears got hot with nervousness. My mouth as dry as sand. More chuckles from my classmates.

"Yes, yes, I have. If you could just . . . give me a second," I said, frantically flipping through digital notes on my tablet trying to come up with something to say.

"Each student was supposed to research a topic about a technological science and its effects, for better or worse, on the human body," she said. "So, are you ready? I think you should go first. Unless, of course, you have nothing prepared," Mrs. Espinoza continued. "I wouldn't want to put you on the spot. I'd just have to give you a zero."

I thought for a second, and then it hit me. Thank *Havens* for the wristbands. "No, I'm good, Mrs. Espinoza," I said. "I've got the perfect topic to discuss."

"Is that so? Well, the floor is yours, Mr. Walker. I can't wait to see how this goes."

I spied Yusuf on the camera giving me a thumbs-up. I smiled. *Here goes nothing, I guess.*

I closed my eyes.

I took a deep breath.

I felt confident, unstoppable. For now, anyway.

This was my happy place.

THE FUTURE IS HERE TO STAY

March 17, 2049

Y ou'd think after all the trouble over the last few months at Futureland that park owners Dr. and Mr. Walker would be ready to give up. But that's not even close to the truth.

Futureland came under intense scrutiny after arriving in New York last month and getting in trouble with the state government and community members alike over safety issues in the park. But the phoenix of Futureland has once again risen from the ashes, proving itself worthy of our support and trust, even in the most confusing of circumstances.

Cameron Walker, son of the park owners, recently led an effort to expose a slew of heinous crimes committed by corrupt ex-government official Clare Whitebourne. Whitebourne had been using her government position to unfairly sanction Futureland and other businesses in New York, as well as owning and operating several private interest companies in the city, violating the terms of her elected office.

One such company, Haventech, was recently found to be at the center of a scandal involving unsafe silicone wristbands, marketed as fitness trackers. These trackers sent damaging electrical signals to the brain, causing delirium, memory loss, and physical illness. There has been a nationwide recall on Haventech wristbands. Clare Whitebourne's representative was not available for comment.

The investigation into Clare Whitebourne's property holdings, tech companies, and other misdoings during her

CONTINUED ON NEXT PAGE

term in office will continue. Rumor has it that Futureland is set to depart from New York City soon, and who could blame them? A fresh start may be in order. We at the *New York Crimes* will keep following the story. Like we always say, *Crime doesn't pay, but it sure does make for good entertainment.*

HOWARD T. TOWERS II
Editor

The New York Crimes *daily newspaper,*
Government Division

EPILOGUE

FAR FROM OVER

Thursday, March 18, 2049
3:33 a.m.

I jolted awake in bed, lifting straight up and gasping for air. My clothes were soaked through with sweat and the knocking in my head made me dizzy. I fumbled in the dark on my nightstand for a glass of water, grabbed it and drank it down. Took a deep breath.

Tonight's nightmare: me, desperately trying to escape Whitebourne's Holo-pet firehawk by sprinting through New York City, block after block after block. Of course, I got lost. I could feel myself holding my breath in my sleep.

I always wake up right before the end. Right before it's too late.

Even though things were better, even though

everyone was safe for now . . . I knew in my heart that our troubles weren't done. When we beat Southmore in Atlanta, I thought maybe the Walkers had had our share of bad luck and the dark cloud had moved past us. I wasn't that naïve anymore. Whoever these people, these Architects, were . . . they wouldn't stop until they got what they wanted.

Or until we stopped them.

Buzz. Buzz. Buzz.

Yusuf's Haventech prototype wristband vibrated on my nightstand. *But how?* The government had deactivated all of them. No LifeBuddy in the world should have been working. Unless . . .

I reached over and took the vibrating wristband in my hand. Clenched my jaw and stared at it. One by one, tiny blinking lights started to pulse around its circumference. Then the entire band illuminated.

Deet deet deet da-deet-deet da-deet.

My eyes shot over to the nightstand again, where the face on my corrupted Futurewatch was backlit. I scooped it up and held it in the palm of my other hand, side by side with the LifeBuddy band. My heart pounded so loudly I could hear it between my ears. Slow, tense. Line by line, a message began to populate my screen.

Cameron

This nightmare . . . is far from over.

You've bested two of our best.

But you can't prepare for the rest.

No matter where you go, we will find you.

This is personal now.

See you soon. . . .

Sooner than you think.

The Architects

CAM'S GUIDE TO THE PARK

So, you wanna know how to make your way around Futureland and have the most fun? Well, you came to the right place. I've been keeping this place "kid-approved" since . . . hmm , , , since I learned how to spell *approved*!

BEFORE YOU GO

Futureland is huge! So you're gonna want to wear some comfy shoes. Sure, the Jet-Blur pods will zip you across the park skies wherever you want to go, but personally, my favorite way to explore Futureland is on foot. You get to see much more. Speaking of, make sure you bring your phone, your camera—stuff like that. Futureland is one of a kind—the pictures and video you'll be able to get inside the park are top-quality content. There are streamers who have entire channels dedicated to Futureland!

GETTING INSIDE FUTURELAND

First things first: you have to get *into* the park. And there's no cooler way to arrive in style than by floating up to the entrance in our antigravity beam. It's basically like a warm green light that picks you up off the ground and makes you feel like you're flying. You'll get so high in the air that you'll be able to see the whole city! But don't worry—if you're scared of heights, you can always take the stairs.

BY ANY DREAMS NECESSARY

You *have* to experience these things.

#1 Future Falls and the Future Ring: Everybody loves our nature-based destinies, but here's some insider advice if you want to have real fun: Head over to Future Falls and the Future Ring. Take a tube around the ring with a couple of buddies. Or splash-dive from the top of the waterfall if you're brave!

#2 Snacks! After all that adventuring, you'll probably need some refreshments. Stop by one of the vendor stands in the park (they're everywhere, you can't miss 'em) and grab a chocolate sky—a Futureland-shaped block of pure milk chocolate—and my favorite drink, a fizzy flow. It's like a bubbly tropical explosion. Top-secret recipe, of course.

#3 Holo-pals and Holo-pets: Interested in making your own Holo-pal? Of course you are. We'll have to get you a Futurelink band first. None of those pesky Haventech bands, either! You'll be surprised at how cool your Holo-pal looks, but don't worry. All you have to do is relax and clear your mind. Itza will take care of the rest. Start thinking about what you might want for your Holo-pet, too. I'm still growing on Sarafina. I'll win her over one day. Pick an animal you've never had a chance to see in real life. That'll make it more fun!

LAST BUT NOT LEAST

We've been on some wild adventures together, huh? Believe it or not, New York City is pretty awesome when it's not in the middle of a Glider crisis. You can catch unbelievable music acts in the subway. High Line Park has the best stargazing. And, I mean, how could you not visit the Alice in Wonderland statue in Central Park after knowing what we went through!

Whether you're uptown, in Queens, or in the Bronx, each part of the city has something cool to offer. You'll meet some of the most interesting people you've ever known. My grandma likes to say that big places make big people. She means that sometimes, even if a place seems overwhelming at first, you can grow into it. Each and every one of us is capable of growing more than we realize. You just have to go for it! Have fun, friend. See ya around.

Your friend,
CJ

ACKNOWLEDGMENTS

First and foremost, I have to continue to express my gratitude to the entire team at Cake Creative for sticking with me on this wild ride. Dhonielle, Shelly, Haneen, Carlyn, Clay, and everyone else without whom there would be no Futureland.

I'd also like to thank Suzie Townsend, Sophia Ramos, and the whole team at New Leaf Literary & Media for keeping the Futureland train rolling with all their excellent advocacy, support, communication, and passion.

Same goes for the Random House #TeamFutureland squad. My editor, Tricia Lin, and her editorial team. Jen Valero and her design team, the marketing and public relations teams, and everybody who is working hard when I don't even realize it. Thanks to Kris Kam, Futureland's publicist, for helping readers all over the continent join the Futureland journey.

Thanks once again to the indomitable Khadijah Khatib for the art that continues to astound everyone!

Personally, there are more folks for me to thank than I could successfully name. I wrote this book during one of the hardest, most painful years of my life. My head could not have remained above water without my community and their love and support. Tiffani A., Madison W., Taylor Byas, Huyen N., Hannah Lee Kidder, Jamar J. Perry, L. P. Kindred, Yvette Lisa Ndlovu, Shingai Njeri Kagunda, Alicia, Epiphany K., Ryenne C., Kendra J., Antwan Eady, Ravynn Stringfield. All of ESA. All of PiDD. Everyone who took care of me. Made sure I ate. Made sure I breathed. Thank you.

Much appreciation to the bookstores, schools, librarians, teachers, reviewers, and students who helped me kick off Futureland back in 2022. Thank y'all for getting in at the ground floor.

And finally, thanks to the kids—the readers. You're the most important part of this. Always have been. Always will be.

P.S. Never thought I'd ever, *ever* say this—but thank you to New Yorkers. Consider this novel my peace offering. Thank you for letting me write about your city. I took it seriously, and I hope I did it some justice.

WITHDRAWN